Chicana Voices: Intersections of Class, Race, and Gender

Chicana Voices:
INTERSECTIONS OF CLASS, RACE, AND GENDER

National Association for Chicano Studies

Editorial Committee

Teresa Córdova, *chair*
Norma Cantú
Gilberto Cardenas
Juan García
Christine M. Sierra

University of New Mexico Press
Albuquerque

 University of New Mexico paperback edition published 1993. Second printing 1997

Originally published: Center for Mexican American Studies, University of Texas, Austin, 1986.

Cover Art
Sylvia Orozco

Cover Design
David S. Cavazos

Library of Congress Cataloging-in-Publication Data

Chicana voices: intersections of class, race, and gender / National Association for Chicano Studies; editorial committee, Teresa Córdova, chair ... [et al.].
p. cm.
English and Spanish.
Papers presented at the Twelfth Annual Conference of the National Association for Chicano Studies, held in 1984 at the University of Texas Austin.
Originally published Austin Tex. Center for Mexican American Studies, University of Texas, 1986.
Includes bibliographical references.
ISBN 0-8263-1404-X (paper)
1. Mexican American women—Congresses. I. Córdova, Teresa. II. National Association for Chicano Studies. III. NACS Conference (12th : 1984 : University of Texas at Austin)
[E184.M5C42 1993}
305.4' 886872'073—dc20 93-21784
CIP

This volume is dedicated to
the many Chicanas
who made it possible.

Contents

Foreword to the Third Printing

This volume exemplifies the emergence of historically repressed voices. These proceedings from the 1984 annual conference of the National Association for Chicano Studies (NACS) represent a plateau in the fight for Chicana voices to be heard, and display the range of scholarship that Chicanas are producing. *Chicana Voices: Intersections of Class, Race, and Gender* remains an important historical document and a significant moment in the history of NACS. The history of struggle, of finding our voices, is integral to the Chicana experience.

In 1993 the themes and essays in this volume continue to be relevant. The first section of the volume contains the statements that were given at the plenary session on Chicana feminism. Christine M. Sierra spoke on the qualities of the university that reinforce inequality; Norma Cantú debunked the Adelita image; Cynthia Orozco discussed the previous role of Chicanas in Chicano studies, how gender explains the Chicana experience, and how feminism can play a role in change; and Alma García raised issues regarding the relationship of Chicana studies to Chicano studies.

Chicanas still are taxed by institutional inequality, still are struggling for increased presence in Chicano studies, and still are insisting on the intersection of class, race, and gender. Chicanas now are invoking "Chicana(o) studies" as a more suitable label. The final paper in part one is the tribute paid by the association to two labor activists: Emma Tenayuca and Manuela Solis Sager.

The second section on labor and politics contains several articles that lay the foundation for analyses of Chicanas/Mexicanas in the workplace. Denise Segura uses demographic data to describe the labor-force segmentation of Chicanas and calls for additional research on the disadvantaged position of Chicanas in the workplace, the barriers that they experience, and the conflicts in which they engage. Segura continues some of her current research.

Marta López-Garza, in her article on informal economic activity of Mexicanas, shows that the way social scientists construct categories is inadequate to depict the experiences of Mexicanas/Chicanas. She calls for the development of concepts that more adequately reflect the economic activities of Mexicanas, especially working class, single heads of households, and older women. López-Garza continues to study the "informal labor" work of Mexican and Central American women in Los Angeles.

Devon Peña offers an important analysis of maquiladora workers in the export-production zones along the U.S./Mexico border. He describes the patriarchal controls used on the predominantly female workers, and their forms of resistance. He, too, continues this research and is writing a book in which he uses the voices of women who are working in conditions that are no less oppressive today than when the maquiladoras first appeared in the early seventies.

The article by Teresa Carillo points to an integral connection between Chicanas and Mexicanas. The identities of many Chicanas are closely intertwined with Mexicanas and the Chicano movement reinforces historical and contemporary roots to Mexico. It is no surprise, therefore, that Chicana feminists are interested in feminist developments in Mexico. Carillo traces the 1982 presidential campaign of Doña Rosario Ibarra de Piedra. Though the long-term impact of this campaign is uncertain, it signals the potential of a feminist agenda to permeate Mexican national politics. This will be a uniquely third world feminism. Carillo's current work examines the basis for connections between grassroots movements among Chicanas and Mexicanas. Her initial results suggest that counterparts in each country are hard to find, making difficult the development of a transnational movement.

The articles in part three remain a useful guide to archival and bibliographic sources on Chicanas. The main purpose of the section is to encourage Chicanas to conduct more research on themselves by providing hard-to-find information. Angelina Veyna uses notarial documentation as a source of rich historical insight. Barbara Driscoll offers excellent advice on how to explore the many uncatalogued archives about Mexican women, which are located in Mexico City. She also gives some leads on where else in Mexico to find archival sources. Richard Chabrán provides a critical review of bibliographic and reference material on Chicanas in the humanities and the social sciences. For a good bibliographic review since the initial publication of *Chicana Voices,* see Lillian Castillo-Speed's essay "Chicana Studies: A Selected List of Materials since 1980." This essay, by one of Chicana(o) studies' most prominent librarians, is published in *Frontiers: A Journal of Women's Studies* special issue on Chicanas, vol. 11, no. 1, 1990.

The final section of *Chicana Voices* contains articles on language, literature, and the theater. Each of the authors critically reviews examples of these cultural forms to suggest ways that power and patriarchy are intertwined in the written word. The analysis of Teatro Campesino by Yolanda Broyles is an important example of how sexism permeates even a self-proclaimed progressive group. Broyles's critique is an important assessment of the limited roles for Chicanas in theater and the ways that men, especially influential ones, perpetuate those roles. The essay is a classic among the limited number of critiques of Chicano theater.

Poetry and literature are important vehicles Chicanas use to redefine themselves. In addition to rejecting imposed depictions such as passivity, Chicanas are claiming increased control and power over their lives through their literary productions. The essay by Clara Lomas, in Spanish and English, analyzes a poem by Margarita Cota-Cárdenas, "A una Madre de Nuestros Tiempos." The poem redefines "mother" at the same time that it empowers her and justifies her control of her own body. Literary criticism has become an important tool in Chicana studies.

In addition to the work by Clara Lomas, *Chicana Voices* contains an analysis by Elba Sánchez of the short narrative, "Un Paseo" by Luz Garzón. This story juxtaposes the journeys of two mothers traveling with two sons down the same road but in different vehicles. Sánchez's analysis draws out the complexities of the narrative and the commentary that indicts the treatment of all migrant laborers. The continued (im)migration of Mexican workers and their families still makes this theme relevant to the Chicana experience.

Language and power is the topic of the final article in this section. Alvina Quintana, in "Women: Prisoners of the Word," depicts the use of patriarchal language and the imposition of male-created identity on the representation of the Chicana. Noting how the written work can imprison, Quintana focuses on two Latina writers to show how Latinas are limited through depictions of history and ideology. Drawing upon French structuralist analysis, Quintana also argues that words have the power to transform. Indeed, she uses the words of two Chicana writers to make the point that Chicanas, writing for themselves, have the possibility of transforming sexist representations and replacing them with a more "holistic" approach to a "gender-balanced ideology of the future." Quintana's work is an early example of cultural studies done by Chicanas. More of her work can be found in a special issue of *Cultural Studies* vol. 4, no. 3, October 1990. The title is *Chicana/o Cultural Representations: Reframing Alternative Critical Discourses.*

Chicana Voices: Intersections of Class, Race, and Gender reflects the personal and political struggles of Chicanas to establish their rightful place within the National Association for Chicano Studies and within academia generally. The 1984 annual conference of NACS, *Voces de la Mujer,* signaled the arrival of Chicana scholars. In addition to the articles in this volume, Chicanas presented excellent papers on a wide array of topics too numerous to mention here.

Since the 1984 conference, the annual NACS gathering has been a means for Chicanas to present their research, to network, and to organize. Chicanas continue to produce work that not only challenges stereotypes but adds to the documentation of Chicana experiences and emotions. Most of these writings are listed in the bibliographic work of Lillian Castillo-Speed. An overview of Chicana feminist writings during the last twenty years can be found in Teresa Córdova's "Roots and Resistance: The Emergent Writings of Twenty Years of Chicana Feminist Struggles" forthcoming in *Hispanic Culture in the U.S.: The Sociological Volume,* edited by Felix Padilla and published by Arte Público Press.

The Chicana Caucus is an important vehicle for networking among Chicanas within NACS. Each year, Chicanas at NACS meet for an early morning breakfast during which issues relevant to the women in the association are raised. Proposals may emerge from this session, which are then sent to the business meeting for approval. Since 1984 the caucus has submitted proposals that eventually resulted in a permanent seat on the coordinating committee for the Chicana Caucus, guaranteed childcare during the annual meeting to its members, and established the annual Chicana plenary.

Many Chicanas from NACS are founding and current members of Mujeres Activas en Letras y Cambio Social (MALCS), an academic organization that formed at approximately the same time that Chicanas became visibly strong within NACS. The group meets during the summer for its annual workshop, has a working paper series, and recently initiated a journal of Chicana Studies. The MALCS preamble conveys the philosophy of the organization:

> We are the daughters of Chicano working class families involved in higher education. We were raised in labor camps and

> urban barrios, where sharing our resources was the basis of survival. Our values, our strength, derive from where we came. Our history is the story of working people—their struggles, commitments, strengths, and the problems they faced. We document, analyze, and interpret the Chicano/Mexicano experience in the United States. We are particularly concerned with the conditions women face at work, in and out of the home. We continue our mothers' struggle for social and economic justice.
>
> The scarcity of Chicanas in institutions of higher education requires that we join together to identify our common problems, to support each other and to define collective solutions. Our purpose is to fight the race, class and gender oppression we have experienced in the universities. Further we reject the separation of academic scholarship and community involvement. Our research strives to bridge the gap between intellectual work and active commitment to our communities. We draw upon a tradition of political struggle. We see ourselves developing strategies for social change—a change emanating from our communities. We declare our commitment to seek social, economic, and political change through our work and collective action. We welcome Chicanas who share these goals and invite them to join us (Mujeres Activas en Letras y Cambio Social 1984).

The 1984 NACS conference, "Voces de la Mujer," was a hallmark in the Chicana struggle for voice and presence. Still, outside the association Chicana academics speak of marginality, harassment, and ostracization from institutions of higher education. Chicana lesbians experience these with even more intensity.

Chicana lesbians have always participated within NACS, but not always comfortably. As they "come out" they bring with them a demand for the end of homophobia, a lesbian caucus which now has representation on the Coordinating Committee, and a social-sexual analysis that challenges patriarchy and male-centered identities. These messages are exemplified in two particularly exceptional plenary presentations: Emma Pérez's paper in 1990 in Albuquerque, and Deena Gónzalez's in 1992 in San Antonio. These papers represent the strength and sophistication with which Chicana lesbians are bringing forward new concepts, critiques, and challenges to Chicana(o) studies.

The title of Pérez's talk was "Sexuality and Discourse from the

Margin: A Chicana Lesbian Historical Materialist Perspective," and was later published as "Sexuality and Discourse: Notes from a Chicana Survivor" in *Chicana Lesbians: The Girls Our Mothers Warned Us About,* edited by Carla Trujillo and published by Third Woman Press, 1991. As a lesbian feminist, Emma Pérez postulates that "sexuality and our symbolic reading of sexuality is the core of the problem," which prevents a successful movement for freedom and justice (p. 160). Drawing upon male psychoanalytic theory (Freud, Lacan, and Foucault) to describe male behavior, and French feminist critics of those theories (Cixous, Duras, Irigaray) Pérez brings in the elements of race, class, and culture to deconstruct patriarchal ideology within colonization. Pérez reevaluates the Oedipal complex, the point when men realize their sociosexual power, and describes what she calls the "Oedipal-Conquest-Complex."

This "conquest triangle" is only one part of the puzzle to understand why Chicanas "uphold the law of the white-colonizer European father, knowing the extent of damage and pain for Chicanas and Chicanos" (p. 169). Pérez finds the answer in the perpetrator/victim dynamic, which for women begins with "the molestation memory," the point when "girls realize that they do not have sociosexual power in relation to men" (p. 162). The result is an "addiction" to patriarchy where one fears "violating the father's orders" and where an "entire social structure" betrays her if she refuses to succumb to patriarchal mandates.

This relationship is symbolized in Luis Valdez's theater production *Corridos,* which Pérez says reveals his male centrist anxieties and "eroticizes women's victimization." The story of "Delgadina" shows a young woman who has refused the *advances of her father, is placed in a tower without food or water and eventually dies*. Despite her pleas to her mother, sister, and brother, "Each one fears violating the father's order, his sexual laws, so they each ostracize Delgadina" (p. 171).

The incestuous language and behavior already was operating by the time the father commands Delgadina to allow his "penetration." According to Pérez, that "penetration" was not necessary to create "a memory of molestation" that enters her psyche and leaves the pain of inappropriate behavior unchallenged—by anyone.

> Like Delgadina, women live in this cycle of addiction/dependency to the patriarchy that has ruled women since the precise

> historical moment that they become aware that women's bodies are sexually desired and/or overpowered by the penis (p. 172).

This "memory of molestation" may result in rejection of the molester but often "victims continue to repudiate and embrace the perpetrator in a persistent pattern through relationships until that addictive/dependent cycle is broken" (p. 173). The answer, argues Pérez, is to "resist the perpetrator" in order to abandon "phallocentric law and order." Letting go of capitalist patriarchal notions of sexual law and order is necessary in order to create a collective in the common good. ". . . Social sexual relations between men and women condoned by the patriarchy are inherently unhealthy and destructive most of the time" (p. 173).

Pérez is concerned with fundamental social change and believes that it is impossible without fundamentally challenging the social sexual ideology of patriarchy. Chicanas defy this patriarchy when they can find "a specific moment of consciousness when they can separate from the law of the father into their own *sitio y lengua,*" rejecting "colonial ideology and the by-products of colonialism and capitalist patriarchy—sexism, racism, homophobia, etc." (p. 161).

In 1992 the title of the Chicana Plenary at the annual NACS conference in San Antonio, Texas, was "Racism, Misogyny, and Homophobia: Chicana Resistance to 500 Years of Denial." In her presentation, Deena Gónzalez brought her lesbian critique to the NACS members, challenging the homophobia of men and heterosexual women. In her opening she said:

> My statements are a strategic intervention, partially a by-product of previous battles waged within our National Association for Chicano Studies and founded on an understanding of a homophobia so deeply rooted, so pervasive within this association, that the needs, desires, ideas, and skills of gay and lesbian Chicanas/os are systematically overlooked, denied, and trivialized. I want to talk today by example, through story, of a discrimination so rampant that it defies dialogue, defies representation, and is continuous.

Gónzalez noted that in Texas, the site of the conference, she could be arrested if she and her lover publicly were to hold hands, kiss, or indicate that they were intimately involved. This oppression, Gónzalez said, is connected to patriarchy and the refusal to challenge it. Yet, she argues, the fear of challenging male authority may underlie the response by closeted lesbians and many heterosexual women and men.

Instead of expressing sympathy for the lesbian who has made the choice to be "closeted," she asserts that the choices of women are connected by a "continuum of oppression and repression." This is especially the case for the woman who refuses to "abide male authority." This continuum is founded upon "the twin devils of patriarchy and misogyny, and is supplemented in steady doses today by the heterosexism—that ideology that says all people are heterosexual—of most straight Chicanos and Chicanas." Meanwhile, it is she, and other out lesbians who bear the burden of "interrupting heterosexism."

The lesbian analysis says that the eradication of oppression at its most intimate level, i.e., as it relates to sexuality, is necessary so that we can "get on with it." A homophobic message conveys that some differences are acceptable while others are not. Gónzalez, on the other hand, calls for embracing the differences and imagines a NACS conference that addresses the question of "queer theory and its impact on the discipline" and a conference that lesbians and gays actually look forward to attending. She ends by asking, "let us stop being so fearful, watchful, abiding of patriarchy and of heterosexuality."

During this same powerful plenary in 1992, Inés Talamantez and Inés Hernandez presented perspectives on our indigenous roots as Chicanas(os). In her talk entitled, "Notes from the Homeland: On the Construction of Chicana Identity," Inés Hernandez began with a poem that she wrote for her mother in which she celebrates her mother's Nimipu background at the same time that she laments the denial of those "whose reveries are not of this land, but of Spain." At this conference that recognized 500 years of survival and resistance, Hernandez poignantly told the audience, "Since I was a child, I have noticed the internalized racism, the Indian-hating that goes on in the Mexicano community." In place of this internalized rejection of our "Indianness," Hernandez offers a reconceptualization of the Chicana. Reading from one of her letters she said, "I feel that within each Chicana/Mexicana/mestiza there is that indigenous aspect, which is connected with the collective consciousness of the red tradition of this continent. . . ."

Yet Hernandez suggests that "coming out" as a "self-identified

Native American" can be as difficult as "coming out" as a lesbian. She asks, "Why do those who proudly carry their Indianness, their womanness, their lesbianess and gayness elicit so much (and often violent) reaction in our community?" Why, she asks, with regards to the quincentennial, "have Chicanos/as been, in large part, silent on the subject of the celebration of the so-called conquest? Why have so many of us accommodated so easily to the term 'Hispanic?' "

Hernandez urges us to look to Native American perspectives to create a synergetic construction—not just intersection—of Chicana identity that begins by "unmasking patriarchy." She herself rejects misogynist notions of a Supreme Being as "lord and master" and instead urges us to pay attention to indigenous constructions of Supreme Beings. In doing so, we can "begin to come into balance" with a Mother/Father Tierra, and a Father/Mother Sol rather than just a Mother Earth and a Father Sun. "Las mujeres también son soles [Women, too, are suns]."

This revived Chicana identity also is connected to the land base, argues Hernandez. That connection to the land is an essential connection to our indigenous roots in the hemisphere.

> I am calling for us to declare our solidarity by not distinguishing ourselves from Native American peoples. I am calling for us to stand with and amongst toda la gente indígena de América, Norte a Sur. . . .

The Chicana experience, says Hernandez, did not begin in either 1965 or 1848 but extends to our indigenous roots, to our herstory, to our women's stories. When we search for these stories, we find that we have a history of feminism here and in Mexico, and even within the "movimiento." "There are and have been, within the Chicana scholarly as well as grass roots community, leaders and elders. As Chicanas, we must look to ourselves first for our models—we must recognize each other and we must recognize each other's work."

The Chicana identity is also a rebellion against "patrón politics" that will "devour" us, and against "popular masculine cultural notions" that define women in terms of male fantasies. In rebellion, Hernandez proclaimed, the Chicana finds "not only pleasure and fulfillment, we find our dignity, our face and heart, our sense of humor and our creative energy."

Our resistance continues but our silence is forever broken. We are telling our stories and we are recording our triumphs and, by virtue of our presence, we are challenging our surroundings. Chicana writing has developed out of personal and political struggle, a fact that shapes the nature of that writing and the impact that Chicana writers have had in political, literary, and social science circles.

Chicana Voices: Intersections of Class, Race, and Gender is an important historical moment for Chicanas, particularly within NACS. We know, however, that Chicana voices are deep within our herstory and contain significant messages for our future.

Teresa Córdova
University of New Mexico

Preface

The 1984 conference of the National Association for Chicano Studies (NACS), held at the University of Texas at Austin, was truly ground-breaking. For the first time in the Association's twelve-year history, its annual meeting focused on women. The theme of the conference, *Voces de la Mujer*, generated an unprecedented number of panels and papers that addressed the question of gender in the Mexican community.

The conference witnessed a dramatic increase in the number of women participants. Chicanas chaired panels, presented papers, and attended conference activities as never before. Most importantly, a growing feminist consciousness marked the increased involvement.

Based on outstanding papers from the 1984 conference, this book is also an historic first. It is the first NACS publication devoted totally to scholarship on *la mujer chicana/mexicana*. Further, it is the first time women scholars and their work predominate in the proceedings of the Association. This volume stands as the culmination of years of effort to place Chicana involvement at the center of our scholarly endeavors.

In the past, when Chicanas, individually or collectively, raised their voices to be heard—as women—in Chicano studies circles, floodgates of reaction broke open. Chicana challenges to their underrepresentation and misrepresentation in NACS, Chicano studies programs, and other arenas drew a variety of responses. In some cases, serious attempts were made to address these issues. But much more likely were the all-too-familiar responses of resistance to change.

Token efforts, if they were made, to invite (not recruit) Chicanas to serve on panels, in faculty and administrative positions, and so forth, constituted a common "defense" for sins of omission. Other responses involved countercharges that Chicanas were distractive, divisive, or duped: distractive because Chicana demands took time and energy away from the more important issues at hand; divisive because such demands disrupted efforts at unity and appealed only to "special interests"; and duped because Chicanas were essentially being used to promote the interests of white women.

Still other responses entailed appeals to "reason" (yes, there are problems, but change can come only incrementally); cries of confusion ("what is it you want?"); or requests for prescription ("tell us what to do").

At the same time, Chicanas themselves were struggling to define their own positions, increase their numbers in academia, and devise strategies for articulating their interests as women of color. Conflict and change marked these efforts as well.

If we as Chicana/o scholars sought to address issues that affected Chicano people as a whole, then addressing the issues of half of our population could not be considered irrelevant or distractive. We also began to recognize that the so-called disruption of unity and harmony meant the disruption of systems of domination that were harmonious as long as they were not challenged. Further, Chicanas indeed were voicing issues and concerns that were distinct from those of middle-class white women.

The increasing Chicana presence in NACS coincides with the development of the Association. In fact, women's participation has furthered the development of the organization. A vital, albeit small, Chicana presence was part of NACS during its formative years. As Chicanas mobilized, Chicana participation in NACS conferences and in leadership positions within the Association strengthened accordingly. Certainly, numerous individuals and particular events could be singled out for clearing the pathways to women's involvement in NACS. Here, two key events are noted.

Mujeres en Marcha from the University of California, Berkeley, presented a panel at the Tenth Annual Conference (1982, Tempe) entitled "Unsettled Issues: Chicanas in the 80's." This session raised the topic of sexism for discussion among women and men and, in doing so, promoted a collective consciousness of *mujeres* in the Association. The following year a group of women met informally at the NACS annual meeting in Ypsilanti, Michigan, and formed resolutions that would be submitted to the site committee. The most notable of these requests was that the upcoming conference to be held in Austin, Texas, have as its theme *Voces de la Mujer*. The proposal was accepted, and thus the twelfth annual conference of the

National Association for Chicano Studies was dedicated to the world as seen and articulated by Chicanas.

Sixty-one panels were held at the conference, twenty-five of which were related to gender. Topics addressed included labor, politics, research, language, literature, theater, art, and the family. The most notable panel was a plenary session on higher education and the problems of gender inequality. "An Open Discussion on Sexism: Constructing a Chicana Feminism" had as its purpose to bring women together to see where we stood in our movement to create a feminism that is uniquely our own, as women of color. "Chicana Political Activity: The Role of Women in La Raza Unida Party and Politics" was a session highlighted by the participation of Chicanas who had been active in La Raza Unida party in Texas. On a more intimate and emotional level, the daughters of Sra. Aurora E. Orozco paid a loving tribute to their mother.

Special events were numerous, among them poetry readings, art displays, and discussions of art programs. On the first evening of the conference, the Association honored Sras. Manuela Solis Sager and Emma Tenayuca for their commitment and dedication to labor organizing. Approximately one hundred Chicanas met to form the Chicana caucus. Caucus concerns served as the basis for action taken during the business meeting of the Association, where the most controversial issue was the composition of the editorial committee. The victory of increased Chicana participation on the editorial committee enhances Chicana representation and the diversity of perspectives.

The events of the conference signify a new era for the National Association for Chicano Studies in which we can expect increased Chicana presence and participation. That participation will be accompanied by the development of Chicana feminism that is the outcome of struggle for our rights. As we continue to struggle, so will our feminism continue to develop. The issues of class, race, and gender are combined in our experience; thus, the challenge that we pose is the challenge to domination itself. In opposing power based on domination, the efforts of Chicanas within NACS will improve the very nature of the Association itself.

It is, thus, with great pride and excitement that we present these proceedings of the Twelfth Annual Conference of the National Association for Chicano Studies.

Acknowledgments: The NACS Editorial Committee would like to extend its appreciation to Rosalinda Diaz for her help in proof-reading the final galleys of this volume. We would also like to acknowledge the Institute for the Study of Social Change at the University of California, Berkeley, for making their facilities available during our editorial conferences.

Chicana Voices:
Intersections of Class,
Race, and Gender

Part I. Plenary Statements and Special Tribute

Introduction

The conference and its proceedings are important political moments in the history of the National Association for Chicano Studies. Women in the Association challenged power relations based on gender so that they would no longer by relegated to a status of inferiority and invisibility. The plenary panel of the conference was a particularly significant forum for raising issues and questions regarding the position of *la mujer chicana* within Chicano studies. Each of the four plenary statements presented in this volume was intended as a political position statement designed to encourage discussion. They are also working papers designed to be a first step to more developed analyses.

The panel was introduced by Margarita Melville, University of Houston, who offered five preliminary assumptions: (1) sexism means domination for the women who experience it; (2) changes are possible for a culture; (3) socializing processes result in differences among racial groups; (4) consciousness raising is relevant for men as well as women; and (5) "everyone can be saved."

This volume opens with the work of Christine M. Sierra, whose paper discusses the ways in which institutional power is based on values, attitudes, and behavior that foster inequality. Chicanas experience, perceive, and respond to institutional inequality in ways that are unique to their experience. Sierra's paper is important in emphasizing the challenge to the very nature of the university itself and the principles of domination on which it is founded. The question for us is: how do we respond to this institutionally reinforced inequality and meet the challenge of fighting domination?

Norma Cantú insists that Chicanas should be seen as leaders and as thinkers. These images, however, are not those commonly found in the field of Chicano studies. She responds to the Adelita image of Chicanas, which she asserts has worked against a more positive image of Chicanas as thinkers, philosophers, and workers for social change. Cantu reminds us that there are few Chicanas publishing and that their work is not taken seriously. Instead, she argues that Chicana writers and Chicana literature must become more salient in Chicano literature courses.

Cynthia Orozco addresses three topics: previous treatment of women's issues by the Chicano movement and Chicano studies; the role of gender in explaining the oppression Chicanas experience as women and the role of feminism for social change. Antifeminist ideologies were prevalent during the height of *el movimiento*. Orozco argues that only through additional analysis of gender can we more fully understand the oppression of *la chicana*. While Orozco is calling for the saliency of a feminist analysis of power relations based on gender, it is important to note that this is an addition to analyses based on race and class and not a replacement.

The paper by Alma García suggests that the study of Chicanas should be brought "into the frame" of Chicano studies and that this can best be accomplished through a synthesis of three current approaches to the study of Chicanas: Chicanas as "Great Women," "Workers," and "Women." Each perspective, according to García, "represents a component of a larger whole," and the key for advancement of literature on Chicanas is the integration of fragments into the whole of Chicano studies. As a result of García's paper, we ask questions about the infusion of Chicano studies with a Chicana consciousness. Should the Chicana perspective be "integrated" into and redefined within a previously established field of study? Or, rather, should the new Chicano studies be an emergent, creative product of interaction between and among men and women as they seek a redefinition of what constitutes legitimate knowledge about Chicanas/os?

The plenary papers and the ensuing discussion constituted a success in the continuing efforts to bring a feminist challenge to the National Association for Chicano Studies. For Chicanas, as for other women of color, the discussion that we offer is one that combines analyses of class, race, and gender. We cannot separate any of the three from our experience. It is the combination that makes our experience unique.

The final paper in part I is a tribute to Manuela Solis Sager and Emma Tenayuca by Roberto R. Calderón and Emilio Zamora. These two labor activists were honored by the Association for their undying commitment to improved working conditions for Chicano/a laborers in the Southwest. Calderón and Zamora have made an important contribution to the historical documentation of the dedication of two women, whose work serves as a model for Chicano/a activists. The selection in this volume contains highlights of the lives and political efforts of the honored women. The text of their presentation at the award ceremony is also included.

The University Setting Reinforces Inequality

Christine Marie SIERRA

Academia and its institutions foster inequality. Class, race, and gender inequalities permeate institutions of "higher learning." The power of academia rests upon the control or monitoring of ideas (what goes in and what comes out of academia) and its hierarchical, elitist ("selective") structures which promote rich over poor and working-class, whites over people of color, and men over women.

When we as Chicanas and Chicanos assaulted institutions of higher education more than a decade and a half ago, we recognized some of these inequities. We demanded fundamental changes within higher education. Our attention then focused on racial inequities. Class inequities were obviously present as well, but it took us a while to address that dimension of inequality head-on.

Certainly, such inequities persist. But currently, we are recognizing the incomplete agenda of our previous movement for equality. Attention is now turning to the pervasiveness of yet another dimension of inequality: the question of gender. I want to address our role in higher education as well as the question of gender in these remarks.

We can recall easily how the goals of our student *movimiento* were to change the structures and processes of higher education. Was this an idealistic movement? Yes, no, maybe? It certainly has been problematic. Many would question whether our collective struggle to foster equality *and* fundamental change in higher education has vanished; it certainly has diminished. Perhaps that aspect of challenge to the status quo has diminished partly because Chicano studies have now undergone an initial phase of institutionalization. To be sure, as compared to twenty years ago, there are more of us as students, Ph.D. candidates, faculty, and administrators. But how do we define our role in higher education? What is our political responsibility in academia? Do we still have political commitments?

Much of that desire for change in higher education has yielded to different notions of what we are about. Institutional power and control loom as the guiding principles of who we are, what we want. Carefully examined, the current quest for institutional power and control is based upon criteria well accepted by institutions of higher education. Some illustrations:

(1) Personal power and authority are sought; power is seen as resting in individuals and what they control, that is, their "turf."

(2) Elitist principles go unchallenged; indeed, they are adhered to in some cases. There is, for example, an on-going categorization of each other among ourselves. Such categorizations adhere to the ever-so-hard-to-define criteria that most academics love ("scholarly excellence and objectivity," "an expert second to none," etc.) Rather than helping us appreciate and work with the diversity among us, reaffirming our strengths and strengthening our weaknesses, such categorizations serve other purposes. They tend to discriminate, to exclude, to separate us.

(3) Hierarchically based processes and policies are followed. For example, recruitment into graduate schools, academic departments, colleges, and universities still reflects traditional mechanisms: networks of who knows whom. Such a process is steeped in race, class, and gender biases.

(4) Finally, personal loyalty, allegiances, and commitment are becoming more attached to the institutions in which we work than to the community which supported our integration into those institutions. For example, Chicano/a presence in universities has been attributed more to university responsiveness than to any political movement of women and men to forge such a presence.

In short, there are certain values, attitudes, and behavior defined, supported, and enhanced in university settings which generate or reinforce inequality. Such values, attitudes, and behavior emerge as a result of the politics of class, race, and, most assuredly, patriarchy. Such values, attitudes, and behavior are also permeating our own endeavors. The question is: how do we respond?

Both Chicanas and Chicanos confront inequities in higher education. But I would like to make three distinctions here:

(1) We as Chicanas *experience* inequality differently than men;
(2) We as Chicanas *perceive* inequality differently; and
(3) We as Chicanas *respond* to inequality differently.

Our experiences differ in many ways, for many reasons. On a very basic level, there are simply fewer of us (Chicanas) in higher education, in graduate programs, and on faculties. Also, we occupy lower positions within academia's hierarchy. We are not department chairs, directors of programs, and so forth. As Rosabeth Moss Kanter explains forcefully in *Men and Women of the Corporation* (New York: Basic Books, 1977), a group's numbers and placement within hierarchical structures hold numerous implications for that group's power and status in those hierarchies.

Our perceptions of inequality also differ. Concerns of Chicanas in higher education will be similar, but also significantly different from those of men. Drawing upon feminist dialogue and discussion on inequality, Chicana feminists will tend to confront, to challenge, the separation of our professional world from our community-based commitments and personal responsibilities. We do not accept the artificial separation of our lives into the so-called public and private realms. We as Chicana feminists are calling for altering the basis of power and influence within our communities and places of work.

Because of these different experiences and perceptions of what we want, our responses to inequality also differ from those of men. Feminist dialogue continues to point out that the "personal is political." We must foster equality in our work and personal behavior, and not just publicly support such a principle. In general, a total reorientation is called for: reexamining what we are about, as students, teachers, scholars. What does our intellectual activity entail?

All of these three factors, the different experiences, perceptions, and responses on the part of women, point to the fact that Chicanas have a leading role to play in the articulation of issues for the Chicano community within and outside the halls of academia.

Women, Then and Now: An Analysis of the Adelita Image versus the Chicana as Political Writer and Philosopher

Norma CANTÚ

When I began preparing for this talk I listed various questions that remain unanswered in my mind and that I believe merit scrutiny at a session such as this one. Since my main area of study is literature, questions regarding gender and inequality in higher education and society in regard to literature outnumbered all others. The list included questions such as why, although we have so many Chicanas writing, so few are publishing consistently. Why do we have so many "one-book" writers, as Tillie Olson calls them? Why is it so difficult to find good serious criticism of women's works? Are Chicana writers oppressed in one more way as writers? Are we, in fact, experiencing a "dark age" of Chicano/a literature—one that is producing nothing new and relying on old, trite formulas? Why aren't there Chicana literature classes in Chicano studies programs? You can see where the list was going. Some of the questions, it can be argued, are irrelevant. More Chicanas are publishing than ever before, and there *are* Chicana literature courses offered in *some* Chicano studies departments—or more probably, Chicanas are included in Hispanic women's literature courses.

But the list also included other questions not directly related to literature. Why are there so few, if any, services available for reentry Chicana students? Why isn't child care the rule not the exception at centers of higher education? How can administrators and faculty support Chicana students in a system that inherently prohibits such bonds? I soon realized that the questions on my list were indeed related, if somewhat tenuously at times, because they led directly or indirectly to literature and to Chicano studies in the broadest sense of both terms.

I have chosen to speak about only two major questions, which might explain, not necessarily resolve, some of my more specific and personal concerns. *Primeramente*, how can Chicana studies survive, in places where no such animal exists, officially or unofficially? As an aside, I suggest that all of us might soon be asking this question about Chicano studies in general unless we take some action, but that is for another session, not this one. The second question is: why are Chicana studies relegated to substatus, a subtopic of Chicano studies, and why do we tolerate this situation?

My comments treat both questions together for I believe that they are ultimately one question. I have been grappling with what I call the "Adelita complex," which might account for Chicanas' exclusion from, or secondary status in, Chicano studies. The explanation I offer comes from literature, from history, and from the various personal experiences of Chicanas.

The images of Adelitas and *soldaderas*—from the Mexican Revolution—are, to a degree, false. Unfortunately, the images still live and give life to attitudes about self and others. They are false in that they often connote a follower—a woman following a man, a soldier, as in the case of the Adelita as a provider, nurturer, healer. The *soldadera*, on the other hand, follows but is more actively involved in the man's activities. Not content with merely keeping the soldiers alive, she is herself a soldier, sometimes donning man's attire and fighting along with the men. But the Adelitas and *soldaderas* were not merely followers—they were often military strategists, political thinkers who gave the Mexican Revolution more than tortillas and beans. A revolution may depend on the feeding of its troops but it must have ideas and ideals even to begin. Leona Vicario, Doña Josefa Oríz de Domíngues, and numerous others were instrumental in developing the ideas that fed not the stomachs but the generating forces of the Revolution.

In Mexican films of the Revolution, one image invariably appears. Always—whether as Adelitas or *soldaderas*—the women follow the men. And as Pedro Armendariz rides into the next battle, Dolores del Rio follows—on foot. The image has not been limited to literature and films, but as self-fulfilling prophecy, has made itself a reality in the minds of contemporary Chicanos and Chicanas who feel that women must follow. Women are perceived as followers, not leaders, or thinkers, when in fact women are active in the role which our foremothers also played, that of political and social thinkers, of leaders in various areas throughout our communities. But denying our existence in this arena—by excluding Chicana writers from courses in Chicano literature, for example, we perpetuate the stereotypes, and this exclusion thereby invalidates our work.

The implication of this is that women are not taken seriously because they are not serious. By not reading Chicana literature, by not supporting our work in any academic or professional area, our organization—by not taking women seriously—follows the pattern of other professional organizations that by exclusion invalidate the work of certain groups. Chicano studies cannot exist without acknowledgement of Chicanas and our work; to do otherwise would betray the spirit of our organization. One cannot claim to be in Chicano studies and continue to ignore Chicanas. As leaders, thinkers and above all partners, whether in academia or in the larger community.

The pejorative image of Chicanas as Malinches or Adelitas must be replaced by one not assigned to us by patriarchally defined categories. Their "new image" is not new in our history, nor in our literature. Chicanas must be seen as positive forces—leaders, workers—for change with all the positive characteristics that women at all levels of our stuggle have demonstrated and continue to demonstrate.

Sexism in Chicano Studies and the Community

Cynthia OROZCO

Acknowledgments: I would like to thank members of Raza Women's Organization, UCLA for their moral support and help. Particular thanks to Luz Calvo.

I would like to address the significance of gender and its relationship to sexism in the Chicano community and Chicano studies. Three questions are discussed: (1) How did the Chicano movement deal with women and how did Chicano studies treat the category of gender? (2) What is the significance of gender for understanding and ending the oppression Chicanas experience as women? and (3) What is the relationship between gender and feminism, and what does this mean for social change?

The Chicano movement was a nationalist struggle for the liberation of the Mexican people in the United States, though class struggle was a conscious component among various sectors. It must be clear that this movement did *not* attempt to end patriarchy, the system by which men dominate women.

Though we can speak of a Chicana movement in which women argued that women's life experiences and oppression were different and worse than men's and acted against this particular oppression, lack of ideological clarity on what gender meant hindered the Chicana movement.[1] At the time, Chicana activists did not recognize patriarchy as a system separate in origins and in everyday life and quite distinct from racism and capitalism. Chicanas struggled against the interconnectedness of this triple burden, but largely battled racism and capitalism on the ideological front. For instance, Anna Nieto Gómez, California's best-known and most controversial feminist, argued in 1977 that sexism "is part of the capitalist ideology which advocates male supremacist values."[2]

When Chicanas raised the issue of male domination, both the community and its intellectual arm, Chicano studies, put down the ideology of feminism and put feminists in their place. Utilizing ideology and its corresponding actions, Chicanos continued to manifest the sexism feminists sought to eradicate.

Various sexist ideologies about feminism (and feminists) emerged from the Chicano movement. Four common ones can be discerned: (1) "El problema es el gabacho no el macho." (2) Feminism was Anglo, middle-class, and bourgeois. (3) Feminism was a diversion from the "real" and "basic" issues, that is, racism and class exploitation. (4) Feminism sought to destroy "la familia," supposedly the base of Mexican culture and the basis for resistance to domination.[3]

These ideologies raised some legitimate concerns, but blurred the feminist vision. Machismo was disregarded. Activists defined racism and capitalism as fundamental problems, but such issues as equal pay for equal work, sex segregation in employment, and rape were hardly considered "basic." Many feminists were Anglo and middle-class, but there were also black and other Third World working-class feminists. Chicanos stereotyped feminism to mean liberal feminism; radical feminism was ignored. Moreover, Chicana radicals had begun to redefine feminism to fit their particular triple oppression when the case against feminism was made. Similarly, while the family has embodied essential emotional and human relationships, the idea that it did not sustain oppressive or hierarchical relationships, especially for women and girls, was asserted.

While the attack on feminism in community action was overt and conscious, Chicana feminism was also undermined in Chicano studies. Chicano intellectuals argued that race and class were the determining factors in understanding the subordinate position of Mexicans in the United States.[4] They interpreted the condition of Mexican men and women to be synonymous; gender was irrelevant in determining life experience and power. Most intellectuals were unconscious of their exclusion of the category of gender, since male thought permeates our thinking and does not allow for the female perspective and opinion. In community life, Chicano activists like César Chávez advanced male thought: he proudly asserted, "We are not beasts of burden, we are not agricultural implements or rented slaves, we are men."[5]

Rodolfo Acuña's *Occupied America*, perhaps the most widely read book about Chicanos—a work which should be considered the

"Chicano Bible"—epitomizes the lack of a conceptualization of gender.[6] Acuña cogently describes racial and class oppression, but he does not mention gender oppression.[7] In not doing so, he suggests a male ideology: sexism is not a problem, and therefore feminism is irrelevant to Chicanas. We must not underestimate the power of Acuña's book: teachers have organized courses around it, and it has taught thousands how to think about the oppression Mexicans experienced.

In the Chicano studies document "El Plan de Santa Barbara," the theoretical rationale for Chicano studies, a lack of consciousness about sexism and gender can be inferred.[8] Sociologist Mary Pardo's analysis of "El Plan" shows that not once did it make reference to women, female liberation, or Chicana studies. Indeed, "El Plan" was a "man"-ifesto.[9]

College course offerings by Chicano studies centers exemplify a lack of awareness about the problem of sexism and the importance of gender. Most small centers offered the token "La Chicana" (usually as a result of Chicana feminists' annual struggle to ensure it) which usually covered all topics briefly and none thoroughly.[10] At some schools, even this class has not been institutionalized. The women teaching these courses have overwhelmingly been part-time workers.[11] The omission of courses on women and the lack of Chicana faculty help to explain the weak feminist consciousness among students and the lack of support systems for young women.[12]

In short, feminism has been suppressed and feminists have been repressed. What is the significance of this? Many lack an understanding of male domination in society; therefore, the oppression that Mexican women suffer which is specific to their gender has hardly been challenged. Moreover, Chicana studies today are underdeveloped. It is time to study problems specific to Chicanas and to rectify them.[13]

To do so, we must understand the significance of gender. It determines life experience, power, and privilege, and the division of labor is created on the basis of it.[14] Our identities are formed by work. Thereby, men learn to be men and women learn to be women; gender is largely a social construction.[15] This varies according to historical period and culture and is subject to change.

Society gives social significance to gender, and a system of power is organized around it. This system is partriarchy or male domination or machismo, if we extend its usual connotation. Its origins are different from those of racism and capitalism, and it is the most universal and historical system.

Patriarchy is sophisticated: it has both structural and ideological features.[16] The key structural feature is the division of labor by sex. Arising from this is the ideological feature of femininity and masculinity, our gender identities. Femininity must not be seen solely as a female-creation; it complements masculinity, which also serves as a foundation for male dominance.[17]

In contrast to patriarchy is feminism. Feminism is a recognition of the domination of men over women and attempts by women to end male privilege. It also seeks to redefine female-to-female relations. Feminism is all-encompassing since it is a theory, a method, and a practice which seeks to transform human relations.[18] Feminism is necessary for liberation.

How can feminism affect social change? How does it relate to women and higher education? To begin, "higher education" demands redefinition, since only 6 percent of our Latina population attend institutions of higher learning.[19] We must broaden our strategies to include the majority of our community.

Schools alienate and exclude women and men, girls and boys. Alternative institutions and mediums must be created, and we must take higher education to common people. Here, higher education is defined not as institutions, but as the realm of thought. We must disseminate our knowledge and progressive perspectives to the community by presenting strategies for change. At the same time, we must listen to the community, for it speaks to us. We must move beyond the barriers that the university seeks to maintain between a privileged sector and the mass of exploited and oppressed Mexicans. Sexism has no geographical barriers—it thrives at the university—nor should feminism stay in the college setting. Feminism belongs in the community.

Higher education promotes the liberation of the oppressed and rejects hierarchy. Feminism as theory and daily practice should be an integral feature of this higher education so we can end the exploitation of women in the home, sexual harassment on the job, sex segregation in employment, wife abuse, and rape.

These strategies imply a vision of the future, a vision of hope. In the spirit of change, visions are revisions. Today, we revise "El Plan de Santa Barbara'' to encompass the feminist voice it lacked in 1969.[20] We have appropriately called it ''El Plan de Santa y Barbara'' since it is a proposal written to Chicano studies across the nation in hope that feminism will reemerge in strength. It follows:

> We will move forward toward our destiny as women. We will move against those forces which have denied us freedom of expression and human dignity. Due to the sexist structure of this society, to our essentially different life style, and to the socio-economic functions assigned to our community by male society—as suppliers of free labor and a dumping ground for male aggression, the female community remains exploited, impoverished, and abused.
>
> As a result, the self-determination of the female community is now the only acceptable mandate for social and political action; it is the essence of Chicana commitment.
>
> Culturally, the word ''feminism,'' in the past a pejorative and class-bound word, has now become the root idea of a new cultural identity for women. Feminism draws its faith and strength from two main sources: from the just struggle of women and from an objective analysis of our community's strategic needs.
>
> It is in this spirit, that we meet in Austin, Texas, in mid-March, over 400 Chicano students, faculty, administrators, and community delegates representing Aztlán.
>
> Let us part with the words of a Chicana feminist named Sra. Josefa Vasconcelos. She said, ''At this moment we do not come to work for Chicano studies and the community, but to demand that Chicano studies and the community work for our liberation too.''

NOTES

1. Carlos Vasquez has pointed to the problem of ideological clarity among Chicana feminists yet subsumes the feminist cause under the Marxist-Leninist struggle and fails to acknowledge patriarchy. ''Women in the Chicano Movement,'' in *Mexican Women in the United States: Struggles Past and Present,* ed. Magdalena Mora and Adelaida R. del Castillo (Los Angeles: Chicano Studies Research Center Publications, 1980), pp. 27-28. For a critique of the so-called ''woman question,'' see Heidi Hartman, ''The Unhappy Marriage between Marxism and Feminism,'' *Capital and Class* 8 (Summer, 1979):1-33.

2. Nieto Gómez was the Chicana movement's eminent intellectual/activist; she waged war on the triple oppression Chicanas suffer. Her writing reflects lack of clarity on the origins and nature of this burden, but to some extent this can be attributed to the interconnectedness of capitalism, racism, and sexism. Adelaida R. del Castillo notes that "Chicana feminism itself was delineated not so much through cohesive political statements as through the focus of issues and activities" (Anna Nieto Gómez, "Sexism in the Movimiento," *La Gente* (February, 1975):10; Adelaida R. del Castillo, "Mexican Women in Organization," in *Mexican Women in the United States,* 11). *This Bridge Called My Back* should be credited with adding new vigor to women's studies and Third World women's studies in particular. (*This Bridge Called My Back: Writings by Radical Women of Color*, ed. Cherríe Moraga and Gloria Anzaldua (Watertown, Mass.: Persephone Press, 1981).

3. Both antifeminist and feminist writings of the Chicano movement and other Third World movements have been collected by Dorinda Moreno, *La Mujer en Pie de Lucha: y la Hora Es Ya!* (San Francisco: Espina del Norte, 1973). A critique of the notion of feminism as an Anglo, bourgeois diversion is Cynthia Orozco, "Feminism: How Chicanos 'Skirt' the Issue," *La Gente* (June, 1983):17, and a critique of the "cult of la familia" has been launched by Beatriz Pesquera. See also Cherríe Moraga, "A Long Line of Vendidas," *Loving in the War Years, Lo Oue Nunca Paso Por Sus Labios* (Boston: South End Press, 1983).

4. Students have transformed intellectual analysis and theory into action, and therefore MECHA's agenda has also reflected the lack of understanding of patriarachy. Mechistas have challenged sexist behavior and attitudes but fail to perceive the systematic nature of women's oppression. See Irene Rodarte, "Machismo vs. Revolution" in Moreno, *La mujer*, 36-40, and Marta Arguello, "Phallic Politics," *La Gente* (March/April, 1984):5.

5. Quoted in Paul Fusco and George D. Horwitz, *La Causa: The California Grape Strike* (New York: Collier Books, 1970), n.p.

6. Rodolfo Acuña, *Occupied America: The Chicano's Struggle Toward Liberation* (San Francisco: Canfield Press, 1972).

7. Acuña made various changes in his second edition but no fundamental change in his conceptualization of women in history. His changes reflect what historians have called "compensatory history." The Mexican American Studies Program at the University of Houston sponsored a symposium on the classic, but no women were invited, nor was gender analyzed. See Rodolfo Acuña, *Occupied America: the Chicano's Struggle toward Liberation,* 2nd ed. (New York: Harper and Row, 1981); Mary Pardo, "Mexicanas/Chicanas: Forgotten Chapter of History," *El Popo* 14/4 (February/March, 1980):8; *Occupied America: A Chicano History Symposium* (Houston: Mexican American Studies Program, 1982); and Cynthia Orozco, "Chicana Labor History: A Critique of Male Consciousness in Historical Writing," *La Red* 77 (February, 1984); and Acuña's sexist and paternalistic response, Rudy Acuña, "Letter to the Editor," *La Red* 79 (April, 1984).

8. Chicano Coordinating Council on Higher Education, *El Plan de Santa Barbara: A Chicano Plan for Higher Education* (Oakland: La Causa Publications, 1969).

9. Mary Pardo, "A Selective Evaluation of El Plan de Santa Barbara," *La Gente* (March/April, 1984):14-15. While it could be argued that the feminist movement in the United States was still at an incipient stage in 1969, recent Chicano studies documents and activities continue to reflect limited consciousness.

10. The fundamental base, Chicana history, has only recently been promoted by some Chicano studies centers. The product of the first symposium on Chicana history is forthcoming; see *Women's History in Transition: Content, Theory, and Method in Chicana/Mexicana History,* ed. Adelaida R. del Castillo (Los Angeles: Chicano Studies Research Center Publications, 1985).

11. Chicano studies must be recognized not only as centers for the production of Chicano ideology, but as workplaces. Female teachers and clerical workers have confronted sex segregation, sexual harassment, and the lack of recognition for their work. Anna Nieto Gómez has become the symbol of the female struggle in Chicana studies as an idealogue and as a worker; she was ousted by the Chicano studies program at California State University at Northridge.

12. See California State University at Los Angeles, Mecha, "Chicano Studies Accused of Fostering Male Chauvinism," in Moreno, *La mujer*, p. 22; and Mujeres en Marcha, *Chicanas in the 80's: Unsettled Issues* (Berkeley: Chicano Studies Library Publications Unit, 1983) for a recent critique. Of more than 500 individuals listed, Julio Martinez's reference work on Chicano scholars listed only 97 women. The National Chicano Council on Higher Education listed 38 women out of 144 members in 1982 (Julio Martínez, *Chicano Scholars and Writers: A Bio-Bibliographical Directory* (Metuchen, N.J.: Scarecrow, 1979); Richard Chabran, "Chicana Reference Sources," *La Gente* (February/March, 1984):18-19; National Chicano Council on Higher Education List of Members, 1982).

13. Chicana feminists made early attempts to delineate Chicana studies but lacked the positions of center directors and professorships to disseminate and distribute curriculum. A rationale, course proposals, outlines, and a bibliography on Chicana history, sociology, literature, and higher education can be found in *New Directions in Education, Estudios Femeniles de la Chicana*, ed. Anna Nieto Gómez (Los Angeles: UCLA Extension and Montal Educational Associates, 1974); and Odalmira L. García, *Chicana Studies Curriculum Guide, Grades 9-12* (Austin: National Educational Laboratory Publishers, 1978). For a summary of recent literature, see Cordelia Candelaria, "Six Reference Works on Mexican American Women: A Review Essay," *Frontiers*, 5/2 (1980):75-80.

14. *Women, Culture, and Society*, ed. Michelle Zimbalist Rosaldo and Louise Lamphere (Stanford: Stanford University Press, 1974); *Towards an Anthropology of Women*, ed. Rayna Reiter (New York: Monthly Review Press, 1975); Heidi Hart-

man, "Capitalism, Patriarchy, and Job Segregation by Sex," *Signs: Journal of Women in Culture and Society*, 1/3 (Spring, 1976), part 2:137-169.

15. Joan Kelly-Gadol, "The Social Relations of the Sexes: Methodological Implications of Women's History," *Signs*, 1/4 (Summer, 1976):809-824; Nancy Chodorow, *The Reproduction of Mothering: Psychoanalysis and the Sociology of Gender* (Berkeley: University of California Press, 1978).

16. *Capitalist Patriarchy and the Case of Socialist Feminism*, ed. Zillah R. Eisenstein (New York: Monthly Review Press, 1979).

17. Susan Brownmiller, *Femininity* (New York: Linden Press/Simon and Schuster, 1984).

18. Catharine A. MacKinnon, "Feminism, Marxism, Method, and the State: An Agenda for Theory," *Signs*, 7/3 (Spring, 1982):515-544. See also Cynthia Orozco, "Crónica Feminista," *La Gente* (February/March, 1983):8.

19. Current issues on Chicanas and higher education can be found in the Stanford newsletter *Intercambios Femeniles*. Pioneer Chicana feminists raised the issues facing Chicanas and their access to education. See Corinne Sánchez, "Higher Education y la Chicana?" and Anna Nieto Gómez de Lazarín, "The Chicana—Perspectives for Education," *Encuentro Femenil*, 1/1 (September, 1973): 27-33, 35-61.

20. Chicano Coordinating Council on Higher Education, "Manifesto," *El Plan de Santa Barbara*, pp. 9-11.

Studying Chicanas: Bringing Women into the Frame of Chicano Studies

Alma M. GARCÍA

Acknowledgments: I would like to thank the following individuals for their helpful comments and criticism: Richard A. García, Ramon D. Chacón, and Christine M. Sierra.

Chicano scholars have yet to critique Chicano studies systematically as a discipline in and of itself. Questions concerning the nature, scope, and parameters of Chicano studies are crucial to this endeavor. Accordingly, a discussion of Chicano studies as a discipline requires an examination of the discipline's past analysis of Chicanas as women. Indeed, dialogue concerning the integration of women into Chicano studies can serve as a starting point for a systematic and critical assessment of the discipline.

Various approaches have been provided by both Chicano and Chicana academics to examine Chicanas in American society. The focus of this paper is to outline these approaches, assess their strengths and weaknesses, and provide suggestions for scholars engaged in Chicano studies concerning the study of Chicanas.

A growing body of literature focusing on the historical and contemporary experience of Chicanas reflects the concern that Chicanas have been "outside the frame" of investigation and research (Smith, 1977). While Octavio Romano's essay (1968) criticizes the biases and sterotypes within social science views of Chicanos, Maxine Baca Zinn's review essay (1982) accomplishes the same for Chicanas. Baca Zinn first outlines the distorted images of Chicanas that exist in the literature and then critically analyzes the recent scholarship on Chicanas. Underlying Baca Zinn's essay is a strong challenge for Chicana scholars to continue to write and research their own history.

Three major approaches have been developed to bring Chicanas into the frame of Chicano studies. First, Chicanas have been studied from the perspective of "Chicanas as Great Women," a perspective representing a counterpart to the "Great Man" theory in historical investigations. Chicanas have been examined as "Workers" within the context of their participation in a capitalist labor force. Third, Chicanas have been analyzed as "Women," focusing on the dynamics of hierarchical relations between males and females. Each approach attempts to integrate Chicanas into the frame of Chicano studies. Each has its own particular strengths and weaknesses. Without a critical synthesis of these approaches, the study of Chicanas and the integration of women into the frame of Chicano studies will remain fragmented.

Chicanas as Great Women

Chicanas as a topic for research have been "elusive beings" (Cotera, 1976:1). To correct the error of omission, attempts have been made to bring Chicanas back into history. A pattern has thus emerged of providing examples of outstanding Mexican women or Chicanas who were then included in the historical record (Cotera, 1976; Blanco, 1977; Del Castillo, 1977; Sweeney, 1977; Mirandé and Enríquez, 1979; Gallegos y Chávez, 1980; Gonzales, 1980; Zamora, 1980; Elsasser, MacKenzie, and Tixier y Vigil, 1980). As with its counterpart—the "Great Man" theory of history—this approach views history as an unfolding story of great individuals who shape and influence the course of history.

This perspective challenges the stereotypes of Chicanas as passive, docile, and submissive. Herein lies both the strength and the weakness of such a framework. On the one hand, a focus of individual Chicanas, either contemporary or from Mexican or Chicano history, dispels damaging and distorting images of Chicanas. Such a focus also provides a window into history. An examination of these women in Chicano history represents a starting point for revising a history that has largely ignored women. In addition, a perspective that documents the struggles and resistance activities of individual Chicanas provides Chicana students with positive role models through the use of such biographical histories. Inclusion of such individuals is, therefore, a major contribution to the integration of women into Chicano studies.

The "Chicanas as Great Women" approach, nevertheless, falls into two traps. Such accounts often remain at a basically descriptive level, lacking a theoretical framework with which to analyze the specific experiences of such women. More importantly, however, this approach fails to analyze the lives of the majority of Mexican women or Chicanas who were the contemporaries of such individuals. The social conditions that affected the masses of Chicanas as such receive very little attention, if any. As one undergraduate student asked after reading an article that used such an approach: "What were all the other women doing?" An analysis of these "other women" and the social worlds within which they lived has led to a second perspective attempting to integrate women into Chicano studies: "Chicanas as Workers."

Chicanas As Workers

One of the major areas of research that has contributed to the growing literature on Chicanas focuses on their labor force participation. Historical studies of the development of Chicano communities contain sections dealing with the incorporation of Chicanas into the paid labor force (Barrera, 1979; Griswold del Castillo, 1979; Camarillo, 1979; García, 1981; Romo, 1983). Issues underlying this research include: (1) the social conditions influencing the entry of Chicanas into the paid labor force; (2) the occupational distribution of Chicana workers; (3) the structure, process, and maintenance of a dual labor market; and (4) labor agitation and strike activities organized by Chicanas. Researchers thus continue to revise Chicano history by including the labor force activities of Chicanas. The "Chicanas as Workers" approach sets out to "present the history of the Chicana and the Chicano in light of the capitalist development that permeated the United States and the world" (Apodaca, 1977:88).

Historical investigations of the capitalist development in the Southwest all reveal general patterns characterizing the labor force participation of Chicana workers (Barrera, 1979; Camarillo, 1979; García, 1981; Griswold del Castillo, 1979; Romo, 1983). Chicanas became concentrated within certain occupations and industries, occupying positions as unskilled and semiskilled workers. As domestics, laundresses, and cannery, garment, and agricultural workers, Chicanas made "significant contributions to the growth of a Chicano working class" (García, 1980*a*:315).

The "Chicanas as Workers" approach provides an insightful and valuable contribution to the study of Chicanas. By focusing on a specific social class of women, this approach goes beyond the "Chicanas as Great Women" approach. Its strength lies in tracing the experiences of Chicanas within the capitalist economy, specifically, the occupational hierarchy. Moreover, it delineates the historical patterns of structural constraints that have operated to keep both Chicanas and Chicanos at the lowest levels of the stratification system. The social world of Chicanas is therefore reconstructed from such a historical perspective.

While these historical studies have provided data on Chicana workers, they have done so largely within an analytic framework that focuses on the male labor force. Although attention is paid to the female labor force, the primary thrust of such investigations involves the Chicano working class. In an attempt to fill this gap, several studies have specifically investigated the historical labor force experiences of Mexican women in the United States (García, 1980*a*; García, 1983). Moreover, studies concentrating on the contemporary labor force participation of Chicanas continue (Arroyo, 1973; Cooney, 1975; Sánchez, 1977; González, n.d.; Berstein et al., 1980; Coyle et al., 1980; Monroy, 1980; Mindiola, 1981).

In general, researchers using the "Chicanas as Workers" perspective have attempted to go beyond the largely descriptive works on Chicanas. Some have focused exclusively on building theoretical models to explain the economic roots of Chicana exploitation (Apodaca, 1977). While ground-breaking, the "Chicanas as Workers" approach also suffers some limitations. This type of analysis brings Chicanas back into the frame of history, but only to the extent that they have become wage earners. Those Chicanas who have not entered into the paid labor force, therefore, continue to reside outside this frame. Oakley (1974:ix) states that "the work of women (housewives) has received very little serious sociological or historical attention. Their unpaid work in the home has scarcely been studied at all." Oakley's assertion applies to the study of Chicanas inasmuch as Chicano studies contain a serious gap concerning the nature of a system of hierarchical relations between the sexes. The third approach, "Chicanas as Women," sets out to fill this gap.

Chicanas as Women

By focusing on Chicana "femaleness," the "Chicanas as Women" perspective begins to formulate a response to the question of gender inequality. A large number of studies examining the conditions and experiences affecting Chicanas as women have concentrated primarily on their role within the family. A substantial body of literature on the Chicano family in general has emerged over the past fifteen years. Less attention, however, has been given to the relation between women's domesticity and gender inequality than to the role of Chicanas as the nurturers of family members within a hostile Anglo society. Challenging the stereotypical view of Chicanas as passive and docile, these studies portray Chicanas as active resisters to the encroachments of Anglo society. Chicanas, as wives and mothers, protect and support family members by providing "warmth, support and affection" (Mirandé and Enríquez, 1979:116).

The literature on the Chicano family has produced evidence, both historical and contemporary, to challenge the distorted social science view of the Chicano family and the role of Chicanas within it (Mirandé, 1977). Nevertheless, many of these studies of the Chicano family are characterized by a fundamental weakness. Much of this research lacks a critical and systematic analysis of male/female relationships within the family. The issue regarding the source of female oppression and inequality within the context of the Chicano family has not been fully examined. This constitutes a major gap in Chicano studies. As one Chicano scholar states in his study of the Mexican immigrant family during the period 1900-1920:

> If the family unit through its cultural and economic support system was the most essential factor in the ability of Mexican immigrants to adjust to life north of the border, at the same time it represented an oppressive condition for women. Women not only maintained and reproduced male workers through their roles as housewives and mothers, but some also had to labor outside the home to supplement family income and in so doing experience a "double day." (García, 1980*b*:129)

Chicana social scientists have recently attempted to go beyond a descriptive study of Chicanas within the Chicano family. They have now started to focus on the sources of gender inequality within the family. Such works highlight the dynamics and patterns of male/female relations as a source of gender inequality and oppression (Baca Zinn, 1975, 1980; Ybarra, 1982; Zavella, 1982). As a result, these efforts have raised the inquiry to a more theoretical and analytic level.

New Chicana researchers as well as black women scholars have drawn on feminist scholarship on gender inequality to explain the societal position of women of color (Zimbalist, Rosaldo,1974). It should be noted, however, that minority women scholars have recognized some limitations inherent in white feminist models of inequality when applied to women of color. Critiques and revisions of the "public versus domestic sphere" model, for example, have developed within the scholarship produced by women of color (Lewis, 1977).

The "Chicanas as Women" perspective goes beyond the cultural interpretation offered to explain the role of Chicanas within the family. The major focus is now on the patterns of male domination within the family. This approach is largely responsible for generating key questions not raised in either of the first two approaches used to integrate women into Chicano studies. The "Chicanas as Great Women" approach tells the story of those Chicanas who served as examples of outstanding women. The "Chicanas as Workers" perspective investigates Chicanas as wage earners in a capitalist economic system. The "Chicanas as Women" approach explains the social location of Chicanas by emphasizing gender as a major explanatory variable. More importantly, such a view calls for a theoretical synthesis of race, class, and gender. The major question raised is no longer which is the greatest source of oppression: race, class, or gender? Rather, the "Chicanas as Women" approach raises a different question: what is the intersection of race, class, and gender in analyzing Chicanas in American society? Although one Chicana scholar reaches the conclusion that "the study of Chicanas must be as far-reaching as the study of all women in society," the view that all three variables are needed in order to locate Chicanas in society remains explicit (Baca Zinn, 1982:272).

Teaching about Chicanas within the discipline of Chicano studies in both a historical and contemporary perspective requires a focus, therefore, on the intersection of the structures of racial subordination, capitalist exploitation, and the hierarchical relations between the sexes. In addition, such structures must be seen as mutually reinforcing and interdependent (Eisenstein, 1979:23). Taken together, then, race, class, and gender form the major axes with which to analyze the experiences and conditions affecting Chicanas in the United States. As such, the integration of women into Chicano studies rests on the continued development of a systematic analysis of the structures of racism, capitalism, and patriarchy.

Towards the Incorporation of Women into Chicano Studies

A major question remains. How can Chicano scholars actively contribute to the incorporation and integration of women into the discipline of Chicano studies? More importantly, what obstacles are blocking such a process of integration and how can they be overcome?

The following are offered as preliminary suggestions. First, "integration" has to be specifically defined. By integration is meant the incorporation of an analysis of Chicanas as an equal and integral part of Chicano studies. That is, such integration requires more than the inclusion of the study of Chicanas as merely a topical addition to a given course. On the contrary, integration rests on the explicit understanding that the discipline of Chicano studies will remain limited without an analysis of women based on the theoretical framework that stresses the intersection of race, class, and gender. For example, a basic element in the Chicano studies curriculum is the introductory course. When and in what manner have Chicanas been discussed within such a survey course? A general trend has been to cover the major topics such as race relations, identity, education, the community, employment, and immigration, and then deal with the topic of "La Chicana." Such a treatment of Chicanas represents a "tacked on" approach. An alternate approach would make the study of women a vital component of this type of course.

Such an integration requires and will ultimately reflect a changing consciousness among all Chicano scholars, male and female. Chicano social scientists need to develop—or, in some cases, continue to develop—a consciousness of Chicanas as women. The shaping of such a consciousness involves the recognition that

Chicanas as women have been largely though not entirely outside the frame of Chicano studies. The development of this changing consciousness will begin to bring Chicanas into the frame of Chicano studies.

A final problem presents itself. Once this study of women—Chicanas—becomes integrated into Chicano studies, the issue of description versus critical analysis will still persist. Any discipline has to define what is essential and then determine how such areas are to be investigated. As indicated in this essay, Chicanas have been included in Chicano studies as "Great Women," and "Workers," and as "Women." Each approach contributes to the overall literature on Chicanas. None, however, can stand alone. Each perspective represents a component of a larger whole. Thus, a synthesis of the three approaches will begin to redefine the social location of Chicanas and, above all, will redefine the study of women within the discipline of Chicano studies.

REFERENCES

Apodaca, Maria Linda. 1977. "The Chicana Woman: An Historical Materialist Perspective." *Latin American Perspectives* 4 (Winter/Spring):70-89.

Arroyo, Laura E. 1973. "Industrial and Occupational Distribution of Chicana Workers." In *Essays on La Mujer*, ed. Rosaura Sánchez and Rosa Martínez Cruz (Los Angeles: University of California, Chicano Studies Center Publications, 1977), pp. 150-187.

Baca Zinn, Maxine. 1975. "Chicanas: Power and Control in the Domestic Sphere." *De Colores* 2/3:19-31.

———. 1980. "Employment and Education of Mexican-American Women: The Interplay of Modernity and Ethnicity in Eight Families." *Harvard Educational Review* 50 (February):47-62.

———. 1982. "Mexican-American Women in the Social Sciences." *Signs: Journal of Women in Culture and Society* 8 (Winter):259-272.

Barrera, Mario. 1979. *Race and Class in the Southwest: A Theory of Racial Inequality* (Notre Dame: University of Notre Dame Press).

Bernstein, Alan, Bob De Grasse, Rachel Grossman, Chris Paine, and Larry Siegel. 1980. "Silicon Valley: Paradise or Paradox?" In *Mexican Women in the United States: Struggles Past, Present, and Future*, ed. Magdalena Mora and Adelaida R. Del Castillo (Los Angeles: University of California, Chicano Studies Center Publications), pp. 105–112.

Blanco, Iris. 1977. "Participacíon de las Mujeres en la Sociedad Prehispanica." In *Essays on La Mujer*, ed. Rosaura Sánchez and Rosa Martínez Cruz (Los Angeles: University of California, Chicano Studies Center Publications), pp. 48-81.

Camarillo, Albert. 1979. *Chicanos in a Changing Society: From Mexican Pueblos to American Barrios, in Santa Barbara, and Southern California, 1848-1930* (Cambridge, Mass.: Harvard University).

Cooney, Rosemary Santora. 1975. "Changing Labor Force Participation of Mexican Wives: A Comparison with Anglos and Blacks." *Social Science Quarterly* 56 (September):252-261.

Cotera, Marta P. 1976. *Diosa y Hembra: The History and Heritage of Chicanas in the U.S.* (Austin: Information Systems Development).

Coyle, Laurie, Gayle Hershatter, and Emily Honing. 1980. "Women at Farah: An Unfinished Story." In *Mexican Women in the United States: Struggles Past, Present, and Future*, ed. Magdalena Mora and Adelaida R. Del Castillo (Los Angeles: University of California, Chicano Studies Center Publications), pp. 117-199.

Del Castillo, Adelaida. 1977. "Malintzin Tenipal: A Preliminary Look into a New Perspective." In *Essays on La Mujer*, ed. Rosaura Sánchez and Rosa Martínez Cruz (Los Angeles: University of California, Chicano Studies Center Publications), pp. 129-149.

Eisenstein, Zillah R. 1979. "Developing a Theory of Capitalist Patriarchy and Socialist Feminism." In *Capitalist Patriarchy and the Case for Socialist Feminism*, ed. Zillah R. Eisenstein (New York: Monthly Review Press), pp. 5-90.

Elsasser, Nan, Kyle MacKenzie, and Yvonne Tixier y Vigil. 1980. *Las Mujeres: Conversations from a Hispanic Community* (Old Westbury, N.Y.: Feminist Press).

Gallegos y Chávez, Ester. 1980. "The Northern New Mexican Woman: A Changing Silhouette." In *The Chicano*, ed. Arnulfo D. Trejo (Tucson: University of Arizona Press), pp. 67-79.

García, Mario T. 1980*a*. "The Chicana in American History: The Mexican Women of El Paso 1880-1920—A Case Study." *Pacific Historical Review* 58 (May):315-337.

______. 1980*b*. "La Familia: The Mexican Immigrant Family, 1900-1930." In *Work, Family, Sex Roles, Language*, ed. Mario Barrera, Albert Camarillo, and Francisco Hernandez (Berkeley: Tonatiuh-Quinto Sol), pp. 117-139.

______. 1981. *Desert Immigrants, The Mexicans of El Paso 1890-1920* (New Haven: Yale University Press).

García, Richard A. 1983. "Mexican Women in San Antonio: A View of Three Worlds 1929-1941." Unpublished paper delivered at the Organization of American Historians, Pacific Coast Meetings.

Gonzales, Sylvia Alicia. 1980. "The Chicana Perspective: A Design for Self-Awareness." In *The Chicanos*, ed. Arnulfo D. Trejo (Tucson: University of Arizona Press), pp. 81-99.

González, Rosalinda M. 1976. "A Review of the Literature on Mexican-American Women Workers in U.S. Southwest 1900-75." Unpublished paper, Berkeley: University of California Chicano Studies Library.

Griswold del Castillo, Richard. 1979. *The Los Angeles Barrio, 1800-1890* (Berkley and Los Angeles: University of California Press).

Lewis, Diane K. 1977. "A Response to Inequality: Black Women, Racism, and Sexism." *Signs: Journal of Women in Culture and Society* 3 (Winter):339-361.

Mindiola, Tatcho. 1981. "The Cost of Being a Mexican Female Worker in the 1970 Houston Labor Market." *Aztlán* (Fall):231-247.

Mirandé, Alfredo. 1977. "The Chicano Family: A Reanalysis of Conflicting Views." *Journal of Marriage and the Family* 39 (November):747-756.

Mirandé, Alfredo and Evangelina Enríquez. 1979. *La Chicana: The Mexican-American Woman* (Chicago: University of Chicago Press).

Monroy, Douglas. 1980. "La Costura en Los Angeles, 1933-1939: The ILGWU and the Politics of Domination." In *Mexican Women in the United States: Struggles Past, Present, and Future,* ed. Magdalena Mora and Adelaida R. Del Castillo. (Los Angeles: University of California, Chicano Studies Center Publications), pp. 171-178.

Oakley, Ann. 1974. *Woman's Work: The Housewife, Past and Present* (New York: Vintage Books).

Romano-V, Octavio I. 1968. "The Anthropology and Sociology of the Mexican-Americans," *El Grito* 2 (Fall):13-26.

Romo, Ricardo. 1983. *East Los Angeles: History of a Barrio* (Austin: University of Texas Press).

Sánchez, Rosaura. 1977. "The Chicana Labor Force." In *Essays on La Mujer*, ed. Rosaura Sánchez and Rosa Martínez Cruz (Los Angeles: University of California, Chicano Studies Center Publications), pp. 3-15.

Smith, Dorothy. 1977. "Some Implications of a Sociology for Women." In *Woman in a Man-Made World*, 2nd ed., ed. Nona Glazer and Helen Youngelson Waehrer (Chicago: Rand McNally), pp. 15-29.

Sweeney, Judith. 1977. "Chicana History: A Review of the Literature." In *Essays on La Mujer*, ed. Rosaura Sánchez and Rosa Martínez Cruz (Los Angeles: University of California, Chicano Studies Center Publications), pp. 99-123.

Ybarra, Lea. 1982. "When Wives Work: The Impact on the Chicano Family." *Journal of Marriage and the Family* 44 (February):169-178.

Zamora, Emilio. 1980. "Sara Estela Ramirez: Una Rosa Roja en el Movimiento." In *Mexican Women in the United States: Struggles Past, Present, and Future*, ed.

Magdalena Mora and Adelaida R. Del Castillo (Los Angeles: University of California, Chicano Studies Center Publications), pp. 163-169.

Zavella, Patricia. 1982. "Women—Work and Family in the Chicano Community: Cannery Workers of the Santa Clara Valley" (Ph.D., University of California at Berkeley).

Zimbalist Rosaldo, Michelle. 1974. "Woman, Culture, and Society: A Theoretical Overview." In *Woman, Culture, and Society*, ed. Michelle Zimbalist Rosaldo and Louise Lamphere (Stanford: Stanford University Press), pp. 17-42.

Manuela Solis Sager and Emma Tenayuca: A Tribute

Roberto R. CALDERÓN and Emilio ZAMORA

Acknowledgments: We wish to acknowledge the valuable assistance of Leticia Lopez, Oscar Marti, and Maria Ortiz. We also appreciate the support by the Chicano Studies Research Center, UCLA, the sponsor of this effort. We also are grateful to Manuela Solis Sager and Emma B. Tenayuca for sharing with us those distant yet inspiring moments in the struggle.

One of the most memorable highlights of the annual conferences of the National Association for Chicano Studies (NACS) has been the formal recognition of such scholars as Américo Paredes, Ernesto Galarza, Carey McWilliams, and Julian Samora. In recognizing and honoring the accomplishments and contributions of such men, NACS has also paid tribute to the purpose and will that guided their scholarly and political contributions to Mexican people.

The 1984 NACS conference extended this tradition by honoring Manuela Solis Sager and Emma Tenayuca, labor activists who organized and led Mexican workers' movements in Texas during the 1930s.[1] As such, NACS emphasized the key role of women in our history of struggle and underscored the need actively and effectively to acknowledge this fact in our classrooms and in our research. This emphasis was possible due to the daring commitment and unswerving dedication that Solis Sager and Tenayuca demonstrated to our community of Mexican workers. They were also the first women to be thus honored and recognized by NACS since its inception twelve years ago.

Manuela's and Emma's intellectual formation was tied to important developments that the Mexican community of South Texas shared with other communities in the Southwest and with the greater societies of Mexico and the United States. Their families nurtured the pride, love, and concern that conditioned their specific experiences as individuals and as Mexicans during the early decades of this century. This is evident when they speak.

Both Solis Sager and Tenayuca credit their relatives for inspiring in their minds and sensibilities the ideas and concerns they would later elaborate on behalf of the Mexican worker in Texas. Moreover, self-help, cooperative, and protest activity in Mexican communities influenced the cultural milieu and political environment around them. Political and cultural experiences with Mexico and conditions of discrimination and inequality in the United States reinforced a national and working-class identity which they shared. Their memories are clear on this.

A short note on the conditions that gave rise to Mexican labor activity during the 1930s is in order. The first three decades of the twentieth century registered the dramatic rise and urbanization of the Mexican population, in part the result of immigration from Mexico. By 1930, approximately 40 percent of the total Mexican population lived in Texas and 30 percent in California.

The significant expansion of the U.S. national economy, particularly evident in the industrial development of the Southwest, stimulated this growth and concentration. Discrimination against Mexican workers, however, denied them fair wages and occupations other than laborers. The following illustrates this structural condition in 1930: 41 percent of the Mexican work force labored in agriculture; 11 percent in transportation; 3 percent in mining; 23 percent in manufacturing; and 10 percent in domestic and personal service. That is, 88 percent of all Mexican workers in the United States were employed in these low-paying and low-status occupations.

The participation of Mexican women in the wage labor ranks increased noticeably. Yet, they generally assumed even lower-paying, segregated positions that represented extensions of housework. In 1930, 20 percent of Mexicana workers were farm laborers; 45 percent were domestic and personal service workers; about 5 percent were saleswomen; and the remainder worked in textiles, food processing, and packing industries.

As in earlier periods, opposition to discrimination and inequality gave rise to increased labor organizing and strike activity among Mexicans throughout the United States. Independent Mexican workers' organizations sought affiliation with national labor unions. They were welcomed by the more progressive labor federations such as the Workers' Alliance of America and the United Cannery, Agricultural, Packing, and Allied Workers of America (UCAPAWA). Although precise Mexican membership figures are not yet available, Mexican participation in these progressive labor groups registered more significant increases than in the American Federation of Labor (AFL). Consequently, Mexican workers' organizations were prominent in the important political challenge led by the Congress of Industrial Organizations (CIO) against the exclusive, craft-oriented AFL. Significantly, the Mexican labor movement of the 1930s was also characterized as never before by increased numbers of Mexicana workers. Women such as Manuela and Emma assumed key leadership positions in this historic struggle.

Manuela's long history as an activist began in Laredo during 1932 and 1933, when she helped organize unions and strikes among garment and agricultural workers. By 1934, she had attracted the respect and admiration of fellow agricultural workers sufficiently to be awarded by Asociacion de Jornaleros a year-long scholarship to attend a highly respected leftist labor school in Mexico City, the Universidad Obrera. Upon her return to Laredo, she joined her husband, James Sager, and other Laredo unionists in consolidating local efforts into a statewide Mexican Labor movement. This resulted in a statewide conference held in 1935 at Corpus Christi that attracted delegates representing numerous Mexican community organizations including labor unions and other community collectivities.

The Corpus Christi conference established the South Texas Agricultural Workers' Union (STAWU), which was to coordinate organizing work among Mexican workers, particularly field and packing shed workers. Manuela and James were appointed official organizers for the STAWU. The decision by the STAWU to assign Manuela and James to organize in the Rio Grande Valley indicates the respect their ability and dedication had earned. The area was known as one of the most difficult places to organize, principally because of strong anti-Mexican and anti-uinion sentiments held by growers, packing shed owners, and law enforcement officials.

Despite strong opposition that included violent union busting tactics, Manuela and James managed to assist workers in organizing several Mexican unions with a total membership of over 1,000 field and packing shed workers. Recalcitrant bosses, however, made it almost impossible to translate labor organizing success into gains at the workplace. Manuela and James, having considered the situation, decided to join other organizers from throughout the state at San Antonio, where the possibility of realizing a major Mexican labor victory seemed tenable.

Manuela and James became an integral part of a veritable labor upheaval among Mexican pecan shellers, the majority of whom were women. They immediately joined ranks with union members and popular, effective leaders, such as Emma Tenayuca, with whom they had maintained direct communication since the early 1930s. Since Emma was so intimately tied to these early labor movements, it is impossible to speak about one without the other.

Emma joined the labor movement at the age of sixteen when she read about the 1932 and 1933 strikes against the Finck Cigar Company of San Antonio. She walked the picket line and subsequently joined the strikers in jail. During 1934 and 1935, Emma was also prominent in the formation of two locals of the International Ladies' Garment Workers Union. By 1937, she had become a member of the Executive Committee of the Workers' Alliance of America, a national federation of unemployed workers' organizations. She had also assumed the position of general secretary of at least ten Alliance chapters in San Antonio. Many of the Alliance members were affiliated with local unions of cigar, garment, and pecan shelling workers.

When at the end of January, 1938, approximately 2,000 pecan shelling workers decided to strike against the local industry, they asked Emma to act as their strike representative. As a result, her participation increased and her popularity soared to the extent that by the time Manuela and James arrived in San Antonio, Emma had become one of the most respected and dedicated unionists in San Antonio. It was at this time that she earned the name of "La Pasionaria."

Strikers were teargassed on at least six occasions, as about 150 San Antonio city police officers were deployed to prevent the strike from being thoroughly effective. Over a thousand strikers were eventually jailed and sent to both the city and county penal facilities. Trivial and even ludicrous charges such as obstructing the sidewalk were trumped up to arrest strikers. Repression and intimidation were intended to instill fear in pecan shelling workers and thus keep them from joining in the work stoppage. These tactics were only partly successful. From six to eight thousand pecan shellers, most of them women, did heed the strike call. Soup kitchens were established, and thousands received their meals there. The Texas Women's International League for Peace and Freedom assisted in the operation of the soup kitchens and extended additional help in other areas. Had it not been for threats hanging over their head, numerous Mexican-owned and-operated business also would probably have offered significant assistance. City politics allegedly promised they would find cause to shut down establishments known to render assistance to the strikers.

The Texas Industrial Commission began a series of hearings into the strikers' grievances. The governor of the state intervened and attempted to persuade the pecan shelling industry to arbitrate. The industry finally joined the bargaining table and agreed on a settlement that ostensibly favored the workers' demands.

The strike, while restoring wages to pre-strike levels, saw its nominal gains whittled away a few months later when the industry remechanized.[2] Thousands of pecan shellers were displaced, and only about a thousand youthful employees were retained in the city's entire pecan shelling industry. In the meantime, just as the Depression seemed to be easing up on Mexican workers, war loomed large on the horizon, spelling a hiatus for Mexican participation in the Texas labor movement.

The leadership and membership of the strike and pecan shellers' unions consisted mainly of women. The Comisión Pro-Conferencia had three members, two of them women, Manuela Solis Sager and Juana Sanchez. And two of the three members of the Strike Committee were women, Emma Tenayuca and Minnie Rendón. Thus, four out of six major strike leaders were women in the front lines working directly with the rank and file.

After the victorious strike and abrogated settlement, both Emma and Manuela maintained a political course that awaits a more deliberate and detailed examination than this short note can accommodate. Some observations, however, should be made. In 1939, Emma assumed the position of chair of the Texas Communist Party. In the same year she also co-authored what is still the most lucid and accurate analysis of Mexican people ever produced by a Communist party representative. Her effectiveness and popularity as a Mexicana labor leader often made her the focal point of anti-union and anti-Mexican hysteria, which eventually forced her to leave Texas to ensure her safety and economic well-being. Years later, she returned to San Antonio as a certified teacher and taught until her recent retirement. She still substitutes as a teacher occasionally.

Manuela, on the other hand, remained with her husband in San Antonio, where she has continued her involvement in progressive causes related to the Chicano movement, the women's movement, immigrant rights, electoral politics, and opposition to U.S. interventionist foreign policy. She has received numerous awards of recognition, including the one that she and Emma received from the National Association for Chicano Studies.

Both women are an inspiration and no doubt will continue to provide examples of courage, dedication, and purpose. As Mexicans, their history of involvement and accomplishment underscores the struggle and the search for justice and equality among our people. Upon listening to Manuela's and Emma's presentations, the NACS conference participants enthusiastically upheld two things. On the one hand, they made evident the still vital example established by Manuela and Emma, and, on the other hand, they confirmed the wisdom in honoring them. The following is the text of the presentations they made during the 1984 NACS conference.

Manuela Solis Sager

Voy a leerles algo en español porque me parece que es la lengua mía y quisiera dejar un mensaje a ustedes y les voy a tener que leer porque estoy muy nerviosa y *excited* con todo esto.

"El mensaje que debemos dejar con los educadores es muy simple. Al investigar la clase obrera mexicana hay que estudiarnos como lo que somos, *obreros*, y al estudiar a los obreros hay que entender nuestras luchas contra el imperialismo, nuestras luchas contra las industrias, nuestras luchas contra las universidades y en las áreas agrícolas. Pero al estudiar también hay que participar en esas luchas—no se debe estudiarlas solamente."

Fuera con Reagan en el '84! Abajo con la intervención imperialista en Centroamérica! Y empleos para todos nosotros y paz.

Manuela Solis Sager, 1937, photo taken during organizing efforts for UCAPAWA in the Harlingen, Texas area, courtesy of M.S. Sager.

También quiero decirle algo a la mujer mexicana y a la mujer en general. Esto no lo escribí, lo estoy diciendo de mi corazón. Esto quiero decirles a ustedes—que así como nosotros luchamos, ustedes tienen que seguir esta lucha y seguir adelante y ayudarnos porque nosotros....Yo ya tengo, voy a cumplir 73 años el 29 de abril y estoy en la lucha desde hace más de cincuenta años y quisiera que cada uno do nosotros, siguiéramos adelante sobre ese mismo tema y ayudar a la clase trabajodora, a las luchas del pueblo trabajador!

Emma Tenayuca, 1937, photo taken at Bexar County Jail after an arrest for protesting worker cuts in the rolls of the Works Progress Administration, courtesy of E. Tenayuca and Tom Shelton.

Emma Tenayuca

The first thing I would like to do is thank you very, very much. During the thirties when I was working in San Antonio I never attached any importance to my work. I never kept newspaper clippings. Actually, I was too busy organizing and working.

I was born in San Antonio, and on my mother's side of the family I am a descendant of Spaniards who came to Texas and settled in one of the colonies on the Louisiana border. There was a mission established there. On my father's side, we never claimed anything but Indian blood, and so throughout my life I didn't have a fashionable Spanish name like García or Sánchez, I carried an Indian name. And I was very, very conscious of that. It was this historical background and my grandparents' attitude which formed my ideas and actually gave me the courage later to undertake the type of work I did in San Antonio. I had wonderful parents and wonderful grandparents.

I remember since I was about five watching the Battle of Flowers parade in front of Santa Rosa Hospital, right in front of the Plaza del Zacate. I also remember, and I was quite young, the election of Ma Ferguson. Here was the occasion for quite a discussion in my family between my grandfather and my mother's uncles. My father had voted for Jim Ferguson, even though Ferguson had been forced out or impeached for having taken some money from the University of Texas. My parents, my grandfather, and his family voted for Ma Ferguson and the reason for that was because she had stood up against the Ku Klux Klan in Texas.

I have a vision right now, a memory comes back to me of hooded figures. I also remember one particular circular, and it read "one hundred percent White Protestant Americans." That left me out. I was a Catholic and also I was a Mestiza, a mixture of Indian and Spanish. During the time I was growing up, it was very difficult to ignore the conditions in San Antonio. Ours was a close-knit family, and I didn't remember any discrimination, actually, until I started school. A lot of people found out that it was hard to push me around. But during the time that I was growing up here in San Antonio, my home, I had deep roots there and I felt a strong attachment with the past. I went to the mission when I was quite young. I remember we used to hold confessions on the eighth of December, which is the day of Our Immaculate Conception. I remember kicking up the dust and discovering my first Indian arrow, and that of course excited my imagination. My father taught me to fish in the San Antonio River, and it was that river that almost brought about my drowning. I was pulled out of that river with water rushing out of my nose and my mouth. I never learned to swim after that.

I witnessed a lot of discussion on topics such as Carranza and the Cristero Movement. I could not help but be impressed by the discussions inside of my family, my family circle. Also, the Plaza del Zacate was the type of place where everyone went on Saturdays and Sundays to hold discussions. If you went there you could find a minister preaching. You could also find revolutionists from Mexico holding discussions. I was exposed to all of this. I was also exposed to the nature of politics and to the form of corruption. I have mentioned this to some of you whom I know. I remember as a youngster attending a political rally with my father. Sandwiches were distributed and inside the sandwich was a five-dollar bill. I didn't get one, neither did my father. I would like you to know that.

Let me give you an idea of what it meant to be a Mexican in San Antonio. There were no bus drivers that were Mexicans when I was growing up. The only Mexican workers employed by the City Public Service and the Water Board were laborers, ditch diggers. I remember they used to take the leaves from the pecan trees and they would put them on their heads in order to go out and dig ditches. I came into contact with many, many families who had grievances, who had not been paid. I was perhaps eight or nine years old at the time. On one occasion while at the Plaza with my grandfather there was a family of poor migrant workers who came and a collection was made for them. I learned that while the family had harvested a crop, the farm owner who lived somewhere in the Rio Grande Valley had awakened the family at two or three in the morning, and he and his son ran the family from the land with shotguns. I remember this discussion at the Plaza on a Saturday and they decided to go down to the Mexican Consul and place charges against the farmer. People from the Plaza accompanied the family to the Mexican Consul. It turned out that the family was Texas-born. This made quite an impression on me as a seventeen-year-old, a recent graduate from high school.

One of the first groups of organized workers that I remember were women and it is with them that we saw the beginning of the breakup of the type of political organization that existed in San Antonio. And I saw those women herded and taken to jail. The second time that happened, I went to jail with them. These were the Finck Cigar workers on strike. In both the Finck Cigar and pecan shelling strikes there was a desire to keep the Mexican population, the Mexican workers, as a reserve labor pool which could be used in case of strikes. There was poverty everywhere.

My city enjoyed the dubious reputation of having one of the highest tuberculosis rates in the country. My San Antonio also had the reputation of having one of the highest infant mortality rates. It was these things and also the fact that I had a grandfather who lost his money when the banks were closed in 1932 that made a deep impression on me. I think it was the combination of being a Texan, being a Mexican, and being more Indian than Spanish that propelled me to take action. I don't think I ever thought in terms of fear. If I had, I think I would have stayed home.

We had demonstrations of 10,000 unemployed workers demanding employment. We visited the mayor's office. We staged a strike at City Hall, and it was there that I was arrested. I went to jail many times. A nun friend used to write to me and tell me, "Emma, I have to read the papers to see whether you are in or out of jail."

I believe that what was done there and what had to be done was confronting the power structure. It was the struggles of the Workers' Alliance, the bringing in the people of mutual aid organizations, some of whom had been anarchists. I read all about the Wobblies and in my mind I also became an anarchist.

I had the idea of actually beginning with the Finck Cigar strike, of actually attacking the power structure, but at the same time doing it in such a manner that we did not get beaten up. We didn't go to jail too often you see. It was much easier for twenty or thirty of us to go to jail for three days or seventy-two hours. It was easier doing that than to fight. And we had many demonstrations in San Antonio. We have now a COPS (Citizens Organized for Public Service) organization, and I assure you that it is one of the most democratic and progressive organizations. And a very active organization too.

So in giving thanks I am thinking of the Finck Cigar strikers. I'm also thinking of the garment workers who went to jail and whose strikes were broken. I'm thinking also of men such as Maury Maverick, Sr., of San Antonio. I'm also thinking of the then Texas assistant attorney general, Everett Looney, who came to San Antonio and defended me on a charge of inciting to riot and therefore I was able to spend my twentieth, twenty-first, and twenty-third birthdays out of jail. I thank you very much.

NOTES

1. The NACS conference program honoring Manuela and Emma was sponsored by the Chicano Studies Research Center and organized by the authors of this note. The accompanying reception was sponsored by the Center for Mexican American Studies, The University of Texas, Austin, and the Mexican American Chamber of Commerce, Austin, Texas. The program included a slide presentation on the condition of Mexican workers and the history of Mexican labor activity in Texas during the 1930s as well as introductory remarks by Calderón and Zamora. The slide presentation and accompanying materials have been deposited at the Chicano Studies Research Library, UCLA, for public use.

2. Prior to the beginning of the Depression in the early 1930s, the San Antonio pecan shelling industry had been mechanized. But the Depression made hand labor more profitable than mechanical labor during most of the 1930s.

Part II. Labor and Politics

Introduction

Of fundamentai importance in the new scholarship on women is the delineation of patterns of power and inequality based on gender. The problem of power and its attendant inequalities, of course, had engaged Chicana/o scholars for some time. Indeed, Chicano studies scholarship developed from the need to examine systematically patterns of power and inequality that characterized the experiences of Mexicans in the United States. Whereas, the dynamics of race and class have received the most attention, Chicana/o scholars are increasingly addressing the question of gender.

The following four articles elucidate how power and inequality take form in the experiences of women of color. The authors present a compelling picture of the forces of domination, division, resistance, and solidarity that permeate the lives and struggles of Mexican women. The articles focus on Chicana workers in the United States and Mexicana workers in the border areas and interior of Mexico. Also depicted are diverse struggles for power, among maquiladora workers on their shop floor and among *mujeres* involved in a national campaign for the presidency of Mexico.

To be sure, Mexican women are examined in different contexts. However, despite differences among the case studies, these papers reveal parallels and interconnections that exist in the work and political experiences of Mexican women on both sides of the U.S.-Mexico border. Indeed, these articles raise numerous questions concerning power and inequality, labor and politics, that hold implications for women of color across the world.

In the first article, Denise Segura, from the University of California, Berkeley, focuses on the Chicana population in the U.S. labor market to outline new directions for research. Segura explains how scholarship from several major fields has failed to address the particular experiences of women of color. Her central concern is with the concept of "triple oppression" and its delineation. Utilizing this notion, she outlines approaches for integrating the factors of class, race, and gender in work on Chicanas. A brief demographic analysis of Chicana labor force participation in recent years serves well to illustrate her arguments. Her call for more empirical study of the Chicana experience is a challenge that must be heeded.

Marta Lopez-Garza, from the University of California, Los Angeles, explores the complexity of women's work in developing countries through a case study of Mexico. Like Segura, she questions the adequacy of social science assumptions and constructs in accounting for women's experiences.

Her study illustrates the great extent to which women in urban Mexico are "economically active," despite academic studies and government pronouncements that contend otherwise. She calls attention to the myriad of activities women perform as "informal" labor. As she argues, there is a "genuine need to reconceptualize" what constitutes employment or economic activity in light of women's work in the informal labor sector. She suggests that additional considerations, such as sexual, class, and age divisions of labor, must enter analyses of women's labor force activity. In the end, Lopez-Garza reminds us how social science is "intrinsically entrenched politically," in this case, how inadequate data can promote the interests of government and capital over those of women workers.

With Devon Peña's article, analysis proceeds to the international economic system and the location of female labor within it. Peña, from Colorado College, focuses on one "transnational, cross-cultural labor process," the Mexican maquiladora or twin plant, to depict a system of capitalist controls over workers. Largely through his own primary research in Ciudad Juárez (Mexico), Peña reveals how capital fuses "Fordist principles" of production with patriarchal forms of control to subordinate its female labor force. The use of male supervisors and sexual harassment of women workers are only two of the elements in the patriarchal system of manipulation.

Importantly, Peña also tells the "other side of the story," that is, the ways in which maquila workers resist capital's efforts to control them. He expounds on this issue more extensively in other work (see Peña, "The Class Politics of Abstract Labor: Organizational Forms and Industrial Relations in the Mexican Maquiladoras," Ph.D. dissertation, University of Texas at Austin, 1983). But this article also describes the "terrains of struggle" for maquila workers on the shop floor and in their communities.

Teresa Carrillo, from Stanford University, develops the theme of women's struggle by focusing on electoral politics in Mexico. Mexican presidential elections paradoxically stir the emotions of the populace yet seldom present unexpected results. Looking beyond voting outcomes, however, Carrillo finds new significance in Mexico's most recent presidential contest.

In her article, Carrillo points to the introduction of a feminist agenda in national presidential politics through the unprecedented campaign of Doña Rosario Ibarra de Piedra. Doña Rosario is the first woman ever to seek the presidency of the Republic. Carrillo explores the significance of Doña Rosario's campaign for party politics of the Left and the women's movement in Mexico.

She notes how class and gender-specific concerns compete uneasily in the framing of electoral strategies for women. The Ibarra campaign impacted upon thousands of working-class and marginalized women, who began to see their concerns as women addressed. However, how the Left was to organize these women, along class lines or gender-specific issues, remained a source of tension among male and female activists. Carrillo concludes that, in spite of these unresolved tensions, women's issues, organization, and participation remain dynamic elements in national politics that will not be ignored.

Although Mexico provides the context for this case study, implications emerge for the forging of feminist politics into national struggles in other countries as well, including class and racial movements in the United States.

Chicanas and Triple Oppression in the Labor Force

Denise A. SEGURA

Acknowledgments: I would like to thank Tomas Almaguer and Beatriz Pesquera for their constructive criticism and support through several drafts of this paper. Also, the helpful comments of Lupe Friaz, Don Mar, and Patricia Zavella are gratefully acknowledged. Finally, this paper benefited greatly from the careful editing and substantive suggestions of Christine M. Sierra and the NACS Editorial Board.

The concept of triple oppression has been used by several feminist and minority scholars to describe the unique class, race, and gender subordination of women of color.[1] Ill-defined and misunderstood, triple oppression is a controversial issue that begs for further analysis. As one critical step in this direction, this essay defines triple oppression and reveals the extent to which it limits the options of Chicanas in the labor force.[2] Implicit in this analysis is the understanding that this essay is written to initiate a dialogue to provide one way for Chicanas to locate the structural limitations they face in order to overcome them.

The major dilemma in defining triple oppression is the complexity of the variables involved. Insofar as class is an economic category, it can be defined according to the common positions of individuals in regard to the social relations of production.[3] Although class provides the base wherein political and social privileges are differentiated, it cannot explain fully the variations in the status and power of different groups in our society. This inadequacy is particularly acute for women and racial/ethnic minorities.

Race, as a social category, exercises an independent influence on the social location of individuals according to a racial hierarchy. Chicanos as a subordinated minority group in the United States historically have been denied political power and relegated to inferior jobs relative to the white population. This racial hierarchy has been manifested economically and legitimized ideologically.[4]

Although class and race bestow and/or limit access to political and economic power, women within each class category and racial/ethnic group are subordinate relative to men. Gender, as a unit of analysis, acknowledges the fact that a specific (and unequal) set of socially prescribed behaviors and expectations has been attached to one's biological sex. The content of the definition of gender expands the options men have—at the expense of women in our society. The pervasiveness of gender inequality transcends class and points to the necessity of incorporating gender into social analyses of women, including Chicanas.

Consideration of any one aspect of the triple oppression of women of color is insufficient to explain the pervasiveness of their social inequality. Triple oppression, then, refers to the interplay among class, race, and gender, whose cumulative effects place women of color in a subordinate social and economic position relative to men of color and the majority white population. The significance of this concept for Chicanas lies in the recognition of their limited options compared to white men and women as well as minority men. Their inferior status is reproduced concurrently in the home and in all other social arenas.

One critical arena where all three aspects of triple oppression intersect is the labor market. The occupational distribution and earnings of Chicanas are important to examine because of their relevance to socioeconomic status and power in our society. The fact that Chicanas historically have been concentrated in low-paying jobs traditionally relegated to women and/or minorities suggests that the triple oppression thesis needs to be considered and developed.

To clarify the necessity of examining this concept with respect to Chicanas, the inadequacy of prevailing explanations of Chicana occupational distribution is discussed, based on research whose focus is the Chicano/a population. Second, relevant analyses of the structure of the labor market are assessed to determine their utility with respect to the Chicana population. Coupled with a brief empirical analysis, these examinations demonstrate the inability of each perspective to account fully for the limits in the range and scope of the occupational distributions and incomes of Chicanas.

It is suggested here that the concept of triple oppression can be useful in the reformulation of each perspective scrutinized. Although this paper is too brief to operationalize this process, suggestions are provided for future research that, if addressed, will expand our data and knowledge of the manner in which triple oppression is realized in the lives of working Chicanas in our society. Furthermore, an understanding of the various manifestations of this interplay will enable us to begin to construct alternatives to bring an end to unequal power relations in society.

To begin our analysis of Chicanas in the labor force, it is necessary briefly to review relevant literature on the subject. To facilitate this task, the literature is organized into research on Chicanos/as and theoretical work in the fields of labor and gender. While the latter category does not utilize evidence from the Chicana experience, a certain universality is posited within each theoretical orientation that must be taken to its logical conclusion with respect to Chicanas. Furthermore, there is an unknown degree of explanatory power within each perspective that may be uncovered within the context of such an analysis.

A Legacy of Triple Oppression in the Labor Market

Recently, studies of Mexican origin women and/or Chicanas have begun to examine critically the labor force participation of this population. Historian Albert Camarillo (1979) describes the work of Chicanas in the Santa Barbara area within the context of an emerging capitalist order at the turn of the twentieth century. He presents data that point to the development of a segregated work force that relegated Chicanas to low-wage, low-status jobs as laundresses and domestic and agricultural workers. Political scientist Mario Barrera (1979) has utilized historical evidence similarly to demonstrate the subordination of Chicanos (including women) in the southwestern part of the United States. He argues that convergence of political, social, and economic factors has formed the basis of Chicano subordination in the United States. This process resulted in the creation of a colonial labor force composed of subordinate labor "segments" that are hierarchically defined by race, class, and gender.

Both of these studies have provided valuable information on this small but economically critical segment of the U.S. population. Most importantly, each has demonstrated that the contemporary lack of occupational options for Chicanas has historical antecedents that developed in the late nineteenth century.

With respect to studies of contemporary Chicanas, the scope and range of their labor force participation and their occupational distribution have been explained in several ways. The most popular approach discusses the limitations on Mexican women to enter the paid labor force as integrally related to their higher fertility (Alvirez and Bean, 1976; Fogel, 1967). This approach suggests that the higher fertility rates of Chicanas cause them to leave the labor force—sometimes for years at a time. This may cause reluctance on the part of employers to train them for career mobility.

Another approach attempts to locate various "cultural" patterns from Mexico that relegate women to the home and do not encourage them to seek career options (Mirandé and Enríquez, 1979; Grebler, Moore, and Guzman, 1970). Other scholars point out that entry and participation in the paid labor force depend upon a variety of factors, including acculturation and educational levels (Gandara, 1982; Vásquez, 1982; Melville, 1980). The role of discrimination based upon race and gender that effectively prevents high degrees of occupational mobility for Chicanos, male and female, forms the crux of still other analyses (Romero, 1979; Briggs et al., 1977).

The explanations presented tend to suggest that certain cultural and linguistic characteristics must be acquired for occupational integration in the larger society to occur. The applicability of acculturation approaches is questionable, given analyses which suggest that a "job ceiling" may exist for Chicanos (Tienda, 1981; Briggs et al., 1977; Ogbu, 1978). This means that Chicanos seek employment in those few job categories in which they have historically suffered less discrimination. Inasmuch as occupational and income mobility seems to level off to that acquired by the second-generation (native-born population), the job ceiling thesis should be carefully considered by scholars interested in the social and economic mobility of this population. For the implications of a job ceiling are extremely unfavorable for future generations of Chicano workers in the United States.

Persistent and unfavorable income differentials often are linked to educational achievement and aspirations. The "human capital" school of thought (e.g., Becker, 1975; Mincer, 1974) is devoted to closer examinations of this principle. The human capital argument asserts that an open labor market operates where all applicants compete on an equal basis for jobs. Thus, to acquire better-paying jobs (where the competition is much keener), unskilled and semiskilled workers must increase those skills which will add to their job productivity and make them more attractive to employers. Theoretically, this can be done by investing in greater amounts of education and on-the-job training.

As an examination of the structure of the labor market, human capital theory fails to discuss those processes that inhibit the quest for acquisition of marketable criteria. The amount and quality of education in particular differ according to race, class, and gender, with women and minorities prepared for a relatively limited range of careers (U.S. Commission on Civil Rights, 1978). In the same vein, Bowles and Gintis (1976) have presented evidence that educational success, including high school and college completion, is linked to the class backgrounds of different populations. Thus, the relatively poor economic backgrounds of the majority of Chicanos often will be reflected in their low level of education—which in our society is critical to gain entry into the higher-paying white-collar and professional jobs.

Other economists (e.g., Reich, 1981; Edwards, 1979; Sackrey, 1973; Gordon, 1972) argue that labor markets themselves have certain characteristics that make it difficult for significant numbers of women and minorities to improve their job options. Labor market segmentation theorists (Gordon, Edwards, and Reich, 1982) go to great lengths to establish what these characteristics are. These theorists posit the existence of a ''primary'' labor market containing relatively well-paying, stable jobs with promotional ladders. Historically, white males have predominated in this sector, which includes professionals, managers, and skilled crafts jobs. On the other end of the spectrum is the ''secondary'' labor market, which includes various semi- and unskilled jobs that are low-paying and offer few promotional opportunties. Until fairly recently, minorities and women have been limited to this sector, which includes seasonal factory operatives (including cannery workers), janitors, and other part-time workers.

Labor market segmentation theorists show that movement from the secondary to the primary labor market is rare.[5] Gordon (1972) notes that only white males seem to make this move successfully.

This can be illustrated by the case of high school students who work at fast-food establishments and then move on to jobs in the primary sector once they complete their education and seek full-time career jobs. Minorities and women, on the other hand, tend to become locked into these types of jobs, since historically they have not had the same job options as white males. Their lack of mobility between labor markets is verified by their continued overrepresentation at certain wage and occupational levels and an unemployment rate higher than the norm.

It should be pointed out that, although labor market segmentation theory describes the greater vulnerability of minority and female workers, race and gender are not the focal points of analysis for this theoretical orientation. The primary focus of this approach is tracing the development of a working-class divided within an occupational hierarchy. Race and gender within this model are mechanisms to divide the working class within and across occupational categories. Inasmuch as race and gender are subsumed under the larger "class" question by labor market segmentation theorists, the range of the processes whereby Chicanas are subordinated cannot be explained except insofar as they occupy a certain job or market sector. The processes leading to Chicanas' point of entry in the labor market, which is the culmination of the interplay among class, race, and gender variables, cannot be addressed without major revisions in this model.

Heidi Hartman (1976, 1981) in her examinations of the close connection between patriarchy and capitalism provides us with a key to understanding one aspect of triple oppression that labor market segmentation theorists have not analyzed. Although Hartman agrees that the interests of a capitalist mode of production have been served by the hierarchical organization of the labor force, she points out that this ordering was based upon the principle of male privilege, or patriarchy. All women, according to Hartman, share an inferior social status relative to men that is reflected in the lower wages produced by their occupational segregation into female-dominant jobs. This disadvantageous situation for women will not change, according to Hartman, unless women challenge the principle of male privilege in all social arenas, including the family.

Each perspective outlined above provides possibilities for the present task of understanding the triple oppression of Chicanas, particularly their limited occupations and income. The information provided on Chicanos clearly articulates the historical and contemporary reality of their limited labor force opportunities and chances for mobility. Because of the pervasiveness of race, Chicanos are not viewed as "professionals" and usually are consigned to "unskilled" or "semiskilled" labor. This labeling process is disadvantageous to all Chicanos. But within this limited labor market are additional subdivisions, or domains of lesser status and/or lower pay. I refer, of course, to the female labor force (e.g., cannery "sorters" rather than line supervisors; garment "sewers" instead of pattern cutters, etc.). The existence of this domain points to the saliency of gender in affecting the labor market positions and job options of Chicanas. Thus, race, class, and gender at the same time impact on the reproduction of Chicanas as a subordinated labor force.

The other theoretical approaches presented can be extended to include the Chicana experience as well. The major postulates within each perspective need to be tested for their usefulness in articulating specific outcomes with respect to Chicanas in the paid labor force. A logical starting point for such an analysis is an overview of the income and occupational profiles of Chicanas in comparison to Chicano males, white women, and white males. This four-way comparison is necessary to demonstrate the importance of the relationship among the structural variables of race, class, and gender. In addition, this type of comparison will lead, necessarily, to questions for future work on Chicanas as the concept of their triple oppression becomes linked to their struggles for parity with the majority population.

Chicanas in the Labor Force: A Demographic Profile

According to the U.S. Bureau of the Census, the past decade has witnessed a significant growth in the labor force participation of all women, including Chicanas. In 1970, 39.4 percent of all Chicanas over the age of sixteen and 41.7 percent of all white women worked for wages in California.[6] White males and Chicanos had labor force participation rates of 78.0 and 79.0 percent, respectively.[7] These figures rose in 1980, to a 51.3 percent labor force participation rate for Chicanas in California—a ratio slightly smaller than the 51.7 percent of white female labor force participants.[8]

Although the labor force participation rates of all women registered major gains, it does not necessarily follow that their occupations and incomes were similar. The preceeding theoretical overview suggests, in fact, that this would not occur. To demonstrate this view, I briefly examine empirical evidence from the U.S. Bureau of the Census on women with respect to their last job and full-time earnings.

Table 1: Median Earnings of Full-Time Workers 15 Years and Over by Sex and Spanish Origin in the U.S.: 1981

	White		Spanish Origin	
	Male	Female	Male	Female
TOTAL Private Wage and Salary Workers (numbers in thousands)	27,880	15,043	1,813	909
Professional, Technical, and Kindred Workers	$26,954	$16,681	$24,376	*
Managers and Administrators	27,290	14,998	20,981	*
Sales Workers	22,306	11,307	*	*
Clerical and Kindred Workers	17,794	11,687	11,962	11,471
Craft and Kindred Workers	20,812	13,133	17,066	*
Operatives (Including Transport)	17,650	10,464	14,361	8,739
Laborers	15,415	10,470	11,422	*
Service Workers	11,687	8,101	9,762	7,561
in Agriculture	10,583	*	10,738	*
TOTAL MEDIAN EARNINGS	$21,087	$11,805	$14,383	$10,500

SOURCE: U.S. Bureau of the Census, "Money Income of Households, Families, and Persons in the United States: 1981," *Current Population Reports*, Series P-60, No. 137.

*According to the Census Bureau, there was an insufficient data base (less than 75,000) to provide accurate income information.

Table 2: Occupational Distribution of Full-Time Workers 15 Years and Over by Sex and Spanish Origin in the U.S.: 1981

	White		Spanish Origin	
	Male	Female	Male	Female
TOTAL Private Wage and Salary Workers (numbers in thousands)	27,880	15,043	1,813	909
Professional, Technical, and Kindred Workers	16.2%	13.7%	6.8%	8.1%
Managers and Administrators	18.6	11.0	7.3	5.5
Sales Workers	8.1	6.1	3.3	4.0
Clerical and Kindred Workers	5.8	41.3	6.5	34.7
Craft and Kindred Workers	24.0	2.7	21.8	3.0
Operatives (Including Transport)	17.2	12.6	30.0	25.4
Laborers	4.4	1.2	7.3	1.3
Service Workers	3.9	11.0	11.6	17.5
in Agriculture	1.7	*	5.4	*

SOURCE: U.S. Bureau of the Census, "Money Income of Households, Families, and Persons in the United States: 1981," *Current Population Reports*, Series P-60, No. 137.

NOTE: All figures were rounded off to the nearest tenth. Approximately 60 percent of the Spanish origin population is of Mexican origin.

*Less than 1 percent reported working in this occupational category.

Chicanas earn lower wages than white women. In 1981, the median income of Spanish origin women in full-time, year-round employment was $10,500, and that of Spanish origin men was $14,383. During this same year, the median income of majority-group men working full time was $21,087, and that of white women was $11,805 (U.S. Department of Commerce, Bureau of the Census, 1981).

To understand why Chicanas have lower incomes, it is necessary to look at the types of jobs in which they work. This examination provides one outcome of their triple oppression as well as leading to further inquiry into the process resulting in their limited labor force experiences. In 1981, the incomes of Spanish origin and white women in full-time, year-round employment in the United States can be compared only in three categories: operative, clerical, and service work (see table 1). Apparently the data base in the other occupational categories was too small for the Census Bureau to delineate income.

Table 2 indicates that in 1981, 17.5 percent of all Spanish origin women who were employed in full-time, year-round employment were service workers; 29.7 percent were blue-collar workers; and 52.3 percent were white-collar workers.[9] Only 13.6 percent of Chicanas worked at the better-paying white-collar administrative and/or professional levels. This is similar to the ratio of Chicano men in these jobs. Over 34 percent of Chicanas were clerical workers. When these job distributions are compared to those of white women, the contrasts are plain to see. White women have a much higher participation rate in the professional and the better-paying white-collar fields than do Chicanas and Spanish origin women. This demonstrates that Chicanas are more limited than white women in their range of careers.

In clerical jobs, Chicanas earned 98 percent of the wages of both white women and Spanish origin men; however, they earned only 64 percent of white male income. A similar pattern existed among service jobs. In operative jobs, the wages of Chicanas were 83 percent of those of white women, but only 42 percent those of white men. Overall, Spanish origin men and women were paid 68 percent and 49.8 percent, respectively, of the earnings of white men. White women earned 56 percent of the income of their male counterparts in full-time employment.

This income pattern is significant at several levels. First, the overall income statistics place Chicanos and women in similar situations relative to white men. Second, the income at each comparable level demonstrates a closer relationship among women than exists within each ethnic group under consideration, except at the clerical and sales worker levels. Further, the occupational distribution in the professional, managerial, and operative categories is more similar within each ethnic group than by gender.

With respect to unemployment, Chicanos, male and female, have much higher rates of unemployment than the majority-group population (see table 3). In 1980, 6.1 and 6.5 percent, respectively, of white men and women were unemployed as opposed to 9.7 and

Table 3: Unemployment for Selected Years in the United States

	White		Chicano	
	Male	Female	Male	Female
1980	6.1	6.5	9.7	10.7
1976	5.9	8.7	11.1	14.9
1970	3.6	5.0	6.4	9.1
1960	4.7	4.7	8.1	9.5

SOURCES: For 1980: U.S. Department of Labor, Bureau of Labor Statistics, "Employment and Unemployment: A Report on 1980, Unemployment Rates by Race and Hispanic Origin," in *Special Labor Force Report 244* (Washington, D.C.: U.S Government Printing Office, April, 1981). For 1960, 1970, and 1976: U.S. Commission on Civil Rights, *Social Indicators of Equality for Minorities and Women* (Washington, D.C.: U.S. Government Printing Office, August, 1978).

10.7 percent, respectively, of Chicano men and women. The levels of unemployment for white women were closer to those of white men than to those of Chicanas. Similarly, the high unemployment levels of Chicanas are closer to those of Chicano men. This illustrates that Chicanas are affected by labor market processes to a greater degree than the other populations examined. This vulnerability is linked to the types of jobs in which they predominate, such as operatives or service workers in declining or unstable sectors of the economy (e.g., canneries, garment factories, hospitals, child care centers, etc.).

Statistics such as those presented above need more development than I can provide here, but they do clarify some of the issues involved in an analysis of the occupations and low income of Chicanas in the labor force. These data seem to verify labor market segmentation in that Chicanas are concentrated in limited occupational categories. Many of these jobs are in the "secondary" labor market, whose inherent instability leads to a higher level of unemployment as well as lower wages. High Chicana concentration in the gender-specific clerical work force also acts to limit their income levels Thus, the wage levels of Chicanas are lower than those of Chicanos or white workers. Whether these differences are due to structural factors or individual choice and ability cannot be told, however, by demographic data. For this type of analysis, we must turn again to the literature to gauge to what extent each perspective explains—or promises to explain—the lower incomes and limited jobs illustrated here.

Chicanas in the Labor Force: Toward an Understanding of the Process of Triple Oppression

In the preceding section, a demographic profile of Chicanas in the labor force established one outcome of their triple oppression in society. As women they have been paid lower wages relative to men and limited to gender-specific jobs. As members of an ethnic/racial minority group, they have been relegated to jobs historically assigned to this group. This partially accounts for their limited job options relative to white women. Both factors, race and gender, utilized within a segmented labor market, interact and produce workers whose characteristics place a preponderance of minority female workers in "secondary" jobs or in the clerical sector of the primary labor market. Given the close connection between income and class position in our society, restricted job options within a segmented labor market have direct relevance to the Chicana population.

The present study has been concerned with the outcome of the triple oppression of Chicanas within the context of a segmented labor market. This type of economic structural analysis, although informative, is constrained by a lack of information regarding the process wherein triple oppression is reproduced ideologically and socioculturally. Drawing upon the theoretical positions previously discussed, the remainder of this essay presents possible approaches whereby this process may be unraveled.

To understand the subordination of women within a capitalist mode of production, Heidi Hartman (1976, 1981) examines the linkage of patriarchy (or male domination) to capitalism. She notes that women are subordinate to men within the family, as they continue to bear the major responsibility for unpaid household labor—a category of socially necessary work that both neoclassical and radical economists fail to include in their analyses. This inequality within the family is reflected in the society-at-large. Thus, to understand the inner workings of female subordinate status in the labor market, it is essential to look at the reproduction of the corresponding division of labor at home.

The relationship of family structure to the labor force position of Chicanas is a problematic issue. The reason for the hesitation of some Chicano scholars to confront this issue critically lies in the damaging early analyses of some researchers that depicted the Mexican family as rigidly patriarchal and pathological to a degree (Heller, 1966; Hayden, 1966; Madsen, 1964; Lewis, 1961).

As a response to this line of analysis, Chicano scholars have channeled their energies into analyses of structural factors such as labor market processes, education, and immigration. The maintenance and reproduction of a sex-based division of labor within the Chicano family is often obscured by Chicano/a scholars studying the "rise of egalitarianism" within that unit (Ybarra, 1977, 1982; Baca Zinn, 1980; Cotera, 1976; Sotomayer, 1971). By analyzing the growth of equality between men and women in Chicano families, these scholars can (and do) obscure the unequal gender role dichotomization and socialization practices that can adversely affect future job preferences and aspirations.

It is essential that the process of gender role socialization be scrutinized in order that a critical component of the triple oppression of Chicanas be understood. Chicanas are not "naturally" factory operatives or clerical workers. In addition to occupational segregation that locates them in these job categories, there are other factors, which may be familial, that can limit their job expectations.[10]

Research on Chicana high achievers (Gandara, 1982; Vasquez, 1982) illustrates that familial support (especially that of mothers) is an important factor in Chicana advancement. Even as families encourage high aspirations, they can discourage future expectations. An important task, then, for future qualitative work on Chicanas in the labor force should be to examine familial relationships with respect to their effects upon future job preferences. This type of question, combined with an assessment of institutional constraints and labor market structuring, can reveal a more complete picture of the manner in which gender operates to restrict the arena in which Chicanas compete.

The role of education in screening potential employees for employers makes it a logical point of departure for studies of the occupations and earnings of Chicanas in the labor force. Although lower levels of educational attainment are linked to lower-paying jobs by human capital theorists, class, race, and gender influence the viability of higher education for Chicanas as well as the quality of education available to this population. By reducing the acquisition of education to individual initiative, human capital theory misses the fact that Chicanas, who tend to be working-class, are inadequately counseled in school and suffer various forms of discrimination that often prevents them from completing their education (U.S. Commission on Civil Rights, 1972, 1974a, 1978). Although Chicanas do not have the same tools with which to forge a future as the white population has, their movement within the labor force—whether lateral or vertical—needs to be researched in order that the interplay among the structural variables of race, class, and gender be analyzed.

Racial discrimination by employers is essential to examine and operates to isolate the Chicana experience from that of white women. Although both groups of women are concentrated in the clerical occupations, white men and women tend to supervise, whereas Chicanas tend to be supervised.[11] The consistency of lower occupational and employment levels for Chicanas suggests that discrimination in the labor market, as well as in the acquisition of different educational levels, is critical to the race, class, and gender stratification of this group.

As an alternative to the human capital approach, the labor market segmentation theory deserves a prominent place in this analysis. This model shifts the locus of blame for lower wages from the individual to societal mechanisms. It suggests that the working class is divided by occupations which are themselves stratified by race and gender criteria. This process of segmentation is critical, because it prevents an organized, coherent challenge to the prevailing social order and ensures the continued existence of a reserve army of labor. Although this model lacks historical specificity to the Chicana experience, other works (especially Barrera, 1979) have refined it to emphasize race.

Barrera's (1979) reformulation of the labor market segmentation approach can serve as a point of departure to examine the Chicana experience. In his analysis of the historical development of capitalism in the Southwest, Barrera mentions that at every class or occupational level, Chicanas were among the most disadvantaged laborers in society. He does not, however, integrate this evidence into his theory of race and class inequality. For this theoretical perspective to be relevant to Chicanas, patriarchy within the Chicano community and the society-at-large must be examined on an equal basis with race and class. The development of such an analysis remains for future researchers interested in this relationship.

The literature on the occupational distribution and incomes of Chicanas within a segmented labor market indicates that additional research in these fields is needed. Qualitative data must be gathered with respect to the job histories of Chicanas. This type of information can provide us with insight into the effects of the structural variables of race, class, and gender on their lives. Inasmuch as Chicanas are not passive actors in society, knowledge of the ways they act to modify their social environment can add a critical dimension to structural analyses that often fail to acknowledge the individual will and initiative that has been so important in the history of Chicanas in the United States.

NOTES

1. With respect to Chicanas, Mirandé and Enríquez (1979) refer to this term within the context of Chicanas' oppression due to their colonized status as Chicanos, their gender, and their culture (chap. 1, pp. 12-13). This conceptualization differs fundamentally from the one I put forth in this essay, where *class*, as opposed to culture, is the arena in which triple oppression is organized and expressed.

In her analysis of the historical subordination of black women in the United States, Angela Davis (1981) utilizes a triple oppression framework, but does not specifically define the term. She hints at the linkage of race, class, and gender at various points in the book—ultimately subsuming gender and race to class concerns, as her critique of the sufferage movement demonstrates: "While their men's sexist behavior definitely needed to be challenged, the real enemy—their common enemy—was the boss, the capitalist, or whoever was responsible for the miserable wages and unbearable working conditions and for racist and sexist discrimination on the job" (Davis, 1981:142). My work departs from this conceptualization because I offer a view of triple oppression that stresses the importance of locating and analyzing the interplay among class, race, and gender as opposed to arranging each variable in an hierarchical manner.

2. In this paper, "Chicano/Chicana" refers to persons (male and female) of Mexican descent born in the United States and/or identifying themselves as such. Another, similar label is "Mexican American." The term "Mexican origin" refers to a person of Mexican descent irrespective of resident or citizenship status. "Spanish origin" and "Hispanic" are broader terms often utilized by state agencies to refer to persons of Spanish and Latin American heritage; 60 percent of all Spanish origin persons in the United States are of Mexican origin.

For additional information on the origins and use of the term "Chicano," especially the political implications of the term, see Tienda (1981), Peñalosa (1970), and Barrera (1979).

3. This brief definition is elaborated upon in Wright (1979, chap. 1). Wright also discusses the various perspectives within sociology with respect to defining and refining "class" within this chapter.

4. See Takaki (1979), for an intriguing comparative examination of early linkages between racial ideology and the economic subordination of conquered and enslaved nonwhite people in U.S. history. See also Acuña (1981, chap. 1) wherein the author in "The Rationale for Conquest" describes the power of the ideology of "manifest destiny" with respect to the legitimization of the war with Mexico. Also (in chap. 2), he discusses the subordination of Mexican American rights in the United States that was consistently culturally legitimized.

5. See Reich (1981:248-267), where he describes the occupational segregation of blacks to unskilled, low-paying jobs. See also Barrera (1979, chap. 3), wherein he discusses the establishment of an occupationally stratified colonial labor force occupied by Chicanos in the Southwest.

6. Briggs, Fogel, and Schmidt (1977:28).

7. Ibid., p. 28.

8. Composed from U.S. Department of Commerce, Bureau of the Census (1982:154).

9. White-collar workers include the following categories: Professional, Technical and Kindred Workers; Managers and Administrators; Sales Workers; and Clerical and Kindred Workers. Blue-collar workers include Craft and Kindred Workers; Operatives; and Laborers.

10. In her doctoral dissertation, Zavella (1982) found that patriarchy within the family as well as the organization of work restricted the freedom of Chicana cannery workers to enter the jobs for which they qualified.

11. An example of this hierarchical relationship is provided by employment figures for the civil employees of the State of California for 1978-1979 (California State Personnel Board, 1979). During this year, 30 percent of white clerical workers were supervisors, as opposed to 14 percent of Chicanos occupying similar positions.

REFERENCES

Acuña, Rodolfo. 1981. *Occupied America, A History of Chicanos*, 2nd ed. (New York: Harper and Row, Publishers).

Alvirez, David and Frank D. Bean. 1976. In *Ethnic Families in America: Patterns and Variations*, ed. Charles H. Mindel and Robert W. Habenstein (New York: Elsvier North Holland), pp. 271-292.

Baca Zinn, Maxine. 1980. "Employment and Education of Mexican-American Women: The Interplay of Modernity and Ethnicity in Eight Families." *Harvard Educational Review* 50/1 (February).

Barrera, Mario. 1979. *Race and Class in the Southwest: A Theory of Racial Inequality* (Notre Dame: University of Notre Dame Press).

Bean, Frank D., Russell L. Curtis, Jr., and John P. Marcum. 1977. "Familism and Marital Satisfaction among Mexican Americans: The Effects of Family Size, Wife's Labor Force Participation and Conjugal Power." *Journal of Marriage and the Family* 39/4 (November):759-767.

Becker, Gary S. 1975. *Human Capital* (Chicago: University of Chicago Press; 2nd edition issued in 1980).

Blaxall, Martha and Barbara Reagan (eds.). 1976. *Women and the Workplace, The Implications of Occupational Segregation* (Chicago: University of Chicago Press).

Bowles, Samuel and Herbert Gintis. 1976. *Schooling in Capitalist Society* (New York: Basic Books, Inc.).

Briggs, Vernon M., Jr., Walter Fogel, and Fred H. Schmidt. 1977. *The Chicano Worker* (Austin: University of Texas Press).

California State Personnel Board. 1979. "Report to the Governor and the Legislature, July 1979." Annual Census of State Employees, 1978-1979; Sacramento, Calif.

Camarillo, Albert. 1979. *Chicanos in a Changing Society: From Mexican Pueblos to American Barrios in Santa Barbara and Southern California, 1848-1930* (Cambridge, Mass.: Harvard University Press).

Chacón, Maria, Elizabeth G. Cohen, Margaret Camarena, Judith Gonzalez, and Sharon Strover. 1982. *Chicanas in Postsecondary Education* (Stanford: Stanford University, Center for Research on Women).

Cotera, Martha P. 1976. *Diosa y Hembra: The History and Heritage of Chicanas in the U.S.* (Austin, Tex.: Information Systems Development).

Davis, Angela Y. 1981. *Women, Race and Class* (New York: Vintage Books).

Edwards, Richard C. 1979. *Contested Terrain* (New York: Basic Books, Inc.).

Fogel, Walter. 1967. "Mexican Americans in Southwest Labor Markets." *Advance Report No. 10* (Los Angeles: University of California).

Gordon, David M. 1972. *Theories of Poverty and Underdevelopment* (Lexington, Mass.: Lexington Books).

Gordon, David M., Richard Edwards, and Michael Reich. 1982. *Segmented Work, Divided Workers: The Historical Transformation of Labor in the United States* (Cambridge, Mass.: Cambridge University Press).

Grebler, Leo, Joan W. Moore, and Ralph C. Guzman. 1970. *The Mexican-American People* (New York: Free Press).

Hartman, Heidi. 1976. "Capitalism, Patriarchy and Job Segregation by Sex."

Hartman, Heidi. 1976. "Capitalism, Patriarchy and Job Segregation by Sex." In *Women and the Work Place, The Implications of Occupational Segregation*, ed. Martha Blaxall and Barbara Reagan, pp. 137-169.

———. 1981. "The Unhappy Marriage of Marxism and Feminism: Toward a More Progressive Union." In *Women and Revolution*, ed. Lydia F. Sargent, pp. 1-42.

Hayden, Robert. 1966. "Spanish Americans of the Southwest: Life Style Patterns and Their Implications." *Welfare in Review* 4/10:14-25.

Heller, Celia. 1966. *Mexican-American Youth: Forgotten Youth at the Crossroads* (New York: Random House).

Lewis, Oscar. 1961. *The Children of Sanchez* (New York: Vintage Books).

Madsen, William. 1964. *The Mexican Americans of South Texas* (San Francisco: Holt, Rinehart and Winston).

Marcum, John P. and Frank D. Bean. 1976. "Minority Group Status as a Factor in the Relationship between Mobility and Fertility: The Mexican American Case." *Social Forces* 55/1 (September): 135-148.

Melville, Margarita B. (ed.). 1980. *Twice a Minority* (St. Louis: C. V. Mosby Co.).

Mincer, Jacob. 1974. *Schooling, Experience and Earnings* (New York: Columbia University Press).

Mirandé, Alfredo and Evangelina Enríquez. 1979. *La Chicana* (Chicago: University of Chicago Press).

Ogbu, John U. 1978. *Minority Education and Caste, The American System in Cross-Cultural Perspective* (New York: Academic Press).

Peñalosa, Fernando. 1970. "Toward an Operational Definition of the Mexican American." *Aztlán* 1 (Spring): 1-12.

Reich, Michael. 1981. *Racial Inequality* (Princeton, N.J.: Princeton University Press).

Romero, Fred E. 1979. *Chicano Workers: Their Utilization and Development*, Monograph No. 8 (Los Angeles: University of California, Chicano Studies).

Sackrey, Charles. 1973. *The Political Economy of Urban Poverty* (New York: W. W. Norton and Co.).

Sargent, Lydia (ed.). 1981. *Women and Revolution* (Boston: South End Press).

Sotomayer, Marta. 1971. "Mexican American Interaction with Social Systems." In *La Causa Chicana*, ed. Margaret M. Mangold (New York: Family Service Association of America).

Takaki, Ronald T. 1979. *Iron Cages, Race and Culture in Nineteenth Century America* (Seattle: University of Washington Press).

United States Commission on Civil Rights. 1972. *The Excluded Student, Report 3* (Washington, D.C.: U.S. Government Printing Office, May).

———. 1974*a*. *Toward Quality Education for Mexican Americans, Report 6* (Washington, D.C.: U.S. Government Printing Office, February).

———. 1974*b*. *Women and Poverty* (Washington, D.C.: U.S. Government Printing Office, June).

______. 1978. *Social Indicators of Equality for Minorities and Women* (Washington, D.C.: U.S. Government Printing Office, August).

United States Department of Commerce, Bureau of the Census. 1980. "Persons of Spanish Origin in the United States: March 1979." In *Current Population Reports*, Series P-20, No. 354, (Washington, D.C.: U.S. Government Printing Office).

______. 1981. "Money Income of Households, Families, and Persons in the United States: 1981." In *Current Population Reports*, Series P-60, No. 134 (Washington, D.C.: U.S. Government Printing Office).

______. 1982. *1980 Census of Population*, Vol. I, Chapter B: *General Population Characteristics, Part 6: California.* PC80-1-136 (Washington, D.C.: U.S. Government Printing Office, July).

______. 1983. "Money Income of Households, Families, and Persons in the United States: 1981." In *Current Population Reports*, Series P-60, No. 137 (Washington, D.C.: U.S. Government Printing Office).

United States Department of Labor, Bureau of Labor Statistics. 1981. "Employment and Unemployment: A Report on 1980, Unemployment Rates by Race and Hispanic Origin." In *Special Labor Force Report 244* (Washington, D.C.: U.S. Government Printing Office).

Vasquez, Melba J.T. 1982. "Confronting Barriers to the Participation of Mexican American Women in Higher Education." *Hispanic Journal of Behavioral Science* 4/2:147-165.

Wright, Erik Olin. 1979. *Class Structure and Income Determination* (New York: Academic Press).

Ybarra, Lea. 1982. "When Wives Work: The Impact on the Family." *Journal of Marriage and the Family* 39/1 (February):169-177.

______. 1977. "Conjungal Role Relationships in the Chicano Family." (Ph.D. dissertation, University of California, Berkeley).

Zavella, Patricia. 1982. "Women, Work and the Chicano Family: Cannery Workers of the Santa Clara Valley." (Ph.D. dissertation, University of California, Berkeley).

Toward A Reconceptualization of Women's Economic Activities: The Informal Sector in Urban Mexico

Marta C. LOPEZ

Acknowledgements: I wish to thank Claudia Cuevas, Arlene Dallalfar, John Horton, Richard Chabran, Estevan Flores, Larry Trujillo, Manny Avalos, and my father, Alfredo Lopez, for their helpful comments and criticism. Special thanks to Christine M. Sierra and the other members of the Editorial Committee for their assistance in the revision.

How economic development affects women is increasingly drawing the attention of scholars. Their answers have varied from the argument that the capitalist mode of production and development in general, based on modernization theories, create the arena for women's economic and social participation,[1] to the argument that the expansion of capitalism, in fact, worsens conditions for working women.[2] Not mutually exclusive, these arguments put forth the contradictions of contemporary society and of the role of women within it.

In order to gauge the impact of capitalist relations on the lives of women in developing countries, we need to understand the nature of women's work. However, this very topic is in grave need of reconceptualization and revision. Much of women's work, for example, exists in the informal sector and remains officially invisible. The contradictions between women's crucial role in the economy and their concentration in occupations of low remuneration, which are often not included in the census, raise numerous issues. This essay focuses on a key factor central to the issue—the conceptualization and measurement of women's economic activities.

The Nature of Women's Work in Developing Countries

To understand the specific employment situation of women in developing countries, one must consider at least three analytically separate dimensions: (1) the supply constraints, (2) conditions of the labor market, and (3) economic policies pertaining to women. Supply constraints are linked to the composition of the household—the position of women within the household, the sexual division of labor, and the relationship between domestic and market production. General labor market conditions prevalent in developing capitalist countries today imply, in most cases, a relatively abundant supply of labor, a relatively low absorption capacity in the more dynamic and productive sectors of the economy, high rates of underemployment, and low-wage work. In the case of women, explicit and implicit employment policies include discriminatory practices and sex segregation of occupations.

As a case in point, in the last several decades Mexico has experienced rapid urbanization. Consequently, a large supply of urban-based labor cannot be incorporated into Mexico's increasingly capital-intensive industries. The result has been the development of a highly heterogeneous labor force and the systematic exclusion of women from certain occupational opportunities. Industry has proven to be an important implement of economic growth and change in Mexico. However, very few of the advantages of industrialization are shared equally across gender lines.

One consequence of this pattern of industrialization in Mexico is the proliferation of informal jobs, that is, noncontractual, minimum-wage level, and intermittent employment (i.e., cottage industry).[3] Although difficult to specify, informal activities in developing capitalist economies, such as Mexico's, must be understood as an integral part of the total pattern of employment in a given country. With regard to women's work in developing countries, an understanding of informal labor activity is essential, because women create the bulk of labor within these most precarious areas of employment.

Whether temporary or permanent, informal activities are usually taken when formal jobs are unavailable.[4] However, the dividing line between formal and informal jobs is very tenuous, especially in regard to women's work. On one hand, formal employment implies a long-term, full-time contractual, stable job. For example, textiles and food processing, which have traditionally employed women, are Mexican industries that offer formal employment. Yet, according to the Mexican census, this criterion does not apply to other types of employment, including paid domestic work and small craft production. These jobs are considered informal if they are carried out on an irregular basis regardless of the amount of hours put into production or if they are the primary source of income for the household. These incongruities point to a genuine need to reconceptualize women's formal and informal economic activities.

Even in the informal sector, differences in modes of productive activities—such as regular wage labor, labor in small enterprises, casual wage labor, and self-employment—suggest a multitude of work situations and imply a probable continuum of modes and organizations of production throughout the entire urban economy. It is consequently apparent that just within the informal sector (leaving aside formal employment), there are significant variations in employment patterns, working conditions, and wages of women workers which need to be addressed further.

Participation in the Labor Force—An Issue of Contention

In the late 1970s, women officially represented 20 percent of the Mexican labor force. Anyone with an inkling of what is occuring in Mexico would know that it is absurd to believe that 80 percent of the women are economically inactive. The low figure reflects, in large part, the inadequate conceptualization and operationalization of women's labor, particularly in the informal labor sector, as outlined above. It is unfortunately true that many women engaged in intermittent, precarious economic activities are considered "economically inactive,"[5] when in fact they are active and are creating products, providing services, and thus generating revenue.

Moreover, the Mexican census shows much higher rates of unemployment among women than among men. Again, this is not as much an indication of women's economic inactivity as of their intermittent-type jobs, which are often not officially counted as employment by the census.

In most cases, neither part-time work outside the home nor work for a family enterprise is included in the national census. Since the Mexican census only records women's primary activity, which is assumed to be domestic work, especially if the woman is not head of the household, the frequent and in many cases constant involvement of women in the informal labor sector fails to appear in official statistics.

Studies by Lourdes Arizpe, Susan Eckstein, Lisa Peattie, Janice Perlman, and Saul Trejo Reyes (among others) found "economic inactivity" practically nonexistent in the poverty areas of urban Latin America.[6] Just about everyone who is physically able works. Economically active women accounted for higher employment rates in these studies than in the official statistics of their respective governments. This is partly explained by the different approaches used to characterize work in a family enterprise and work women bring home (e.g., washing or making clothes). Whereas the censuses do not include these and other informal types of occupations in employment statistics, these studies do.

These considerations overwhelmingly imply the need to revise what is meant by "economically active" and to redefine "economically inactive." Because of such inadequate theoretical constructs, there are great difficulties and ambiguities in the measurement of women's economic activity.

While the formal/informal sector dichotomy, widely used in the literature on developing nations, presents serious problems of demarcation, it also allows for potential insights when empirically measuring labor market activity. The distinction between informal and formal work can be useful in highlighting certain important features of women's employment. If these concepts are defined broadly enough to distinguish between regularity/irregularity and security/insecurity of employment, they would be useful in revealing sharp differences in levels of earnings. Such a distinction is important when empirically measuring labor force activity.

Inequality and the Sexual Division of Labor

Another issue of concern is the persistent sexual division of labor. Regardless of whether work is in the formal or informal sector, women more often than not perform tasks which are extensions of their domestic work. In virtually all contemporary societies, men tend to appropriate the governing, more socially important positions, while women are assigned to or voluntarily occupy menial positions. This general tendency for sexual division within labor raises important questions for research.

In general, tasks reserved for women in the wage labor market are often analogous to women's responsibilities in the household.[7] In Mexico, women primarily work in industry related to clothing manufacturing and food production. These two industries include one-third and one-fifth, respectively, of women in this sector of the work force.

During the mid-seventies, studies in Mexico City by IMES (Instituto Mexicano de Estudios Sociales) and a group of social workers indicated that 23 percent of the men interviewed accepted the fact that their wives could work, but only in the following occupations: 40 percent as a dressmaker; 31.4 percent as a servant; 8.5 percent as a factory worker; and 6 percent as a nurse.

Needless to say, in the division of labor there exist class inequalities as well as inequalities along gender lines. The official statistics are alarming. In regard, for instance, to minimum wages, 18.1 percent of active males earn less than the legal minimum wage in Mexico City; the corresponding figure for women is 35.6 percent.[8]

In addition to being occupationally relegated to domestic-type jobs, women by and large acquire employment as unskilled workers. In Mexico, the 1971 statistics indicate that of the unskilled workers in the service sector, 71.8 percent were women, who also comprise 40.2 percent of the stallholders.[9] Excluded from relatively secure areas of work, women occupy employment categories which correspond to the lowest income groups. Of the stallholders, 50.8 percent of the men earned less than the official minimum wage, while the comparable statistic on women stallholders was 80 percent. In the service sector, 41.2 percent of the men and 92.3 percent of the women earned less than the minimum wage. While this is an extremely depressed state of affairs for all concerned, the economic status of women indicated by these statistics is most startling.

In much of the literature on women it is assumed that women's economic role remains primarily within the household and only secondarily in the public realm. This relationship between family status and labor market participation is taken for granted.

Some literature exists on the relationship between female labor force participation and fertility in Mexico. With varying methods of measurement and consequently different findings, Stanley K. Smith, Maria Davidson, and Alvan Zarate,[10] among others, illustrate that empirical evidence on female labor force participation is extremely contradictory. Some of the writers argue that having a family does not preclude women from productive undertakings, while others argue the opposite.[11] The theoretical debate on the interplay between productive and reproductive activities continues.

For example, women who are heads of household are more likely to be employed than women who are not. They are also more likely to be found in the informal sector, where they are paid the lowest wages. This tendency to pay women wages below the value of labor power is justified on the assumption that a woman is at least partially dependent on the wages a man earns. This situation is, in turn, responsible for the plight of single women with families to support. Thus, these female-headed households deserve considerable attention in view of their increasing numbers and their poverty level. The study of women's activities, as determined by their position in the household, requires a characterization of the variety of households according to their position in the class structure, taking into account changes over time.

Class and Age Division of Labor in the Informal Sector

In addition to sexual divisions in labor, hierarchical socioeconomic structures separate women and their interests from other women. The informal activities of women in the cities of Mexico cover a wide range of tasks—from private tutors in foreign languages to dishwashers.[12] However, a definite stratification of such informal tasks exists, which differentiates at least two clearly defined social groups: middle-class women who enjoy educational and social advantages and working-class women with few such advantages. The lower-class women in urban Mexico carry out their activities primarily in their own homes, in other women's homes, or in the streets.

Some women provide part-time or full-time household services, such as washing and mending clothes, preparing food, looking after other people's children, and so forth. Because caring for the children and home is generally assumed to be the "natural" supreme purpose of a woman's existence, paid domestic work is not conceptualized as a job, but merely the extension of her responsibilities.

In the cities of Mexico, and most likely in those of other Latin American countries, women's participation in formal employment declines with age while, conversely, informal activities increase with age. Thus, women who need to work but who cannot find jobs compensate for their unemployment by taking up informal activities. Young working-class women can sometimes find a factory job or employment in small entrepreneurial enterprises. However, middle-aged and elderly women tend to go into low-compensation employment. Data which indicate that the highest rate of female participation in economic activity is found in the age groups fifteen to twenty-nine years reflect the census's inability to acknowledge informal economic activities.[13] I recognize child-bearing and child-rearing as potential causes of nonparticipation in the labor force. Nonetheless, given the economic conditions of the majority of Mexican people, the underrecording of women's participation in the informal labor force is a serious oversight.

Alternative Approaches to Measuring Women's Economic Activities

A multitude of problems confront analyses of women's work in the informal sector. Census categories do not cover the variety of work included in this area. Some activities are never declared, others are not included in census questionnaires, and others overlap with various types of formal work. Perhaps research efforts in this area should proceed on the assumption that everyone has some socially determined activity (time-use survey).[14] An approximation of the time devoted to each of the possible activities and of the changes in time allocation along the life cycle would give a better picture of the social division of labor and would elucidate the various forms of "invisible" labor. Time-use surveys allow for a more valid and inclusive approach to the study of labor supply, especially in regard to women and children.

By following this path, however, another important issue emerges, namely, the degree to which human potential is socially utilized. This issue has usually been discussed in relation to labor productivity or unemployment and "disguised unemployment."[15] Development of criteria for defining these concepts poses a difficult problem; that is, in order to arrive at a proper measurement there must also be some standard of "full employment." However, thus far, it has not been possible to arrive at a widely agreed upon definition for full employment. At the minimum "employment" should be seen as part of a broader concept, "economic activity." It would include occupations in the informal sectors, cottage industries, low-paying service jobs, and unpaid work in a family enterprise.

Conclusion

Economic development itself is problematic to evaluate. It is certainly no panacea to assure improvement of living and working standards, either for women or for men. High underemployment rates and poverty are widespread phenomena in many countries, but overall economic growth does not assure that these conditions will change. The recognition of women's economic value will more likely result from social/political movements and struggles carried out at specific historical conjunctures. Nonetheless, discussion of the participation of women in the labor force, or even of their contribution to growth and development, cannot be isolated from the issues of exploitation and poverty.

Issues I have raised are first, the substantial disregard of women's economic activities, especially those outside the realm of formal labor. Second, working-class, single heads of household and older women fall within the most neglected areas of official statistics. Third, given the neglect of the economic participation of women in the informal sector, there remains the need to examine and redefine terms and concepts which identify the parameters of labor force activities. Science and technology are generally assumed to be the answer to material deprivation. Yet, without simultaneously considering the social and economic inequalities in society, or without paying attention to women's work (over one-half of society's resources) and potential, there is little promise of social development At a minimum, we must point out and acknowledge the existing conceptual and data-gathering limitations and shortcomings. This is a necessary beginning for an adequate scientific investigation into the impact of capitalist expansion on women in developing countries.

Implicit theories and methods of measurement of employment are intrinsically entrenched politically. The manner in which terms are defined and concepts are developed is linked to the existing socioeconomic interpretation and rationalization; these terms and concepts as assumptions are more than merely sociological in nature, but very much political in their practical implementation and application. Specifically, the worsening conditions of workers in the informal sector are made invisible by the data-gathering procedures. This occurs while these very workers are simultaneously experiencing exploitation by the economic system which minimizes their plight in the official statistics.

NOTES

1. Mary Elmendorf, "Mexico: The Many Worlds of Women," in *Women: Roles and Status in Eight Countries*, ed. J.Z. Giele and A.C. Smock (New York: John Wiley and Sons, 1977); Orlandina de Oliveira, *Absorpción de Obra a la Estructura Ocupacional de la Ciudad de México* (Mexico City: El Colegio de México, 1976); M. Young and P. Willmott, *The Symmetrical Family* (Harmondsworth: Penguin, 1975).

2. Alonso Aguilar, "Capitalismo Monopolista de Estado: Subdesarrollo y Crisis," *Estrategia* 2 (July, 1976):30-52; José A. Alonso, "The Domestic Clothing Workers in the Mexican Metropolis and Their Relation to Dependent Capitalism," in *Women, Men, and the International Division of Labor*, ed. J. Nash and M.P. Fernandez-Kelly (Albany: State University of New York Press, 1983), pp. 161-172; Alejandro Alvarez and Elena Sandoval, "Desarrollo Industrial y Clase Obrera en México," *Cuadernos Políticos* 4 (1975):70-83.

3. ILO characterizes the informal labor sector in the following manner: (1) ease of access and flexibility in the creating of new employment; (2) operation outside of social and labor legislation; (3) low productivity, small-scale production, rudimentary technology; (4) low salaries, low income (OIT-PREALC, *La Mujer y Empleo en América Latina* [Geneva, 1976], p. 16).

4. Formal employment signifies high enough wages to live above subsistence level, security of continuous employment, and those positions included in the national and international censuses.

5. "Economically inactive" refers to those individuals not officially considered part of the wage-labor force or producing for the market.

6. Lourdes Arizpe, "Women in the Informal Labor Sector: The Case of Mexico City," *Signs* 3/1 (1977):25-37; Susan Eckstein, "The Political Economy of Lower Class Areas in Mexico City: Societal Constraints on Local Business Prospects," and Lisa Peattie, " 'Tertiarization' and Urban Poverty in Latin America," both in *Latin American Urban Research* 5, ed. W. Cornelius and F. Trueblood (Beverly Hills: Sage, 1975); Janice Perlman, *Myth of Marginality* (Berkeley: University of California Press, 1976); Saúl Trejo Reyes, "Desempleo y Subocupación en México," *Comercio Exterior 22/5 (1972): 411-416; and his Industrialización y Empleo en México* (México: Fondo de Cultura Económica, 1973).

7. Ester Boserup (ed.), *Women's Role in Economic Development* (New York: St. Martin's Press, 1980); Dorothy E. Smith, "Women, the Family and Corporate Capitalism," in *Women in Canada*, ed. M.L. Stephenson (Toronto: Newpress, 1973), and her "Women's Perspective as Radical Critique of Sociology," *Sociological Inquiry* 44/1 (1974); Heidi Hartman, "Capitalism, Patriarchy, and Job Segregation by Sex," and Margery Davis, "Women's Place Is at the Typewriter: The Feminization of the Clerical Labor Force," both in *Capitalism, Patriarchy, and the Case for Socialist Feminism*, ed. Z.R. Eisenstein (London: Verso Editions, 1980); Bonnie Fox (ed.), *Hidden in the Household: Women's Domestic Labour Under Capitalism* (Toronto: Women's Press, 1980).

8. Arizpe, "Women in the Informal Labor Sector," p. 30.

9. Stallholders are essentially street vendors.

10. Stanley K. Smith, "Women's Fertility, and Competing Time Use in Mexico City," *Research in Population Economics* 3 (1981):167-187; Maria Davidson, "A Comparative Study of Fertility in Mexico City and Caracas," *Social Biology* 20 (1973):460-472; Alvan O. Zarate, "Differential Fertility in Monterrey, Mexico: Prelude To Transition?" *Milibank Memorial Fund Quarterly* 45 (1967):93-108.

11. See Smith's work in regard to conflicting views on this issue.

12. Arizpe, "Women in the Informal Labor Sector."

13. Gloria Gonzalez Salazar, "Participation of Women in the Mexican Labor Force," in *Sex and Class in Latin America: Women's Perspectives on Politics, Economics and the Family in the Third World*, ed. J. Nash and H.I. Safa (Mass: Bergin and Garvey Publishers, Inc., 1980), p. 186.

14. This method allows for a wide spectrum of activities in that individuals are asked what it is they do in the course of the day. No one is asked to make a judgment as to whether an activity is within the realm of legitimate work or not (Guy Standing, *Labour Force Participation and Development* [Geneva: International Labour Office, 1978]).

15. "Disguised unemployment" refers to those who may seem unemployed, who are considered "economically inactive." The types of employment they encounter are not within the formal structure of the labor market.

Between the Lines: A New Perspective on the Industrial Sociology of Women Workers in Transnational Labor Processes

Devon PEÑA

Introduction

The on-going dialogue between Marxists and feminists is one of the most critical exchanges of ideas among those concerned with the changing role of women in the international division of labor. One recent collection of essays attempts to develop a synthesis of Marxist theories of class relations and feminist theories of gender relations (Sargent, 1981). Critics of Marxist-feminist scholarship point to a marked failure to synthesize issues related to race and nationality as important features of capitalist patriarchy (see James, 1974).[1] Marxist-feminists face several dilemmas: (1) the relative scarcity of empirically based research, (2) the lack of action-oriented research, and (3) the need for a theoretical synthesis that incorporates class and gender hierarchies and cross-cultural variations.

Perhaps the theoretical impasse in the Marxist-feminist exchange originates in the tendency for both sides to emphasize a particular aspect (i.e., class vis-á-vis gender) of the political composition of the working class. By "political composition" is meant the internal divisions of power within the working class—divisions based on sex and class as well as factors such as age, ethnicity, nationality, skills, education, and industrial location. What is perhaps needed is an approach that gives *relative primacy* to whatever one of these aspects is concretely more important in particular compositions of the working class. The perspective of political composition may allow analysts to overcome the impasse, since the primacy of any particular aspect is determined by the actual composition of workers in real situations of struggle. This perspective is in agreement with Young (1981), who calls for a "culturally-sensitive" Marxism that recognizes the differential interactions of race, gender, and class in specific cultural settings.

This paper examines the dynamics of power relations involving a predominantly female assembly line work force supervised by an all-male group in a transnational, cross-cultural labor process (the Mexican maquiladoras). The goal is to demonstrate the efficacy and theoretical clarity of the political composition perspective in terms of an actual situation involving relations of domination and resistance.[2]

Women and Global Fordism

The process of internationalization of capital involves restructuration of the labor process in terms of a global rearticulation of power relations. The labor process is not simply a material aggregate of instrumental functions, but above all a social process based on a specific set of power relations. Currently, capital's global restructuration depends increasingly on use of female labor in the Third World. The modus operandi of industrial relations in the transnational circuits of capital is based on *Fordism*. As a system of industrial relations, Fordism involves the following principal elements:[3] (1) the so-called "flow-line" principle, that is, use of an automated conveyor belt system which provides management greater control over the speed and intensity of productive activity; (2) use of hierarchical managerial controls over the quality of production and evaluation of worker performance; (3) increasing and continual division of labor, that is, use of workshift and line reassignments, implicit deskilling, and fragmentation of tasks; (4) a systematic link between worker productivity and wages based on quota and quality performance patterns rather than the older Taylorist piecework system; (5) "preconceptualization" of the entire process so that the continuity, accuracy, and intensity of productive activity is established a priori.

In outlining the specificities of global Fordism it is crucial to note that these five elements are universally applicable regardless of national or cultural setting. However, in comparative perspective it is also important to note that the Fordist system must adapt to local nuances in class composition. In a word, an examination of Fordist systems in a particular cultural setting should reveal changes in basic organizational form.

In the case of the Mexican maquiladoras, differences in the sexual division of labor play a major role in the final determination of the system of capitalist control and conversely of workers' struggles. Previous research (Peña, 1983) shows that in the Mexican maquiladoras, transnational capital has had to rely on a synthesis of imported Fordist principles and "native" features of Mexican culture, primarily the traditional patriarchal subordination of women.[4] The synthesis between imported and native features was necessary due to the increasing resistance of women workers to technical and bureaucratic forms of control.[5] Through individual and collective acts of output restriction, sabotage, and wildcat work stoppages, female maquila workers undermined to a considerable degree the effectiveness of a purely Fordist system of organizational control. Disruption of the Fordist system of power relations led to experimentation in which patriarchal modes of domination and subordination were used. Although the subordinate status of maquila workers has always been present, planned use of patriarchal control emerged in the period following the 1973-1975 strike waves. What follows is an analysis of the interaction between Fordist organizational principles and patriarchal modes of control in the maquiladoras of Cd. Juárez, Chihuahua, México.[6]

Class and Patriarchy in the Maquiladoras

A major aspect of capitalist restructuration in the Mexican maquiladoras proceeds on the basis of divisions related to sex stratification. Division of workers includes sexual hierarchies in the internal labor markets (e.g., women are confined below the first-line supervisory level). These divisions based on sex are not unique in themselves. Such fragmentations have been a feature of capitalist restructuration since the development of large-scale industry, as Marx demonstrated. Their uniqueness in the context of the maquilas resides in two related dynamics: (1) a synthesis of "imported"

Fordist principles with traditional patriarchal features unique to the host Mexican setting, and (2) capital's ability to manipulate wage and productivity differentials due to both the transnational character of the labor process and male-centered, male-controlled supervisory systems which manipulate the gender specificities of Mexican culture.

Managerial control of the labor process in the maquilas largely relies on a combination of changes in technical organization and in the forms of managerial supervision. The Fordist assembly line in the maquilas typically combines speed-up with line reassignments, male-administered admonishments, and use of informal surveillance networks to control workers' resistance and productivity. The synthesis between imported Fordist principles and native Mexican features is clear in maquila management's willingness to rely on informal contacts and networks to exert control. While modern, U.S.-based corporations, as Edwards (1979) argues, increasingly rely on bureaucratic forms of control, in the maquilas there is also a marked reliance on informal dimensions of the host culture. That is, management relies heavily on the tendency for Mexican workers to establish work relations on the basis of personal links as opposed to reliance on universal rules and formal role definitions.[7]

The patriarchal structure of the internal labor market in the maquilas owes its existence to the manner in which it provides transnational capital an alternative form of control to supplement and at times supplant more typical technical approaches. Van Waas (1981) has pointed to management's use and manipulation of the sexual demographics of the maquila work force: a predominantly female assembly line stratum is subject to supervision by a predominantly male stratum. Thus, in the maquilas the task of productivity supervision is under control of male technicians, engineers, first-line supervisors, and production managers. Moreover, the unique native features of male/female relations are transferred from the general social milieu to the factory setting: the "maleness" of factory command is partly a transplant from the traditional, patriarchal Mexican household. This study supports Fernandez Kelly's (1983) claim that male managers use traditional value systems to manipulate women into submission, for example, the promise of favoritism (cf. Kanter, 1977).

One example of the synthesis between Fordist forms of control and native patriarchal features is the relationship between female lead operators and male first-line operators.[8] The relationship between lead operators and first-line supervisors is a critical conjuncture in the network of shop floor relations because the interactions and conflicts between these two positions can largely determine the outcome of productivity supervision. If male first-line supervisors are unable to exert sufficient control over female lead operators, then control over output restriction and other types of informal resistance will be undermined.

Thus, whereas traditional forms of Fordist control like line and workshift reassignments are often undermined by female line workers, native Mexican forms of patriarchal control may impede the formation of shop floor networks. A co-opted lead operator is capital's final resort to control in the maquilas. A major feature of capitalist control in the maquilas is based on increasing access to rewards, opportunities, and power for a limited number of women.

Maquila workers' rejection of promotions from line to lead operator may imply rejection of a reward system controlled by men.[9] Yet, among workers accepting such promotions, movement up into the lead operator position increases the level of interaction with males. It also increases sharing by select women in a male-controlled system of admonishments, that is, it gives a select few, co-opted women petty increases in power. But a critical factor seems to be the increased level of female/male interactions, since first-line supervisors are not as involved with primary work groups as are lead operators. This exposes lead operators to a greater risk of co-optation and manipulation under the sway of opportunity and power systems controlled in patriarchal fashion. In a word, men "own" the right to make decisions regarding promotions, seniority, wage increases, and so forth. Women must conform to the male-centered system of managerial control or face expulsion.

The second dynamic at work, that is, productivity and wage differentials, also assumes a unique form in the context of the maquiladoras. Van Waas (1981) and others have already provided an in-depth analysis of the transnational character of production and its implications for productivity and wage differentials.[10] This study is concerned with the unexamined impact of patriarchal relations on productivity and wages in the maquilas.

The division of the maquila work force on the basis of sex has implications for productivity and wage differentials. First is the manner in which supervisors manipulate certain attitudes seen as traditionally held by Mexican females (i.e., respect for male authority, a willingness to perform for attractive males). In the case of a particular plant operation, in 1977, management substituted younger, friendlier, handsomer supervisors for older, more impersonal supervisors. The younger supervisors had more direct interaction with line workers (Oral History 1, Cd. Juárez, November, 1981). Prior to 1977, management relied on older, mixed-ethnic (Anglo and Mexican) supervisors. There were a number of incidents involving conflicts between line workers and supervisory staff. There were also a variety of incidents involving conflicts between Anglo and Mexican supervisory staff. Older, more aggressive supervisors conflicted with Mexican workers and production management staff. Apparently, management based subsequent development of its supervisory styles on the premise that Mexican women appreciate and obey young, handsome, friendly men. Thus, management relies on the ability of these younger male supervisors (an increasing number of them Mexican) to forge friendship and social networks with line operators in order to extract greater productivity and control.

Essential for success in managing the productivity of female line workers in this setting is participation by male supervisors in after-work events, that is, parties, dinners, dances, and the like (Oral History 1). Women, seemingly, work harder for a supervisor who lavishly entertains them after work (often at company expense). Wage hierarchies are also developed partly on the basis of male supervisors' participation in social and friendship networks. Women who join male supervisors for entertainment and perform well on the shop floor are rewarded with wage increases, bonuses, vacations, and the like (see also Fernandez Kelly, 1983). Women who resist the "seduction" are ostracized or threatened with termination. Sexual harassment in this manner becomes a fundamental aspect of control in the maquiladoras.

The same processes characterizing female/male relationships on the floor seem to operate in the traditional, male-dominated trade unions. Only 4 of the 223 workers in the survey taken for this study reported ever being elected or appointed to a union stewardship. Only 12 percent of the workers reported participating in union elections, and 25 percent reported conflicts with male trade union officials.[11] Over 95 percent of the workers rejected established unions as a preferred organizational form, citing male unionist cooperation with management and sexist behavior.

The "classic" case of how male trade unionists cooperate with maquila management is Acapulco Fashions (see De la Rosa Hickerson, 1979). The contract signed between the CROC (Confederación Revolucionaria Obrera y Campesina) and Acapulco Fashions included a clause allowing the company unilaterally to establish production standards without input from the workers or the union itself. Another clause gave the firm total control over work force reductions and production schedules. These clauses were used to eliminate female workers involved in informal struggles.[12]

As on the shop floor, female union members must socialize with union officials in order to gain access to rewards, opportunities, and power. The result is either co-optation or expulsion. One male trade unionist boasted that his female members were a personal "harem" (Field Journal Entry, February, 1982). A critical aspect of the relationship between male union officials and female rank-and-file members has to do with the fact that male unionists often mediate between supervisors and workers. This is particularly true in the case of shop stewards, who play a major role in the settlement of disputes between workers and supervisors. The present study suggests that union stewards admonish, reprimand, and fire workers on behalf of male supervisors (see also Van Waas, 1981).

Women's Resistance in the Fordist Factories

Capitalist labor process organization in the Mexican maquiladoras—based on imported Fordist principles and native patriarchal relations—is not without opposition. Given the features of capitalist restructuration described above, female organizational forms involve tactics and strategies which serve to overcome the divisions imposed by capital.

On the shop floor, female organizational forms tend to revolve around the line operator/lead operator/first-line supervisor conjuncture. This female/female/male triad is the key constellation around which the process of political recomposition in the maquilas revolves. A major challenge for women is overcoming sanctions that male supervisors impose for resisting absorption into social networks. One worker described her fears of being laid off as a consequence of not socializing at dinner parties with her supervisor (Oral History 3, Cd. Juárez, November, 1981). Maquila workers, nevertheless, show a capacity for overcoming divisions imposed through technical or managerial restructuration, that is, line and workshift reassignments.

However, overcoming divisions based on the patriarchal manipulation of social networks is more difficult. Given the personalized character of social networking, resistance to change becomes highly visible, since interpersonal relationships are the governing criteria upon which workers are ultimately judged. Most susceptible to this type of pressure are the lead operators, who depend on male first-line supervisors for their initial job evaluations, promotions, wage increases, and the like. Line operators, on the other hand, largely depend on lead operators for their initial evaluations. This study indicates that line and lead operators cooperate in matters related to output restriction and other issues concerning job performance and productivity. However, the relationship between lead operators and first-line supervisors may become conflictual, particularly if the lead operator is discovered participating in or concealing output restriction networks.

Therefore, female maquila workers focus much of their effort on either trying to free themselves of manipulation by co-opted lead operators or reducing the level of co-optation among lead operators. The first task seems much easier than the second. Reducing lead operator co-optation involves risking the "wrath" of male supervisors, a prospect most line workers prefer to avoid. There are severe limits, in the end, on how successful female line workers are in developing autonomous shop floor networks. The predicament entails having to form primary shop floor networks without the benefit of the vast information in the hands of lead operators. While primary shop floor networks can function without lead operator participation, their effectiveness in the struggle is thereby limited.

Thus, female resistance in the maquilas seems to develop along various tangents of activity: (1) output restriction struggles and other forms of resistance to managerial control and productivity supervision, (2) efforts to prevent co-optation of lead operators and to avoid absorption into social networks controlled by male supervisors, and (3) friendship ties. The primary shop floor network is the principal form of organization among maquila line workers. Yet disruption of these networks through various forms of capitalist restructuration often necessitates networking activity beyond the confines of the factory setting.

It is in the circulation of networking, organization, and struggle from the factory to the community or small groups that female organizational forms attain a greater degree of autonomy and relative success. Autonomy here means independence from patriarchal domination, from male-centered working-class organizations, and from managerial control. COMO (Centro de Orientación de la Mujer Obrera), Despacho Obrero, and the dozen or more independent worker coalitions are emerging as formidable autonomous networks of struggle in Juárez.[13] Prior research demonstrates that former maquila workers, trained as "external promoters" (community and cooperative organizers) at COMO,[14] circulate struggles and organizational initiatives through the CEBIs (intensive primary education centers in marginalized areas),[15] the various self-managed cooperatives in the Juárez area, and strike support groups. External promoters often must confront and transform the traditional views of women held by members of cooperatives and the working-class community in general.

There are a number of terrains of struggle among Juárez maquila workers both inside the factories and in the community that have a distinctly female character: the struggle against reproductive hazards in the workplace, against sex segregation into low-paying and hazardous jobs, the struggle for inclusion of more men in the maquila work force, and various struggles related to the reproduction of the working-class community as a whole (education, health, housing). While these struggles affect men as well, women have initiated demands and developed the organizational resources for conducting self-activity.

Maquila workers are developing their own organizational priorities and struggles. A major issue centers around how best to organize struggles related to the *social reproduction* of the working class. Female maquila workers, particularly those acting through COMO as external promoters, have emphasized networking tactics, which often build on preexisting relationships among other women in the community (e.g., *comadre* networks).[16] An example is the manner in which CEBI instructors organized struggles for more educational resources, better housing, and a sanitary water supply in the southwestern periphery of Cd. Juárez (Colonia Libertad). They appealed to the mothers of children attending the local CEBI to help them organize meetings where educational, housing, and water supply issues were discussed. The mothers, already involved in community networks, accepted the challenge with enthusiasm. CEBI instructors, many of them sensitized to the experience of child-rearing, formulated a strategy which recognized the needs of marginalized mothers and their children. Education, adequate housing, and safe drinking and cooking water were foremost among the concerns voiced by mothers during the CEBI community meetings (Oral History 5, Cd. Juárez, November, 1981; Field Journal Entry, November 20, 1981). In this manner, the CEBI workers circulated organizational activity without imposing an agenda on the women's community, that is, they respected their autonomy.

The findings on decision-making processes in the household are particularly relevant to the consideration of the possible relationship between male/female relationships in the household and the entire range of organizational forms and struggles. The findings suggest that maquila workers are often the primary source of income for many households (see also Fernandez Kelly, 1983; Carrillo and Hernandez, 1982). This occurs in situations where the women are single daughters living with their primary family, in cases involving married couples, and where workers are divorced, separated, or widowed and live with children and/or other relatives and friends.

The economic importance of maquiladora workers within their households has resulted in higher levels of decision making compared to non-maquila workers or women who are confined to the domestic sphere. The data suggest that women are assuming a greater role in many decision-making areas—including areas traditionally reserved for males by Mexican cultural norms. Shopping, bill paying, plans for education and household activities, and discipline of children are all areas in which maquila workers show high levels of participation.[17] This participatory role in decision making and planning has involved considerable struggle within the household. Conflicts with fathers, mothers, brothers, and spouses are reported by some workers (Oral History 1, 6, 8, Cd. Juárez, November, 1981-March, 1982). It seems maquila workers are challenging traditional patriarchal authority within the household. This issue may be of considerable importance for understanding self-activity within the factories.

If women are taking steps to challenge authority relations in the household, does this necessarily mean that they are also likely to challenge them in the factories? This issue is complicated, since it is difficult to establish a causal relationship between household and factory self-activity. This study does suggest that women involved in higher levels of decision making in the household also have proportionately more significant representation in output restriction struggles.[18] However, this study does not determine whether increasing militancy originates in the factory or household. There is little doubt women's entry into the maquila work force transforms traditional gender relations in the household. But the connection between such change and the process of political recomposition in the workplace is ambiguous.

Creative Praxis in the Labor Process

Braverman's (1974) research initiated a debate concerning the thesis that capitalist organization of the labor process results in increased deskilling of workers. The Fordist assembly line certainly strips workers of traditional craft skills and control over the pace of production. However, this does not necessarily imply that workers are also stripped of the capacity for creative activity and technical innovation.

Nearly half of the workers surveyed in this study were involved in one or more skilled activities. In this context, skilled activity involves engineering, repair and maintenance, and innovations which go beyond the formal job training or job descriptions of workers; 45 percent of the workers reported repair and maintenance activities and 48 percent reported engineering activities. To determine the accuracy of these reports, respondents were asked to describe their activities. The largest group of cases (29 percent) reported repairing tools or machinery to continue working. Another 23 percent reported job setups, and nearly 8 percent reported time and motion study. Almost 44 percent of the cases reported inventions and technical innovations: of these, 39 percent reported modifications of tools or machinery; 26 percent, modifications of product or components designs; 14 percent, modifications of two or more types.[19] A strong association was found between worker involvement in these creative activities and the incidence of production speed-ups: chi-square tests of significance revealed associations between speed-up and repair/maintenance activity at $P < .02$, engineering at $P < .003$, and inventions at $P < .001$.

Thus, there are two opposing tendencies in the maquiladoras. On the one hand, line workers are involved in skilled activities beyond tasks formally expected and remunerated—largely in response to productivity pressures. On the other hand, line workers engage in informal types of resistance, such as output restriction and work stoppages. The existence of these opposing tendencies suggests a need for further research on organizational dynamics and worker attitudes. Prior research indicates that workers with more militant attitudes are more likely to participate in output restriction networks (Peña, 1983). These militant workers are also less likely to participate in skilled activities, *unless they result in less work and reduced stress.*[20]

The "creative praxis" of maquila workers—involving both skilled activities and informal struggles—suggests Braverman's theses on deskilled labor are an oversimplification. Deskilling of labor does not necessarily imply depoliticization of workers.[21]

Summary of Implications

The tendencies described above have implications for theories of transnational labor processes and the interaction between class and gender in cross-cultural settings. First, capital's reliance on native patriarchy implies that control strategies under global Fordism must often focus on changes in the social, cultural, and demographic composition of the work force. Changes in the technical organization of the labor process and in managerial supervision are important. However, often the primary and most important control strategies involve manipulation of the social and cultural characteristics of the work force—in this case through patriarchal domination of female maquila workers. This is not meant to imply that Mexican culture is the only patriarchal system interacting with global Fordism. It is merely suggested that transnational labor processes, particularly those operating in cross-cultural settings, may of necessity rely on certain native features for control over workers. Identification of these native features of control and how they are modified and used by capital must become a major theoretical concern in future research.

Second, any theory of women in the labor process that aims at a two-sided class and gender perspective must give equal attention to capitalist restructuration and changes in the *internal* power relations of the working class. In a transnational setting, analysis should deal with local, plant, and community-specific processes and international linkages between home-base and local operations. The circulation of workers' struggles and capitalist restructuration should be analyzed to specify how local processes and class composition impact on the overall constellation of power relations and to understand the effects of global processes on local struggles.

Third, labor process theory has been limited by a focus on industrial workers and factory work. This study suggests a need to focus on the interconnections between the labor process and household/community experiences and struggles. More research and theoretical analysis is needed to understand the significance of women's experiences in the household as a factor affecting workplace experiences and vice versa. Much can be learned about the labor process through analysis of the circulation of workers' struggles from factory to community and vice versa.

Fourth, a theory of the transnational labor process which recognizes the interactions between gender and class must include analysis of international differentials in working-class power, accounting for sex-specific inequities in power. Political economists have focused on the international division of labor as if the working class is only labor power—another factor of production. A focus on the working class as a political and social entity would be more useful, particularly for those concerned with action-oriented research. The political composition perspective provides a theoretical framework for such an analysis in that it understands the internal divisions of the working class primarily as divisions based on differences in social and political power. Future theoretical inquiry might lead to analysis of how women "fall between the lines" of internal divisions based on gender and class relations. Women in the interstices of the transnational labor process face not only class divisions, not only gender divisions, but also the cross-cultural and cross-national inequities which characterize the current situation of the international working class.

Finally, the transnational character of capital and the working class calls for comparative analysis in light of cross-cultural and cross-national differences. The findings of this study have implications for understanding the situation facing Chicanas and other Third World women in the United States. Chicana, black, and Filipino women comprise a large proportion of the labor force in

U.S. electronics and garment operations (Snow, 1983). In California's "Silicon Valley" these women represent close to half of the assembly line work force. Most analyses of Silicon Valley workers have focused on workers' demographic and socioeconomic characteristics or on capital's strategies for control. However, a number of important studies of struggles among Chicanas have found interactions between class and gender relations. For example, Coyle et. al. (1979) studied the El Paso Farah strike and found that garment workers experienced considerable sexual harassment. Workers who refused to socialize with supervisors were punished with high quotas, harder tasks, and other stressful working conditions. Magdalena Mora's (1981) study of the Tolteca workers' strike found that preferential treatment of workers by supervisors created internal divisions. Mora also found that informal resistance to speed-up and efforts to reform the union played critical roles in the workers' struggles.

Future research on women's struggles in the global electronics and garment industries must include further analysis of formal and informal modes of struggle and study of the dialectical interactions between class and gender relations outlined in this and other studies. Issues related to cross-cultural and cross-national divisions must be carefully considered. For example, in the United States, unlike Mexico, there is a pronounced division among workers on the basis of race, ethnicity, and nationality. In southern California, Nalven (1983) found that the internal labor market in an electronics firm was characterized by an *all-Anglo, mixed male and female* supervisor stratum. Assemblers and inspectors were predominantly Third World women. Between these two strata was a group of lead operators and lead inspectors comprised of about half women and men and about half Anglo and Third World workers. Thus, in the U.S. setting, divisions at supervisory and staff levels cut across both gender and nationality lines. In Mexico, by comparison, all positions of first-line supervisor and above are held by males of mixed Mexican and Anglo-American nationality. All women are confined below the first-line supervisor level, and few men are found in operator positions. Thus, in Mexico's maquiladoras there is a more pronounced sexual division of workers compared to the United States, where divisions based on race and nationality figure prominently. This comparison serves to illustrate the significance of cross-cultural and cross-national differences in working-class political composition. Obviously, the implications for struggle are that U.S. workers organize to overcome race, nationality, and gender divisions, while Mexican maquila workers primarily face gender divisions related to the highly patriarchal structure of internal labor markets.

Chicanas and other Third World women occupy a strategic position in the new international division of labor. They are concentrated in key sectors of the global capitalist economy. Comparative studies of women's struggles in the global electronics industry could provide important insights concerning changing power relations, tactics for organization, and the possibilities for linkage of struggles at the transnational level. This study, hopefully, will stimulate such future inquiry.

NOTES

1. In fairness to the collection of essays in Sargent (1981), the issue of racism is acknowledged. However, none of the essays, with the possible exception of Young (1981), attempts to develop such a synthesis. One excellent effort in this direction is the work of Cavendish (1982). Also cf. O'Barr (1982) and Keohane et al. (1981).

2. One of the tendencies in the Marxist-feminist literature is a striking absence of analyses dealing with women workers' actual struggles. There is a marked emphasis on analyses of relations of domination, with much less attention given to relations of resistance.

3. This summary of Fordism is based on a synthesis of various works, including Aglietta (1979), Braverman (1974), Burawoy (1979), Clawson (1980), Cooley (1980), Hales (1980), Palliox (1976), and Sohn-Rethel (1976).

4. Most of this paper is based on my doctoral dissertation. See Peña (1983).

5. For commentary, see Edwards (1979), who outlines three basic forms of control in the development of the capitalist labor process: simple, technical, and bureaucratic.

6. The data for this study are based on a ten-month research project in the Juárez maquiladora sector. Data included 223 survey interviews, 15 oral histories, 11 management interviews, and observations from September, 1981, through June, 1982.

7. For further discussion, see Zurcher et al. (1965).

8. Lead operators, also known as group-chiefs (*jefes de grupo*), are assembly line operators chosen by management to perform supervisory tasks in conjunction

with first-line supervisors. The lead operators are so called because they lead the group in establishing the upper limit on performance or quota standards. In the language of U.S. industrial sociologists, the lead operators may be seen as rate-busters, that is, workers who consistently surpass the quota levels informally established by the primary work group.

9. This study found that over 60 percent of the workers in the survey reported rejecting promotions. The major motive cited by workers for the rejection was fear of disruption of friendship ties.

10. Van Waas (1981) argues that maquiladoras are interested not only in the relatively lower wages paid Mexican workers but also in their considerably higher productivity. The setting of wage policies in the maquilas is based not only on government guidelines but on the unit-output per worker as well. See also Carrillo and Hernandez (1982).

11. See also De la Rosa Hickerson (1979); Carrillo and Hernandez (1982); Gambrill (1983).

12. One worker described her reasons for her discontent with traditional *charrista* trade unions: "The men expect the women to cater their every whim. Make coffee, go get *burritos*, clean the office, arrange the files, deliver the mail to the post office. . . and some, many I would say, expect sexual favors. But if you ask for help, say with making sure a union member is represented by a lawyer at an arbitration hearing, forget it! The only thing they care about is their own power which is a direct function of their good standing with managers . . . " (Oral History 8, March, 1982, Cd. Juárez).

13. For further discussion of COMO, see Peña (1983: chap. 8). This organization, founded in 1969, is an experiment in alternative worker education (utilizing a critical, social problem-solving or neo-Freirean pedagogy) and cooperative self-management.

14. External promoters trained at COMO combine skills in community organizing with social work principles of change agency and advocacy. COMO trains maquila workers in three major areas of activity: public education, public health nursing, and social work.

15. The CEBIs (Centros de Educación Básica Intensiva) are outreach primary education centers serving marginalized communties with high levels of illiteracy.

16. The term *comadre*, literally translated as "godmother," has a variety of meanings dependent on the speech situation and the persons communicating. My use of the term is meant to suggest a network of friends and not kinship ties per se, although in many cases the *comadres* COMO workers referred to were actual godmothers in more than a figurative sense.

17. Shopping and plans for household activities are traditionally areas of decision making for women in Mexico. Bill paying and the discipline of children are traditionally reserved for men. Plans related to education and household activities are often jointly shared areas of responsibility. This survey, however, included many cases reporting participation in the disciplining of children and bill paying.

18. A chi-square test of significance on the relationship between output restriction and worker participation in household planning and decision making revealed that workers with a participatory background in the household had a proportionately greater representation among the output restriction cases as well ($X^2 = 6.79987$, 4 *df*, significant at the $P < .1$ level).

19. For detailed descriptions and commentary on inventions and technical innovations among maquila workers, see Centro do Orientación de la Mujer Obrera (COMO) and Centro de Estudios Fronterizos del Norte de México (CEFNOMEX) (1984). See also Peña (1983: chap. 6).

20. For related commentary on the issue of stress in the workplace, see Gettman and Peña (1984) and Gettman (1984).

21. For a similar argument, cf. Cooley (1980) and Hales (1980).

REFERENCES

Aglietta, M. 1979. *A Theory of Capitalist Regulation* (London: New Left Books).

Braverman, H. 1974. *Labor and Monopoly Capital* (New York: Monthly Review Press).

Burawoy, M. 1979. *Manufacturing Consent* (Chicago: University of Chicago Press).

Carrillo, J. and A. Hernandez. 1982. "La Mujer Obrera en la Industria Maquiladora: El Caso de Ciudad Juárez" (Tesis Professional, Universidad Nacional Autónoma de México, Facultad de Ciencias Políticas y Sociales, Mexico, D.F.).

Cavendish, R. 1982. *Women on the Line* (London: Routledge and Kegan Paul).

Centro do Orientación de la Mujer Obrera (COMO) and Centro de Estudios Fronterizos del Norte de México (CEFNOMEX). 1984. *Primer Taller de Análisis sobre Aprendizaje en la Producción y Transferencia de Tecnología en la Industria de Maquila de Exportación* (Cd. Juárez: COMO/CEFNOMEX).

Clawson, D. 1980. *Bureaucracy and the Labor Process* (New York: Monthly Review Press).

Cooley, M. 1980. *Architect or Bee? The Human/Technology Relationship* (Boston: South End Press).

Coyle, L. et al. 1979. *Women at Farah: An Unfinished Story* (El Paso: Reforma—El Paso Chapter).

De la Rosa Hickerson, G. 1979. "La Contratación Colectiva en las Maquiladoras" (Tesis professional, Universidad Autónoma de Ciudad Juárez, Facultad de Derecho, Cd. Juárez, Chihuahua, México).

Edwards, R. 1979. *Contested Terrain* (New York: Basic Books).

Fernandez Kelly, M.P. 1983. *For We Are Sold, I and My People: Women and Industry on Mexico's Frontier* (Albany: State University of New York Press).

Gambrill, M. 1983. "El Sindicalismo en las Maquiladoras de Tijuana" (Paper presented at the First International Conference on Technology and Culture on the Mexico-U.S. Border, October, La Jolla, Cal.).

Gettman, D. 1984. "Feminist Therapy with Working-Class Chicanas" (Paper presented at the Annual Meetings of the National Association for Chicano Studies, March, University of Texas, Austin).

Gettman, D. and D. Peña. 1984. "Women, Mental Health and the Workplace: Research Issues and Challenges in a Transnational Setting" (Paper presented at the first NASW National Health Conference: Policy Politics and Practice, National Association for Social Workers [NASW], June, Washington, D.C.).

Hales, M. 1980. *Living Thinkwork* (London: CSE Books).

James, S. 1974. *Race, Sex, and Class* (Bristol: Falling Wall Press).

Kanter, R.M. 1977. *Men and Women of the Corporation* (New York: Basic Books).

Keohane, N.O. et al. (eds.). 1981. *Feminist Theory: A Critique of Ideology.* (Chicago: University of Chicago Press).

Mora, M. 1981. "The Tolteca Strike: Mexican Women and the Struggle for Union Representation." In *Mexican Immigrant Workers in the United States,* ed. A. Ríos Bustamante (Los Angeles: Chicano Studies Research Center Publications).

Nalven, J. 1983. "Prophets of Boom, Prophets of Gloom: The Future of Industrial Development in the San Diego-Tijuana Region" (Paper presented at the First International Conference on Technology and Culture on the Mexico-U.S. Border, October, La Jolla, Cal.).

O'Barr, J.F. (ed.). 1982. *Perspectives on Power: Women in Africa, Asia, and Latin America* (Durham, N.C.: Duke University).

Palliox. C. 1976. "From Fordism to Neo-Fordism." In *The Labour Process and Class Strategies*, ed. Conference of Socialist Economists (London: CSE/Phase One).

Peña, D. 1983. "The Class Politics of Abstract Labor: Organizational Forms and Industrial Relations in the Mexican Maquiladoras" (Ph.D. Dissertation, Sociology, University of Texas, Austin, Tx.).

Sargent, L. (ed.). 1981. *Women and Revolution* (Boston: South End Press).

Snow, R.T. 1983. "The New International Division of Labor and the U.S. Workforce: The Case of the Electronics Industry." In *Women, Men, and the International Division of Labor*, eds. J. Nash and M.P. Fernandez Kelly (Albany: State University of New York Press).

Sohn-Rethel, A. 1976. "The Dual Economics of Transition." In *The Labour Process and Class Strategies*, ed. Conference of Social Economists (London: CSE/Phase One).

Van Waas, M. 1981. "The Multinationals' Strategy for Labor: Foreign Assembly Plants in Mexico's Border Industrialization Program," (Ph.D. Dissertation, Political Science, Stanford University, Stanford, Cal.).

Young, I. 1981. "Beyond the Unhappy Marriage: A Critique of Dual Systems Theory." In *Women and Revolution*, ed. L. Sargent (Boston: South End Press).

Zurcher, L. et al. 1965. "Value Orientation, Role Conflict, and Alienation from Work: A Cross-Cultural Study." *American Sociological Review* 30 (August).

The Women's Movement and the Left in Mexico: The Presidential Candidacy of Doña Rosario Ibarra

Teresa CARRILLO

In 1976 there was only one participant in the Mexican presidential elections—José López Portillo. In contrast, the 1982 elections brought both volume and diversity to the list of presidential candidates—eight parties ran six candidates, one of whom was a woman. As the candidate for the Partido Revolucionario de los Trabajadores, (PRT, Revolutionary Workers party), Doña Rosario Ibarra de Piedra became the first woman in Mexican history to run for president of the Republic. This study focuses on Rosario's candidacy and evaluates the impact of her campaign on women's political participation and organization within the Mexican Left. The issues raised define a basic tension between class- and gender-based analyses of women's issues. These issues lead to a more generalized set of questions involving the tension between domination and resistance experienced by progressive women operating within the Mexican Left and the Mexican political system at large.

This study draws heavily from a series of personal interviews with Doña Rosario Ibarra and Susana Vidales, a feminist organizer who worked on Rosario's campaign as the director of the Comités de Mujeres en Apoyo a Rosario Ibarra (Committees of Women in Support of Rosario Ibarra). Additional sources including Mexican periodicals and party publications were also consulted.[1]

To place the campaign in context, this article first presents background information on Rosario Ibarra and the 1982 elections. A short description of women's issues within the elections follows. Finally, three effects of Rosario's campaign on women's politics are outlined. The first was a general increase in women's political participation in Mexico. The second involved a shift in the nature of the demands put forth by women from gender-specific demands such as legalized abortion or voluntary motherhood to a more class-based set of demands oriented toward the situation of working-class women, such as wage increases, controls on the cost of basic foods and rent, and so forth. Finally, as a third effect, the campaign facilitated a reconciliation between independent feminists who were ex-PRT party members and the leadership of the PRT. The campaign provided an opportunity for cooperation between the two groups in pursuit of a common interest in the organization and mobilization of women.

Doña Rosario Ibarra de Piedra

Because of the currents of feminist activity already in motion in Mexico combined with the efforts of the leftist parties to incorporate women into their membership, women's political participation would undoubtedly have increased during 1981-1982 with or without a female presidential candidate. However, Rosario Ibarra's campaign facilitated women's participation, because there was an organized attempt by women to take advantage of the opportunities provided by the campaign. Rosario herself was an important factor because of the platform she presented, her long history of political activism, and her reputation as a strong and determined woman.

Over ten years ago, Ibarra de Piedra's son, Jesús Piedra Ibarra, a politically active medical student, "disappeared." Eighteen months later, the newspaper *El Norte* reported his capture along with three members of La Liga Comunista de Septiembre 23 (the Communist League of September 23). According to the article, the prisoners were delivered to Military Camp No. 1, "physically beaten but alive."[2] Frustrated by the government's refusal to acknowledge her son's imprisonment or to provide information about his condition, his whereabouts, or the charges brought against him, Rosario Ibarra began to organize and activate the families of the many *desaparecidos políticos*.[3] In 1974 she founded the Comité Pro-Defensa de Presos, Exiliados y Desaparecidos Políticos (the Committee in Defense of Political Prisoners, Exiles, and Disappeared People), an organization made up largely of women—the wives, daughters, and mothers of many of the 509 *desaparecidos políticos* who have been documented by the group.

The committee's main objective was (and still is) to bring an end to the government's repressive actions against political activists, with special attention given to the problem of the *desaparecidos políticos.* During the Echeverría administration, Rosario, representing the Comité Pro-Defensa, made contact with the President 36 times—first in meetings, later in any setting or function that provided the opportunity. The committee's most dramatic tactic was to stage a hunger strike outside the cathedral in the Zócalo in Mexico City. On August 28, 1979, Rosario Ibarra and 83 other women began the hunger strike demanding that the amnesty law that the Congress was debating be enacted. On August 31, the eve of the state of the union address, the hunger strike was broken up by police. Yet on the following day, President López-Portillo announed his amnesty proposal, which would benefit those who "have chosen the mistaken path of crime." Once the amnesty law was adopted, the committee put forth demands for its realization. In August, 1979, the López-Portillo administration freed 919 political prisoners (813 of whom were peasants arrested for demanding land) in accordance with the amnesty law. The *Latin American Political Report* said, "The release of the prisoners came after the police had forcibly evicted 30 members of the *Comité Pro-Defensa de Presos y Desaparecidos* from the Swiss embassy."[4]

In 1977 the Comité Pro-Defensa organized a national coalition of leftist political parties and various organizations called the Frente Nacional Contra la Represión (FNCR, the National Front against Repression). Through this coalition Rosario Ibarra began working with the Partido Revolucionario de los Trabajadores (PRT). In an interview, Doña Rosario described the PRT as one of the most active member groups in the coalition. "In everything the Frente has done, the PRT has always been present offering their support, time, and effort."[5]

The PRT was founded in 1975 when four Trotskyite groups in Mexico, the International Communist League, the Marxist Workers League, and two socialist leagues united to form one party. In a threefold strategy to use the electoral campaign as a forum to organize, to gain seats in Congress, and to attract people to the party, the PRT decided to seek legal recognition as an official party in the 1982 elections. The PRT's efforts were successful, and the party joined three other leftist opposition parties (PCM, PST, and PDM) that had won their official party status in the 1979 national elections.[6]

Electoral Reform Law of 1977

Securing official party status for the PRT was possible as a result of the liberalizing reforms called *la apertura*. New party registration in 1979 and 1982 was an important and unprecedented phenomenon in Mexican electoral politics, finding its legal basis in the Electoral Reform Law of 1977. The law, known as the LOPPE (Ley Federal de Organizaciones Políticas y Procesos Electorales), outlines changes in four areas central to the electoral process, the first of which is procedure for party recognition.[7] To become registered, a party must prove an enrollment of at least 65,000 members distributed across the nation and gain 1.5 percent of the total national vote in the election.

The second change enlarged the federal Chamber of Deputies to allow for participation by opposition parties. In 1982, 100 minority party seats were distributed as follows: PAN (Partido Acción Nacional) 50, PSUM 17, PDM 12, PST 11, and PPS (Partido Popular Socialista) 10.[8] The last two areas of change involve material support and access to mass communication provided by the electoral commission. Legally registered opposition parties were given financial assistance for campaign literature, meeting halls, and transportation as well as permanent and regular access to TV and radio time, postal and telegraph privileges, and exemptions from all taxes and duties to help offset campaign expenses.

The electoral reforms represent legislative outcomes of a liberalization process: *apertura*. Although the reforms constitute an official and legal change, there has been little evidence of a consequent shift in the power structure. The Mexican political system remains a one-party authoritarian regime with the Partido Revolucionario Institucional (PRI, the Institutional Revolutionary party) in a clearly dominant position. Many see the effort to incorporate new political forces into the established party system as a way to expand the system's representative capacity and to strengthen its claim to popular consent and legitimacy.[9] This view is supported by the fact that a long-standing trend toward increased voter abstention was reversed in 1982 when 75 percent of all registered voters participated in the elections—the highest rate recorded since 1946.[10]

Nevertheless, for the PRT and Ibarra de Piedra's campaign, the electoral reform laws made at least a small difference. As an officially registered party, the PRT gained access to media time, equipment, and funds that allowed it to expand the campaign to a national level. Official party status also offered a certain amount of legitimacy which ensured regular media coverage and allowed for minimal agenda-setting power within the larger setting of the 1982 election.

Doña Rosario's Campaign

April, 1981, marked the beginning of Rosario's campaign when the PRT asked her to run as their candidate for president. Ibarra de Piedra seeing the potential use of the campaign as a forum to fight more effectively against repression, accepted the nomination. In her acceptance speech she explained,

> This campaign is a call to the workers and all oppressed sectors of Mexican society to organize and unite as the only way toward a resolution of the problems that face us. If after this campaign, the organizations grow in number of militants, if the workers from the cities as well as the country have raised their consciousness and come to identify more exactly their friends and their enemies, if we get even one more person who is outraged at the number of political prisoners, at the torture, at the existence of secret prisons, and if the campaign helps to make strong this contingent of society, we can say that it has been a good fight; a good electoral campaign that has helped to invigorate this "army of the people."[11]

Ibarra de Piedra, along with various groups on the Left in Mexico, was eager to make use of the electoral reform—not to gather votes so much as to amplify more fully the interests and demands of workers, campesinos, women, and other oppressed sectors that have traditionally constituted the politically impotent masses in Mexican society.

Ibarra de Piedra's campaign gained the support of a diverse cross-section of Mexican society, with concentrated support among the rural and urban working class and the marginalized classes. Susana Vidales explains,

> Rosario's campaign resulted in extensive participation among the marginalized population that had never before been ac-

> tive. In these sectors women participated in an important manner—a participation that was unprecedented among marginalized women. This can be attributed to the type of campaign Rosario led and to the personality of Rosario. She is a woman with a long history of struggle and with an impressive talent to speak and to motivate the people.[12]

During the course of her fifteen-month campaign, Rosario Ibarra spoke with hundreds of thousands of Mexicans throughout the country. Traveling in twelve vehicles provided by the Federal Electoral Commission, Ibarra de Piedra and representatives of the PRT visited prisons, factories, ejidos, cooperatives, unions, schools, and any other place where they were likely to find a receptive crowd. Speeches during the campaign consistently addressed the need for revolutionary changes in order to bring about a workers' government. Ibarra de Piedra always addressed the problem of repression and the *desaparecidos políticos.* A march and demonstration at Tlatelolco that closed the campaign drew 50,000 participants.

The campaign can be seen as a product of converging interests. Ibarra de Piedra and the FNCR were quick to recognize the enormous opportunity provided by the campaign for nationwide activism against repression; the PRT saw in Ibarra de Piedra a candidate with tremendous popular appeal to sectors of society that had formerly been politically inactive. Moreover, feminist activists worked to use the first woman's presidential campaign to facilitate women's political participation.

Although Ibarra de Piedra was the first woman to run for president in Mexico, she did not center her campaign around feminist issues. She spoke on women's issues, but only infrequently. Much of the campaign work that focused on women's issues was done by the feminist organizations that got involved. Susana Vidales, commenting on this sparse coverage, explains that the vast majority of Mexicans do not include these issues on their political agenda. "A tendency shared by almost everyone in Mexico, and above all by the people on the Left that are involved in so many other political struggles, is to neglect the problems defined within the women's platforms."[13] This campaign significantly focused on demands of working and marginalized classes, placing both the PRT and Ibarra de Piedra far to the Left on the political spectrum. However, because Ibarra de Piedra was a female candidate and because of PRT's early progressive women's platform, the campaign uniquely oriented itself toward women's issues—an orientation that was developed by feminists working in conjunction with the campaign. A connection between the campaign and women's politics on the Left can be explored within the more general context of women's politics in the 1982 elections.

Women's Politics in the 1982 Elections

Every party to take part in the 1982 elections presented some semblance of a plank on women's issues, including the PRI and the PAN. The PRI, with the aid of the Asociación Nacional Femenil Revolucionario (ANFER, the women's group within the PRI), developed a National Plan for the Integration of Women with Development in 1980.[14] The plan outlined three basic rights that have been denied to women: (1) a right to equal educational opportunities, (2) an equal right to work, and (3) a right to participate in popular politics/elections. A plan of action in the report called for an intense campaign to increase opportunities for women in education and the workplace, and to implement legislative changes to eliminate obstacles to women's opportunities. A previous 1978 program of action developed by the PRI contained a chapter titled "Politics for Women" (Política Hacia la Mujer) in which the party assigns a role to women in national politics,

> The party knows that it can successfully engage women's militancy in tasks for social benefit such as assistance in the schools, in civic organizations, in recreational programs, etc. . . . As partners and collaborators of men, as daughers, sisters, and wives, the woman transmits her civic and political concerns to her family and through her, the family's consciousness is expanded on a social, economic, and cultural level.[15]

In spite of its patronizing role assignment, the PRI's women's platform included demands for state-run child care centers, equality of rights, responsibilities, and obligations within the party, and active promotion of women's political participation.

Feminist reactions to the women's platform put forth by the PRI were mixed—both supportive and critical. Marta Lamas, a feminist and journalist, in a critique of the PRI's platform on women, noted the conspicuous absence of a demand for women's control of their own bodies—a demand which includes rights to voluntary motherhood and protection against sexual violence. Lamas proposed that integration of women into economic and political life must be accompanied by changes within the family and in the traditional division of labor between men and women. She called for a redefinition of the integration of women/family based in social reality and not in the mystification of "the couple" and of the ideal family.[16]

The parties on the Left presented more extensive women's platforms. In addition to those demands voiced by the PRI, the PSUM, and the PST, the PRT addressed the rights of women in the countryside to receive and work land and to own land in their own names; legal protection and unionization for artisans, seamstresses, waitresses, maids, and border factory workers; legal aid for single mothers, abandoned wives, and widows; changes in education and public services to facilitate a redistribution of responsibilities within the home; and legal reforms to change laws that discriminate against women.

The demands raised by the PRT were the most extensive. They introduced a six-part demand for women's right to control reproduction that included: (1) a condemnation of the state's population plan, (2) legal and accessible abortion, (3) prohibition of forced sterilization, (4) dissemination of information on reproduction and birth control, (5) medical research on birth control methods for both men and women, and (6) prohibition of medical experimentation on women without their consent. The PRT also developed a twenty-one-part demand for juridical reforms protecting the legal rights of women, prostitutes, homosexuals, female workers and students, pregnant women, and victims of sexual abuse. Although these demands were selectively and intermittently addressed during the campaign, any characterization of the 1982 elections would be incomplete without an acknowledgment of the attention given women's issues and women's participation.

Feminist organizers, many of whom had once been active in Leftist party politics, decided to work within Ibarra de Piedra's campaign to organize women around women's issues. Within the context of the electoral campaign, feminist politics eased into the discussion. The campaign provided a nonthreatening setting in which women could come together and organize as women without the stigma attached by many to feminist activism.

Susana Vidales, an ex-member of the PRT and a feminist organizer, together with other feminists, approached the PRT with a proposal to form Comités de Mujeres en Apoyo a Rosario Ibarra (Committees of Women in Support of Rosario Ibarra). The PRT agreed and the women began their work. They concentrated their organizational efforts in two districts of Mexico City in support of women from the feminist movement who were candidates for the Chamber of Deputies. They also sought participation as representatives of the women's movement in the campaign tours of Ibarra de Piedra and the PRT. Vidales described the tactics of the Comités as the small groups of organizers began their work:

> First we distributed flyers asking the women to tell us what they perceived to be the problems of the women in their particular barrio. Later, we returned and put up posters with the demands of the women and the names of the candidates. We then distributed flyers from house to house inviting the women to a meeting in their neighborhood during which we would have music and singing. Many women would come. Often while we were distributing flyers the women would come out of their houses and ask where they could get information or who they should contact and we would write down their names and addresses and follow up with a meeting every week for the new women who were just joining. During these meetings we would plan activities and discuss the problems women experienced. The idea was that once the campaign was over, we would be able to organize women as women—not only in support of Rosario but as women.[17]

Vidales noted that the majority of women who showed an interest in the work of the Comités were working-class.

As the Comités de Mujeres began to grow and expand both in and around Mexico City, a group of central organizers began planning a national meeting for representatives from each Comité. The meeting was held March 14, 1982, in the Cine Régis in Mexico City. Vidales, on describing the event, says, "Rosario spoke and the auditorium was packed—there were about 1,500 women—all women. They came not only from the city, but from the provinces and smaller towns that had been successful in organizing their groups."[18] The women, representing workers, campesinas, colonas,[19] and students, focused their discussion and speeches on the role that women play in the workers' struggle and the obstacles they have faced as women in their efforts to participate. Lourdes Uranga, a representative of the Unión de Lucha Revolucionaria, spoke of the sexual division of labor within the revolutionary movement. "We have to start now to change these patterns of subordination. From our compañeros we ask for access to positions in the political organizations and in the unions, and co-responsibility between men and women for raising children and maintaining the household."[20] The meeting of the Comités de Mujeres was unique in two respects. It was the biggest meeting of feminist women ever held in Mexico City, and the women in attendance represented all the popular sectors—urban working women, rural women, students, and marginalized women.

Many factors contributed to an environment conducive to women's organizational efforts during the 1982 elections. Susana Vidales, as the promoter of the Comités de Mujeres, explains that the campaign offered

> a pretext to go to the neighborhoods, the barrios, and the factories—a pretext to go as part of Rosario's campaign but we went with the demands of women. We addressed ourselves solely to women and this sparked an interest. All of our leaflets and flyers dealt with issues directed toward the women, for example, problems of inflation and cost of living since these problems interest mainly women as managers of the household finances. We also took up issues such as the lack of child-care facilities, the difficulties of finding work as a woman, problems of machismo, of household division of labor and even issues concerning sexuality. This attracted a lot of women. It might have happened without Rosario's campaign but the campaign acted as a license for women . . . allowing more women to participate with the permission of their husbands and without problems.[21]

Ibarra de Piedra's campaign facilitated an increase in women's political participation not only through direct organization of women in the committees, but also by offering a certain legitimacy to women's issues. Vidales points out that in Mexico the feminist movement is thought of as very radical and not as pressing as other issues important to the revolutionary movements. The women within the revolutionary parties often adopt that same attitude and view the women's movement as something foreign and divisive. Ibarra de Piedra's campaign made it easier for many women to see the connection between the feminist and class dimensions of their own struggle as working-class or marginalized women. The connection was made explicit through meetings with the organizers of the Comités de Mujeres, through flyers, posters, and literature produced by the committees that specifically addressed these issues, through PRT's extensive women's platform, and through public forums and television programs in which Ibarra de Piedra and women affiliated with the Comités de Mujeres spoke about the women's situation in Mexico.

The novelty of a female presidential candidate also added to the campaign's impact on women. Vidales makes this point, saying, "The men in the rural setting were always the ones to attend political events and meetings and the women never went. When the people saw that Rosario was the candidate, the women went along with the men to the event. For the men it was a bit difficult to say to a woman that she couldn't go hear another woman speak."[22] Most of the women's participation in Ibarra de Piedra's campaign was in the form of attendance at political events and demonstrations or at meetings held in the communities of the working and marginalized classes. A smaller number of women participated as members of a particular women's organization. In addition to the Comités de Mujeres, there were newly formed committees for women within almost all the political parties and unions. Two examples are the Frente Nacional de Mujeres (FNM) of the PRT, and the Grupo de Mujeres de CONAMUP (Comité Nacional de Movimientos Urbanos Populares), two groups that experienced incredible growth following the 1982 elections.

The PRT and other leftist parties saw through the campaign that women were interested in participating and responded by creating women's groups within the political party structure. Their strategy for incorporating women into a popular woman's movement involved concentration on class-based demands that are defined as women's issues largely in accordance with a traditional sexual division of labor. Issues relating to the home and the family, such as rent control, control of basic food prices, transportation, health services, and so forth, became the new women's issues. Working-class and marginalized women could easily identify themselves with the demands of the women's groups within the parties; for the first time, the woman's movement was gaining support as a popular movement.

The women's groups within the parties avoided confrontational feminist demands such as voluntary motherhood or protection against sexual violence even though these demands were part of the progressive women's platforms that were put forth earlier by small but militant feminist groups within the parties. The most progressive feminist demands in the platforms were ignored or postponed as part of the strategy to attract women into a popular, working-class movement. Although more and more women were becoming organized into groups, the support and mobilization behind feminist issues (control of reproduction, equality of rights between men and women, etc.) was declining, and the new women's issues filled the agendas of the women's groups. The woman's movement on the Left shifted its focus from gender-specific demands to class-based demands oriented toward the working-class woman in her traditional role as caretaker of the home and family.[23]

Susana Vidales comments that the women's group in the PRT, like other women's groups within the Left, constitutes "a movement that is a class movement and not necessarily a feminist movement." Summing up the impact of Rosario's candidacy on women's politics, Vidales says,

> The campaign was helpful in that it attracted women to participate, it created conditions needed for women to become more conscious of their oppression as women, and it increased the scope of the movement . . . but the way PRT is changing its platform toward woman's issues by laying off volatile issues such as legalized abortion will slow down the development of the women's movement by not simultaneously raising issues of class and gender.[24]

Vidales's criticism is reminiscent of the extended debate among feminists in Mexico regarding the problem of *doble militancia* (double militancy). Early in 1981, Marta Lamas, a feminist journalist, addressed the problem in a journal article. She refers back to 1976, when the Coalition of Feminist Women was formed, bringing together women from the three different veins of feminism—the

NOW-type reformists, the radical feminists, and the Socialist/Marxist feminists. The Coalition focused its efforts on a campaign to legalize abortion. Within the context of a working coalition, the women alternatively clashed and meshed in the process of defining an autonomous movement of feminists. The problems articulated by Marta Lamas address the relationship between leftist parties and feminists and ask: (1) To what extent can the two groups work together? (2) Is it important strategically to work together? and (3) What does the alliance imply? She questions *how* the two groups could "work together without opportunism, without having one group consume the work of the other and without confusing organizational autonomy with political autonomy."[25]

Lamas's article appeared early in 1981 following the division of the Coalition into two groups—one that would work within the political parties and the other whose members wanted to identify themselves first as feminists and shape their organizing strategies accordingly. Participation in independent feminist organizations declined during 1980. The feminist movement was perhaps becoming better defined but was losing momentum and supporters for its gender-based issues. In mid-1981 Maria A. Rascón published an article in *FEM* entitled "Feminism and Political Reform." In her article, Rascón links the birth of the feminist movement to the process of political liberalization or *apertura*. After presenting evidence of growth and progress in the feminist movement in Mexico, she writes,

> Feminists are faced with options and alternatives to work within the parties while the prospect for historically necessary independent feminist organization doesn't seem to find immediate conditions for its own development. Possibilities for extension and development of feminism as an autonomous political movement are conditioned by Mexico's political and economic development and by the material conditions and the consciousness of the women as well as the political reforms and the possibilities for the advance and integration of Leftist currents at the national level. Faced with the practical and theoretical difficulties in articulation of feminist politics at the national level, our immediate alternative tends toward an integration into party politics, fundamentally Leftist party politics, as the most viable and productive option for feminists in Mexico.[26]

This was the option chosen by the feminists during the 1982 elections. The organizational work that took place within the context of the campaign served the interests of both the feminists and the PRT. Although the relationship between the two groups retains elements of conflict, the reconciliation that took place constitutes a development in that relationship. In a cooperative effort the two groups were able to take advantage of their overlapping interests while acknowledging and respecting the areas of interest which did not overlap.

Reflections

The main questions raised by Rosario Ibarra's campaign go beyond the scope of political participation to ask what significance it has had for the participants themselves, for the women's movement, and for the Mexican political system in general. For the thousands of women and working-class or marginalized people who went through an important politicization process, the campaign will have long-lasting effects at the personal level and possibly beyond. The process of politicization was encouraged by successful efforts at grass roots organization which resulted in registration of the PRT as an official party, formation of the Comités de Mujeres and similar groups, increased party membership in PRT and other leftist parties, and over 500,000 votes cast for Rosario Ibarra. Ibarra de Piedra's campaign and the organizing of women that took place as part of it also helped to ground the women's movement in a popular-based class movement. Thousands of women beginning their process of politicization at a personal level offer great potential for development of a popular, grass roots feminist movement. The campaign raised important questions by defining a tension between resistance and domination as feminists working within leftist party politics.

For the Mexican political system in general, the effects of the campaign are difficult to gauge. Despite increased political participation, women, the working class, and the marginalized classes have been unable fundamentally to alter the existing political structure in Mexico. Even though the electoral reform law has admitted a variety of new actors into the political arena, the PRI still constitutes the dominant actor with an overwhelming monopoly of political power. Nevertheless, Rosario Ibarra and the campaign provided an invaluable opportunity to amplify a message from the Mexican people to the Mexican government. The demonstrations, speeches, television and radio messages, organizational work, and so forth, added to a growing resistance movement that can not be ignored and would be extremely costly to repress. Rosario Ibarra's campaign closed with a demonstration of 50,000 people at Tlatelolco where, fourteen years earlier, demonstrators were massacred under the Díaz-Ordaz regime.

A critical review of the 1982 elections and women's politics also raises questions of strategy. Perhaps a presidential campaign is too temporary a setting for effective organization with long-lasting results, and organizing around something more permanent could be more productive. If after a period of increased participation the women look back on their activity as nothing more than wasted effort that had a legitimating effect for the PRI as an authority resilient to opposition, that type of organizational drive as strategy for women's politics should be questioned. Likewise, if women's organization takes place within the leftist political parties and is misguided by the affiliation, that strategy for organization should also be questioned.

Rosario's campaign had a significant impact on women's politics on the Left, but it remains to be seen whether the impact will have any concrete results measured by social change in conformance with feminist ideals. Presently 2 million illegal abortions are performed in Mexico every year. One-quarter or 500,000 of the operations prove to be fatal for the woman.[27] In spite of this shocking fact, Mexican women have been unable to legalize abortion and have experienced similar problems with many other feminist issues. Nevertheless, despite such difficulties, Mexican women, joined by Third World women across the globe, are working to develop a Third World feminist movement—a movement that is both necessary and inevitable.

NOTES

1. An agenda for further research would necessarily include additional data on the volume and content of women's political participation on the Left in Mexico. Using John Booth's definition of political participation as "behavior influencing or attempting to influence the distribution of public goods," indicators of participation

might include membership in an organized political group or party, attendance at political rallies, demonstrations, or other events, politically oriented union or church activity, participation through voting and electoral politics or individual political activity such as writing, educating, and so forth. (John A. Booth, "Political Participation in Latin America," *Latin American Research Review* 14/3 [1979]:31).

Popular forms of political participation can be difficult to document. I relied on newspapers and periodicals for estimates of popular participation in rallies and marches. Political parties and unions have records on party or union membership for both women and men. I found the most valuable source of information on women to be the *Centro de Documentación* de CIDHAL, Apartado Postal 579, Cuernavaca, Morelos, México. CIDHAL stands for Comunicación, Intercambio y Desarrollo Humano en América Latina and is located at Madero 516, Colonia Miraval, Cuernavaca, Morelos, México, tel. 388-94.

2. Elena Poniatowska, *Fuerte es el Silencio*, (México, D.F.: Ediciones Era, 1980), p. 95.

3. *Desaparecidos políticos* are missing persons, many of whom are most likely political prisoners. Jesús Piedra Ibarra has been missing since 1975, when he was reportedly captured. Rosario Ibarra has spoken with released prisoners who have had contact with her son while in clandestine prisons. He is believed to be alive and imprisoned in Military Camp No. 1 in México, D.F.

4. *Latin American Political Report* 13/33 (1974): 264.

5. From an interview with Rosario Ibarra, September 10, 1983, Mexico City.

6. PCM is the Partido Comunista Mexicana; PST, Partido Socialista Trabajadora; and PDM, Partido Demoncrático Mexicano. The PSUM (Partido Socialista Unificado de México) is a coalition of Socialist parties that was unified during the 1982 elections. The parties that are part of PSUM include the Mexican Communist party (PCM), the Mexican Popular party (PPM), the Revolutionary Socialist party (PSR), and the Movement for Socialist Action and Unity (MAUS).

7. The law was published in the *Diario Oficial de la Federación*, 2nd ed., December 30, 1977.

8. The PRT's share of the proportional representation vote was 1.47 percent—less than the minimum 1.5 percent required to qualify for representation in the Federal Chamber of Deputies. The party gained its registry on the strength of its performance in the presidential voting, where it won 1.8 percent of the votes. Calculations for the proportional vote were questioned by the PRT, which voiced allegations of electoral fraud. PAN is the National Action party, a conservative opposition party with electoral support from the middle classes. PPS is the Popular Socialist party, a pro-government/Pro-PRI Socialist party which supports the presidential candidate nominated by PRI.

9. See Kevin Middlebrook, "Political Reform and Political Change in Mexico,"

in Jack W. Hopkins (ed.), *Latin American and Caribbean Contemporary Record* (New York: Holmes and Meier, 1982), vol. 1, p. 149.

10. Ibid., p. 149.

11. From *Bandera Socialista*, October 12, 1981, p. 7.

12. From an interview with Susana Vidales, December 28, 1983, Tucson, Arizona.

13. Ibid.

14. See E. Boserup and C. Liljencranz, "La Integración de la Mujer al Desarrollo," in *Estudios sobre la Mujer* (México: Secretaría de Programación y Presupuesto, 1982), Serie de Lecturas III, vol. 1, pp. 99-123.

15. Taken from "Patriarcado Político e Integración Feminista," *FEM* 5/19 (June/July, 1981): 20.

16. Marta Lamas, "De la Madrid Recoge Tesis Feminista," *Uno Más Uno*, February 18, 1982, p. 5.

17. From an interview with Susana Vidales, September 5, 1983, Mexico City.

18. Ibid.

19. A colcna, as described by Rosario Ibarra, is a woman who lives in a rundown or abandoned building in an urban setting without paying rent; an urban squatter.

20. From *Bandera Socialista*, March 22, 1982, p. 6.

21. From an interview with Susana Vidales, September 5, 1983, Mexico City.

22. Ibid.

23. There is clearly a need for more theoretical work regarding the feminist movement among working-class, Third World women. Here, feminist issues are issues that directly address both classism and sexism. The experience of Third World women both as workers and as women cannot be compartmentalized into manifestations of, for example, a sexist society *or* a classist society *or* a racist society. These intersecting systems of domination converge upon Third World women who struggle to define and change their situation. A feminist, in this study, is a person who acknowledges sexism as a system of domination and acts to (1) rectify the inequalities that exist between the sexes and (2) change the interpersonal, societal, and institutional relations that perpetuate inequalities between men and women.

24. From an interview with Susan Vidales, September 5, 1983, Mexico City.

25. Marta Lamas, "Feminismo y Organizaciones Políticos de Izquierda en México," *FEM* 5/17 (February/March, 1981):35.

26. Maria Rascón, "Feminismo y Reforma Política," *FEM* 6/23 (June/July 1982): 45.

27. Reported by Dr. Leobardo Ruiz-Pérez, Director del Sistema Nacional de Desarrollo Integral de la Familia, DIF, *Uno Más Uno*, May 20, 1983, p. 1.

Part III. Research: References and Primary Data

Introduction

Traditionally, historical studies have been male-oriented and male-dominated in their content. Because of an archaic emphasis on the accomplishments of Anglo-Saxon heroes, the lives and experiences of people of color have been largely ignored and excluded from the historical record. Efforts to study people of color from traditional social science paradigms have often resulted in distorted and inaccurate images which have served to reinforce existing stereotypes or misrepresentations of their experiences. Although such research was criticized and challenged by Mexican Americans, their demands for reform went largely unanswered.

With the social upheavals that accompanied the 1960s came renewed efforts to make the "system" more responsive to minority concerns and demands. Chicanos and Chicanas joined forces to bring about responsible change in research. In addition to challenging existing scholarship, they began to reevaluate much of what had been written about them and to rewrite it from a Chicano/a perspective. Afterward Chicanos/as stopped allowing the existing literature to dictate their research agenda and began to branch out into other areas which had been largely ignored by social science research. This led to the development of new paradigms and methodologies for studying the Chicano/a experience.

An important outcome of this was to generate discussion, controversy, and more research. Unfortunately, Chicano scholars fell prey to the very practice for which they had so vehemently criticized the Anglo research community. They now became guilty of perpetuating the same sins of omission which had characterized much of the mainstream literature. In essence, they overlooked the role and presence of the Chicana in their work. To date, much of the historical research among Chicanos has failed to include *la mujer*, has remained insensitive to the unique challenges which such research presents, or has continued to reinforce a number of the distortions and misconceptions commonly found in the mainstream literature. It should be noted that women's programs have also neglected Chicanas in their research agendas, and that they are glaringly absent from much of the literature published by and about women.

However, Chicanas and their allies have not been silent on these points. They have developed plans of action which call for a research agenda that is responsive to their needs, and they have called upon their male colleagues to become more conscious of the role of women in the historical process. This was the challenge issued by Cynthia Orozco in her perceptive article "Chicana Labor History: A Critique of Male Consciousness in Historical Writing" (*La Red* [February, 1984]). According to Orozco, "The issue of women's history is not simply a matter of filling in the gaps." Instead it will require "a new conceptualization of history, new categories of analysis, and new periodization schemes . . . "—and of course more historical research.

Chicanas and Chicanos have begun responding to the new challenges in women's history in a variety of ways. Some have begun to seek and identify "new" sources of archival information, while others have assembled and analyzed existing bibliographies in order to assess their relative merits and usefulness. Currently there is a renaissance of Chicana scholarship that will radically alter the existing historical record on *mujeres* and greatly expand the horizons of research in this area. The selections which follow this introduction represent some of the work which is being done in the field.

In the first article Angelina Veyna has admirably combined her training in anthropology with history in order to study the experiences of women in colonial New Mexico. The study describes the power relationships extant in that society by focusing upon the legal battles which women fought in order to settle disputes or receive compensation for wrongs committed against them or their families. The cases discussed in the article involve *mujeres* from different classes and thus provide the reader with insights into colonial society, its structure, and how the legal and social system responded to their respective cases.

In reviewing the cases, Veyna makes it apparent that women were anything but passive in accepting the roles assigned them. Instead they filed their grievances and voiced their views in a public forum. That they were heard and that the courts at times ruled in their favor begins to challenge existing views about colonial society and the place women occupied in it. While in many ways this study is exploratory, it nonetheless raises a number of intriguing questions and ideas that merit further investigation.

The local, state, and national archives of Mexico contain rich but largely untapped sources of information about Chicanas and Mexicanas. A large proportion of this archival material remains unindexed, uncatalogued, and unexplored by contemporary historians, especially as it pertains to research on women. The few existing guides on conducting research in Mexico's archives, including Richard Greenleaf and Michael Meyer's *Research in Mexican History* (Lincoln: University of Nebraska Press, 1973), are useful in that they provide researchers with general content overviews of the various collections housed in Mexico City's archives. However, they do not contain references to materials on women.

In her essay Dr. Barbara Driscoll begins to delineate resources and information on women housed in the Archivo General de la Nación and the Archivo de Relaciones Exteriores in Mexico City. While the materials she discusses are mainly about Mexican women, she argues that they represent an important source for scholars because the cultural and historical legacy of Chicanas transcends the geopolitical boundaries of Mexico and the United States. Furthermore, she points out that the bonds of culture and history between Chicanas and Mexicanas remain strong and that they are reinforced by the contiguity of the two countries and continuous migration.

In discussing the various and sundry resources, she cautions readers that they must go beyond the traditional historical methodologies in documenting the history of women. While some of the collections refer specifically to women, the great majority do not. Thus, much of the information must be extrapolated from historical and statistical records. For those willing to invest the time and effort, however, the fruits of such labor can be very rewarding.

Another source of information for researchers is the bibliography. Bibliographies can generally be classified in two categories: those which list primary and secondary source materials and those which contain a listing of other bibliographies. If properly researched, organized, and annotated, such guides can be an invaluable and time-saving tool for the researcher.

Richard Chabran has undertaken the task of analyzing the organization, contents, and relative merits of research and reference works on Chicanas. In his analysis, he found that most of them were inadequate or too focused in their approach. He also found that a great number of the bibliographies he examined were marred by poor organization, numerous spelling errors, incomplete citations, and a lack of information regarding primary resources. While his own work in this area suffers at times from inconsistencies in format, structure, and analysis, his essay is timely in that it discusses the current status of bibliographies on Chicana research and points out the need for more work in this much neglected area.

Historical research on Chicanas is still in a fledgling state, and much remains to be done if it is to address the issues, directions, and challenges identified by Chicanas. Hopefully the three selections which follow will stimulate further interest in research that is responsive to the unique and important role of Chicanas in our history.

Women in Early New Mexico: A Preliminary View

Angelina F. VEYNA

The vast majority of research on colonial New Mexico has tended to emphasize institutional and ecclesiastical matters. While certain individuals such as Juan de Oñate and subsequent New Mexican governors have received added attention, relatively little has been done to describe the various members of that society. When it comes to describing the women of colonial New Mexico, they seem to become lost under collective terms such as "settlers," "inhabitants," and "colonists." Recent research directed at filling this void has been undertaken by Antonio José Ríos-Bustamante (1976) and by Janie Louise Aragón (1976) via census analyses, and by Ramón Gutiérrez (1980), who has focused on marriage, sex, and family practices in colonial New Mexico. Efforts such as these have begun to shed light on the condition and lives of New Mexican women during this time.

This paper thus focuses on women in early New Mexican society as reflected in notarial documents from Santa Fe and from Santa Cruz de la Cañada. The corpus utilized for this study was taken from the Spanish Archives of New Mexico housed at the New Mexico State Records Center and covers a time span from 1710 to 1733. The Spanish Archives are comprised for the most part of administrative records accumulated between 1621 and 1821. Documents such as reports by local officials, censuses, petitions, military records, litigation proceedings, and auxiliary documents are included. As Beers (1979:20) has pointed out, the Spanish Archives are useful not only for the political and social history of New Mexico, but also for ecclesiastocal history, personal and family history, and as a record of the activities of foreigners in New Mexico.[1]

Some of the documents to be presented were initiated by women, while others refer to women as a result of the litigation. By using notarial documents produced by the people themselves, we can begin to discern how the various elements of that society were interrelated. It is also possible for the historian to begin to reconstruct the day-to-day activities of women.

Obviously, the observations to be offered are quite preliminary based on the limited corpus, but they probably reflect concerns not only of women in Santa Fe or Santa Cruz, but also of women throughout the Southwest during the colonial period. Future research will expand or dismiss some of the ideas to be presented. The core of this presentation consists of summaries of the documents (addressed in chronological order) with an immediate analysis of each and followed by some general observations; first, the documentation must be placed in an appropriate historical perspective.

Historical Perspective

Spaniards reached the New Mexico area by 1540, and Santa Fe was established as the capital in 1609 by Don Pedro de Peralta, New Mexico's first appointed governor. According to Bannon (1974:14), the number of Spaniards increased from a few hundred to a few thousand. This population laid the groundwork for future New Mexican agricultural and sheep-raising activities. Until 1680, Santa Fe was the only formally organized community in the province. During this time, the majority of the population tended to become dispersed throughout the rural areas in isolated farms, ranches, and hamlets (Weber, 1979:102). This tendency apparently continued into the following century.

The Pueblo Revolt took place in 1680, which forced all of the Spanish population south to El Paso del Norte. Reconquest efforts continued for the next twelve years; by 1692, these efforts were considered successful. In 1695, a third villa was founded, Santa Cruz de la Cañada, which is approximately forty miles north of Santa Fe. Though Santa Cruz had been occupied by Spaniards throughout the 1600s, it had been overrun by Tano Indians after the Revolt. This villa was strategically "refounded" to control part of the northern New Mexican frontier. Albuquerque was subsequently established as a fourth administrative center in 1706 and thus served as a way station between El Paso and Santa Cruz de la Cañada.

The documents used in this study were formulated approximately twenty years after the reconquest. The Spanish population of this time can conceivably be described as three-quarters native-born and raised in New Mexico and one-quarter immigrants, who were brought from northern Mexico specifically for settlement purposes or who eventually immigrated for political or economic reasons. According to Scholes (1935:97), by 1680-1681, it was evident that more than 80 percent—perhaps as much as 90 percent—of the population was native to the province itself. A general description of New Mexican society at this time, and of the Southwest in general, has been offered by Juan Gómez-Quiñones (1982:8).

> Early settlers, who may be termed Mejicanos Españoles, were comprised of a small élite of officers, civil officials, and priests; the rest were mostly mestizo farmers or specialized laborers along with Hispanicized Indian retainers and mulattos. Women were part of the migratory and laboring process which initiated settlement: wives, daughters, mothers were involved in establishing frontier society. Settlers were not from the wealthy class; they were principally agriculturists, artisans, skilled laborers and in local cases the majority were mestizo soldiers.

Let us now take a closer look at these settlers, focusing on the women.

Complaint of María Martín

Our first document was initiated by María Martín, the central figure in this paper, against her brother-in-law, Luís Lopes, in 1710. She opens her case by describing herself as a "pobre viuda, sola y sin abrigo." She accuses Lopes of attempting to murder her son. Lopes had previously accused her son of being careless when taking care of some goats which had begun to attack Lopes's horse.

After the initial incident, Lopes went to Martín's home to clarify what had occurred with the animals. When he arrived, one of María

Martín's sons called him a thief, a "cinco dedos," and he became enraged, which led to his attacking the boy responsible for the animals. Lopes called this insult to María Martín's attention, but she did not reprimand the boy. Lopes thus attacked him for being "desbergonzado," or audacious enough to insult him. In defending himself, he notes: "el intento no era más que . . . por castigarle su desbergüenza ya que su madre no se la castigó." When Lopes's represenative summarizes the case, he, too, focuses on the child's ill manners, which, in fact, are the primary theme of the document.

The second woman mentioned in this document is Ana María de la Concepción, who is Lopes's wife. She is first mentioned in passing by María Martín when she describes how Lopes asked his wife for a sword to injure her son and, because she refused to give it to him, "la baño en sangre de un bofetón." But de la Concepción is of further importance in this litigation because she presented a petition requesting permission for her and her husband to pay a bond in lieu of the time her husband might spend in jail during the case. De la Concepción noted that it was time to cultivate the fields and that the time in jail might jeopardize their crops. A direct response to her petition was not provided, but when Lopes's representative summarized the case, he indirectly referred to de la Concepción's petition by indicating that Lopes had already been in jail for eighteen days, which had caused "atraso en la siembra para el mantenimiento de sus obligaciones, como también de sus bienes."

After the testimony was heard and reaffirmed, the verdict was given in favor of Lopes because, it is stated, María Martín could not prove that the incident with the animals took place, and Lopes was freed of charges. A representative was assigned by the court to go to María Martín's home to inform her of the outcome; she subsequently expressed her sentiments in the following manner: "que a todos los que han sido cómplices en su velación, las sitava para el tribunal de Dios porque conocía que todo se había hecho a su contra por ser una mujer viuda, pobre y sola." In other words, God would eventually punish them. It is interesting to note that, in order to gain empathy from everyone, she twice identified herself as a poor, defenseless woman as a result of her marital status.

This document illustrates that by 1710 women in Santa Cruz de la Cañada were already initiating court proceedings. As a head of household, María Martín felt the responsibility to defend the actions against her son. But during the proceedings Lopes in turn accused her of not teaching her boy "buena educación"; she had not taught him to respect his elders, and for this reason he took it upon himself to reprimand the boy. Lopes's wife is noteworthy because she represents a woman who makes a decision, to file a petition, without her husband's intervention; the main concern seems to be their crops.

Distribution of Tools

This document originated in Santa Fe and dates from January, 1712. It reflects orders apparently initiated in Mexico that tools should be distributed to inhabitants of Santa Cruz for their aid; apparently Santa Cruz was experiencing some economic difficulty. The accompanying document lists fifty-six individuals who received the tools, of which twenty-three were female. Each of the citations is similar to the following: "Para María de la Cárdena, guérfana, llevó Roque Jaramillo tres coas, una acha, un azadón." Some of the women listed are distinguished as *doñas* (2), *viudas* (9), and *huérfanas* (4). Only four types of implements, all of them agriculturally related, are being distributed: *coas* (digging sticks), *achas* (axes or hatchets), *azadones* (hoes), and *rejas* (plow shares; the small iron section of the plow which actually creates the furrows). It is interesting to note that only women, twelve of them, were recipients of *rejas*.

The primary importance of this distribution list is that it serves as a census-like inventory of citizens from Santa Cruz. Regarding the female population reflected in this document, we find that only two of them had the title of *doña*, and that almost half of the female population numerated were widows. (Both of these groups are discussed below). As for the orphaned women, we are not informed whether they lacked one parent or both. This listing does not in any way refer to their race or caste.

We can only speculate why the distribution of *rejas* was limited to women. Perhaps some women were devoted only to plowing. Perhaps it was a valuable implement which women might guard more closely than men. Or perhaps these women were meant to be keepers to share them with a given number of local citizens. Future research will, hopefully, shed light on this note.

Criminal Proceedings against Diego Moraga

This third document was initiated in Santa Cruz in 1715 and is comprised of criminal proceedings initiated by Joseph Básquez of nearby Chimayó against Diego Martín Moraga, who "defended the honor" of his sister by attacking Básquez. The document narrates that Básquez had stopped by their house in the late afternoon to ask for a light for his cigarette; he saw Diego Martín's sister and bid her good afternoon.

Diego witnessed the scene from afar, but caught up to Básquez and attacked him with a *coa*. The scene is described as follows: "[Diego Martín] bido que la dicha su hermana estaba bolteando la cara para todas partes y para donde estaba el dicho declarante y que biendo estas demostraciones, le causó malisia . . . " Martín stated in his testimony that his actions were a result of the "selo de la honra de su dicha hermana." Subsequently, Básquez was ordered to leave Chimayó and to take his wife to Santa Fe, "para quitar la ocasión de que buelva a entrar en la casa de Diego Martín."

The document presents a recurring theme, as indicated by other cases previously examined and by the numerous examples cited by Ramón A. Gutiérrez in his dissertation (1980). These proceedings do not clarify whether Diego Martín responded so strongly because he was the sole guardian of his sister. It is interesting to note that Martín's sister did not present her own testimony; she is not named, nor are we informed of her age.

Also interesting is that among the witnesses was María Barba Luján, who mentions that although she was not present at the time, she did offer first aid to Básquez. Through this, we are informed that, as early as 1715, women were afforded the opportunity to serve as witnesses in a case. After presenting her statement, Luján again verified it but did not sign it ("y no firmó por desir no saber"). The *alcalde*, instead, provided her signature.

Power of Attorney

The fourth document surveyed was executed in Santa Fe on October 31, 1715. In it, María de Quiroz, an inhabitant of Santa Fe, gave power of attorney to her *compadre* and his son to bring her own son, Juan Durán de Armijo, from Chihuahua. De Quiroz's husband, who served as *sargento de milicia* and who was also the local barber/doctor, could not personally go to Chihuahua since he was out of town (at Santa Cruz de la Cañada). Apparently her husband's absence involved considerable time, and she wanted her son brought to her for the sake of companionship.

The document informs us that the son was "hacia los reales de minas"; the circumstances surrounding his stay there are not known. De Quiroz's son apparently was with his maternal grandfather, who was trying to impede his grandson's departure for some unknown reason. In her petition, de Quiroz conveyed her concern for the well-being of her son, "que lo traigan y no se bea el dicho [mi] hijo perdido en dichos reales de minas."

Once again, a woman initiated a petition apparently without her husband's assistance. María de Quiroz entrusted her *compadre* with her son, thus indicating that *compadrazgo* was one of the cultural institutions brought by the settlers from Mexico. It might also be deduced that de Quiroz was an immigrant to New Mexico, since her father lived in Chihuahua. Since de Quiroz could not sign her name, the *alcalde ordinario* provided her signature at the end of the petition.

Estate Proceedings

In this document filed in Santa Fe and written in 1716, Doña Micaela de Velasco sued the estate of Don Francisco Cuervo y Valdés on behalf of her daughter, Doña María Francisca de la Rivas. Don Francisco served as governor of New Mexico between 1705 and 1707. Doña María was fighting her deceased lover's inheritors for 10,000 pesos, which he promised to give her in lieu of marriage. He seems to have been promoted to serve in the treasury of Guadalajara and thus never married her. The objective of Doña Micaela's document was to request that two archives be searched to see if the original promissory note could be located. Cuervo y Valdés gave a copy of the note to his intended, but reacquired it from her while they lived in Mexico City. As the mother noted, he acted cautiously and never returned the copy to her daughter.

The search lasted two days and ended with the Secretarios de Gobierno y Guerra noting that, prior to 1713, it was customary to give the executor of a document the original copy. The document in question was apparently completed in 1707 by Don Francisco, who at the time held the office of governor. Since Don Francisco's original document was nonexistent in any file, two witnesses were brought in to testify that they were present when the original was dictated. Their new document was completed and a copy of it delivered to Doña Micaela de Velasco.

Unlike the other documents presented, members of the higher strata of society are clearly represented here. This becomes evident by observing the titles of *don* and *doña* of the individuals involved. In fact, Doña María Francisca de la Rivas gave birth to a child by Don Francisco, who, although illegitimate, was still designated as *don*, his complete name being Don Francisco Antonio Xabier. (After all, he was the son of a governor.) Another indication of their status is the amount of money being requested. The sum of 10,000 pesos is quite large by both today's and yesteryear's standards, especially if we note that governors were paid approximately 2,000 pesos a year (Scholes, 1935:75).

Travel between regions is another point brought out in this document. For example, Doña Micaela seems to have been quite a voyager, living in New Mexico, returning to Mexico City, and filing this petition in Santa Fe. The conditions surrounding this regional travel are not described, but the fact that these individuals did interact with other communities is valuable to note.

Family Dispute

Document F entails a domestic and property dispute in Santa Fe in 1716. The initial document was filed by Pedro Vígil, who demanded an explanation from his sister-in-law, Ana María Romero, as to why she was hiding his wife. Romero testified that she was keeping his wife because there had been some differences between them—hence the domestic dispute.

In the following pages, Pedro Vígil demanded that his father-in-law transfer to him title to some property, since he apparently had not received three rooms in his home at the time he married the daughter. Pedro's father-in-law, Matheo Truxillo, was summoned to testify on the issue. He stated that, at the time of the marriage,

Pedro Víjil was given the option of the three rooms or the property. Víjil apparently chose the property, but he subsequently sold it to a local official. Matheo Truxillo pointed out that Pedro Víjil had lost what he was given through his own fault and should henceforth leave him and his family in peace.

In essence, Pedro Víjil manipulated the situation from the moment he filed the domestic dispute. He apparently used it as a vehicle to convey his immediate objective, to obtain benefits from his father-in-law. Interestingly, three-quarters of the document does not refer to the domestic dispute, nor to his wife's sister, Ana María Romero.

For analysis, Ana María Romero is important because she again illustrates that women were allowed to testify, and also because she serves as an example of a woman who personally signed her name after her testimony. Pedro Víjil's wife did not even appear once to defend herself, nor to discuss the property dispute. Pedro Víjil seems to have been more preoccupied with what he could gain from his father-in-law than with what he could gain from his wife.

Land Litigation

This document is from Santa Cruz de la Cañada and dates from May 12 thru May 30, 1719. The underlying theme is the conflict of land ownership between Cristoval Tafoya Altamirano and Ysavel Gonzales, a widow indirectly related to Tafoya. This feud was apparently ongoing; however, the conflict escalated when Gonzales's son, Diego de Archuleta, supposedly slapped Tafoya's wife while Tafoya was away in Mexico City.

On a subsequent day, the *alcalde mayor* of Santa Cruz tried to bring Tafoya, Gonzales, and witnesses together at the disputed parcel of land to recognize its legal ownership. When everyone was gathered, Tafoya was informed of the previous incident, and a new argument ensued while the land was being examined. Tafoya became very aggressive; the *alcalde mayor* tried to reason with him, but Tafoya would not listen. For having caused such problems, the *alcalde mayor* then fined him the cost of the litigation papers.

After testimony was presented by numerous officials, it became evident that Tafoya's wife was lying; for this, Archuleta was incarcerated for thirteen days. The case was resolved in favor of Ysavel Gonzales. Tafoya was instructed to pay the fifty pesos, which he agreed to do by transacting a *yunta de bueyes*.

This case is interesting because it illustrates a conflict brought to court by a man against a widow, with the defending female party the victor. As is subsequently revealed, the property was being disputed because Gonzales could not initially provide documents which would prove ownership. By extension, this litigation indicates that by 1719 women were already considered property owners; however, it is not clarified whether she inherited the land from her husband or owned it prior to marriage.

Personal Complaint

The last document under consideration dates from fourteen years after the one previously discussed. It is a case brought to court by Antonia de Jirón in Santa Cruz in September, 1733, and focuses on her attempt to clear her name. Though the document appears to be incomplete, it is possible to determine that de Jirón's husband, Francisco Víjil, threw her out of their home because he found Miguel Martín in the environs of their house around midnight, and, as a result, "a echo mi marido mal consepto de mí siendo una mujer honrada." Consequently, she continued, "dise [mí] marido no querer hacer vida conmigo onde me veo hobligada a rescartar mi crédito."

Miguel Martín had arrived on the pretext that there were some animals in her *milpa*. In trying to emphasize that Miguel Martín did wrong to come to her home, she noted that "una mujer casada es un vidrio de Venesia" and, as such, should be dealt with very cautiously. At the end of the unfinished record, Governor Cruzat y Góngora seems to have been convinced that things would work out, since de Jiron's husband reaffirmed that he wanted her and loved her as God ordered and that he would receive her back.

This document again illustrates a case in which a woman's honor is at stake. These pages show that a man's mere presence near a married woman's home was considered sufficient grounds to merit such action. It seems that the responsibility for clearing such a misunderstanding fell on the woman and that, in order for the clarification to be publicly recognized, a formal document had to be filed. Antonia de Jirón personally signed the document, thus providing another rare example of a woman's signature.

Remarks

As a result of reviewing these eight notarial documents, it becomes apparent that during the early eighteenth century, women as well as men were making use of the judicial system of New Mexico to fill their individual needs. Four of the documents were initiated by women: one woman attempted to defend her son, a second attempted to have her son reunited with her; a third attempted to ensure her daughter's economic security; a fourth attempted to improve her public image.

Though women do not seem to form part of the governing or decision-making body, we do find that by the second decade of the eighteenth century, they were allowed to serve as witnesses, and their testimony was just as respected as that of men. (Other documents consulted indicate that the only testimonies questioned are those of individuals fourteen years old or younger, but even they were allowed to speak in a case.)

The two personal signatures of women are important in view of the fact that a great majority of the population was illiterate. After describing illiteracy among men, Scholes (1935:100) notes the following: "In the case of women, the illiteracy was worse. Many women appeared before the agent of Inquisition during the years 1626 to 1680 and more than ninety per cent could not sign their depositions. In 1631, when 33 women testified, not one of them could sign." Taking this into account, these two women formed part of a literate elite.

It is assumed that all of the women were Spanish; not one of the documents refers to their race or caste. (This also applies to the men.) The practice of not identifying them might be reflective of the corpus, or possibly of the time and place in which they were written, that is, during a period when New Mexican society was consolidating itself after the reconquest. It seems that there were other concerns more important than identifying ethnicity.

Though women may not have been strongly distinguished by race or caste, there do exist socioeconomic differences among them, even in the few cases examined. The case in which the mother tried to obtain the document for her daughter gives us a view of women of the upper strata: Doña Micaela de Velasco had the means to travel back and forth between Mexico City and Santa Fe. They were also women who were sufficiently sophisticated to request the nominal sum from the governor's estate.

Antonia de Jirón provides an example of a woman who possessed global knowledge, making the analogy between women and glassware from Venice—this comment almost appears ironic in the context of frontier New Mexico.

María de Quiroz serves as an example of the professional's wife. Within New Mexican society, it would seem that a doctor or barber held status above others who had no specialty. Since de Quiroz's husband was away in Santa Cruz at the time she executed the document, one speculates that there were few doctors at the time or that he excelled in his profession, having been called to tend to another community.

The document which discusses the distribution of tools clearly gives us a picture of the degree of involvement of women in agriculturally related activities. It is unfortunate that an explicit picture of women in this endeavor cannot be pieced together, but perhaps future documentation will provide data on this topic. It can also be speculated that, by 1719, in addition to working the land, women also had the opportunity to own property, both collectively with their husbands and individually.

The women reflected in these documents include *doñas, viudas, huérfanas*, and married women. Regarding the use of *don* and *doña*, Janie Louise Aragón summarizes its use in the following manner (1976:397).

> There is one aspect within the españoles that is exclusive to them and certainly an indication of social standing: the titles *don* and *doña*. While these titles were signs of nobility in the fifteenth and sixteenth centuries, they gradually lost their exclusivity and came to be applied more generally. Their use in the Santa Fe census does not indicate the presence of nobility, but rather a title that denoted a degree of social and economic importance.

As we saw, *viudas* also seem to have been a strong element of New Mexican society. Aragón also notes that one of the most salient features of the female population as reflected in the 1790 Santa Fe census was its large widow element (1976:408-409). Some of the spouses were probably killed in military campaigns, while other women married older men. Aragón believes that remarriage by widows rarely occurred (1976:409).

This corpus also reflects everyday marital life. The first document shows Luís Lopes and his wife, Ana María, concerned about their agricultural endeavors. In the last document, we find marital problems between Antonia de Jirón and her husband. Athearn, in his dissertation on New Mexico (1974), notes that marital difficulties are a frequent topic in New Mexican notarial documents.

The nature of the corpus provides a view of women as witnesses, as defendants, and, generally, as initiators and actors of these proceedings. This series of vignettes offers a preliminary view of women in colonial New Mexico. These documents depict women actively making use of the judicial system available in their community.

The cases just presented illustrate that women played different roles in colonial Southwest society and provide views of women which are contrary to the presiding notion that Hispanic women have always been passive, or at least that they were passive up to the present century. This is an image perpetrated by individuals who do not know of, or who have failed to recognize, the various forms in which women have participated in their local societies. A woman does not need to become a national heroine in order to have made a contribution.

Much of Chicano historiography, in general, has tended to focus on individuals who have overtly "excelled." In the case of women of the colonial period, attention has primarily been given to Doña Marina (La Malinche) and Sor Juana Inés de la Cruz. But very little is actually known of their social counterparts. What little research by social historians does exist tends to focus on women of Central Mexico. To provide data on colonial women of the Southwest, obviously, requires work with archival material, such as has been undertaken here.

Working with notarial documentation is not easy; it usually requires use of microfilmed documents and also the specialized skill of paleography—transcribing colonial written script into a form that can be easily handled. These documents offer intimate insight into the people of this period. They provide a wealth of data which cannot be obtained by consulting general government or ecclesiastical records. Notarial documentation also reflects human interests and concerns not visible in other written forms.

One of the purposes of this paper has been to make other scholars aware of the availability of such data. Archives, whether those of New Mexico, Texas, California, or the Archivo General de la Nación in Mexico City, have enormous collections yet to be touched. Different types of information can be gained by working with such documentation, all to help reconstruct the daily lives of Southwest colonial peoples.

Whereas this paper has examined women in early New Mexico in a general manner, specific areas are yet to be addressed. One approach might be to concentrate on women from a given settlement and to follow them through a given period. Another approach might be to compare and contrast women from different colonial Southwest settlements. Topics yet to be explored include the various forms of interaction between Hispanic and Indian women and the roles of colonial women with regard to men, family, and community. Since this is a relatively new field of inquiry, the possibilities for research are innumerable.

This paper, hopefully, is just the beginning of our understanding of the role of the Mexicana/Chicana woman in the Southwest. As Judith Sweeney (1977:99) has pointed out regarding the history of the Chicana, "in order to understand the functioning of a society in any time period, it is necessary to understand how the elements of that society interrelate." Since Mexicana/Chicana women were a vital element to the founding and settlement of the Southwest, it is crucial that their history be addressed.

NOTES

1. For further information regarding the history of these documents, see Beers (1979: 9-27).

PRIMARY SOURCES

All sources form part of the Spanish Archives of New Mexico (SANM) housed at the State of New Mexico Records Center, Santa Fe, New Mexico. Microfilm copies of these documents were used for the study.

Complaint of María Martín vs. Luis Lopes for Attempted Murder. SANM, Roll 4, Frames 166-195. March 6 thru May 30, 1710.

Distribution of Tools to Settlers of Santa Cruz de la Cañada. SANM, Roll 4, Frames 344-349. January 10, 1712.

Criminal Proceedings against Diego Martín Moraga of Santa Cruz. SANM, Roll 5, Frames 196-213. July 27 thru September 13, 1715.

María de Quiroz, Power of Attorney to Francisco Lorenso de Casados. SANM, Roll 5, Frames 342-343. October 31, 1715.

María Francisca de la Ribas, Santa Fé: Proceedings for Claims against Cuervo y Valdés. SANM, Roll 5, Frames 435-445. January 14 thru 16, 1716.

Ana María Romero vs. Pedro Montes Vígil. SANM, Roll 5, Frames 592-601. August 11, 1716.

Proceedings in Case of Cristoval Tafoya vs. Diego de Archuleta. SANM, Roll 5, Frames 835-860. May 12 thru 30, 1719.

Proceedings in Complaint of Antonia Jirón against Miguel Martín Serrano for Molestation. SANM, Roll 7, Frames 183-185. September 19 thru 21, 1733.

REFERENCES

Aragón, Janie Louise. 1976. "The People of Santa Fe in the 1790's." *Aztlán* 7/3: 391-417.

Athearn, Fredric J. 1974. "Life and Society in Eighteenth Century New Mexico" (Ph.D. dissertation, University of Texas, Austin).

Bannon, John Francis. 1974. *The Spanish Borderlands Frontier, 1513-1821* (Albuquerque: University of New Mexico Press).

Beers, Henry P. 1979. *Spanish and Mexican Records of the American Southwest* (Tucson: University of Arizona Press).

Gómez-Quiñones, Juan. 1982. *Development of the Mexican Working Class North of the Río Bravo.* Popular Series No. 2, Chicano Studies Research Center Publications (Los Angeles: UCLA).

Gutiérrez, Ramón A. 1980. "Marriage, Sex and the Family: Social Change in Colonial New Mexico, 1690-1846" (Ph.D. dissertation, University of Wisconsin, Madison).

Ríos-Bustamante, Antonio José. 1976. "A Contribution to the Historiography of the Greater Mexican North in the Eighteenth Century." *Aztlán* 7/2:347-356.

Scholes, Frances V. 1935. "Civil Government and Society in New Mexico in the Seventeenth Century." *New Mexico Historical Review* 10/2: (April)71-111.

Sweeney, Judith. 1977. "Chicana History: A Review of the Literature." In *Essay on La Mujer*, ed. Rosaura Sánchez and Rosa Martínez Cruz. Chicano Studies Center Publications, Anthology No. 1 (Los Angeles: UCLA).

Weber, David J. 1979. *New Spain's Far Northern Frontier: Essays on Spain in the American West, 1540-1821* (Albuquerque: University of New Mexico Press).

Chicana Historiography: A Research Note Regarding Mexican Archival Sources

Barbara A. DRISCOLL

The historical and cultural legacy of Chicanas, or Mexican women living in the United States, like that of all Americans of Mexican descent, transcends American society and its geopolitical boundary with Mexico. Historic and cultural bonds between Chicanos/as and their kin in Mexico have superseded many obstacles such as geographical distance, political alienation, and societal pressure to "become Americanized"; indeed, these ties have been reinforced by contiguity between the two countries and continuous migration from Mexico and within the United States. Not surprisingly, some of these bonds between Mexico and the Mexican American community in the United States have corresponding historical documentation in Mexican archives.

For the purposes of retrieving documents in Mexican archives, it is important to consider Chicanas in two groups—those Mexican women who lived in the American Southwest before the Treaty of Guadalupe Hidalgo (i.e., during the colonial and early independence periods) and those who were or became residents of the United States after the Treaty. Moreover, while many Mexican women became residents of the American Southwest by virtue of the Treaty of Guadalupe Hidalgo, many others over the years have migrated to the United States. Whether by choice or necessity, migration to and within the United States has brought Mexican women to many areas beyond the Southwest, into the Midwest and even the Northwest and Northeast, helping to make Mexican Americans a national minority.

Moreover, as in the case of documenting the history of women in general, we must often look further than the more traditional historical methodologies to identify relevant documents and to assess their usefulness. To be sure, there are some documents in Mexican archives which refer specifically to "mujeres mexicanas en los Estados Unidos," but most do not. We must consider, then, the full context of the circumstances surrounding the experiences of Mexican women in the United States and their past and present legal and cultural relationship to Mexico to be able to retrieve pertinent documents in that country. For example, it is often necessary to extrapolate material about Chicanas from statistical material that does not even mention females directly, much less Mexican women living in the United States.

For the purposes of this discussion, I use the terms "Chicanas" and "Mexicanas" interchangeably. This is not to say that the terms are synonymous, only that to identify documents in Mexican archives it is necessary to consider all women of Mexican descent living in the United States within the same general category, regardless of nationality. Terms such as "Latinas," "Mexican American women," and "Chicanas" obviously did not come into use until after the Treaty of Guadalupe Hidalgo and were not recognized by Mexican archival documentation until very recently. Documents generally available in Mexican archives are usually at least thirty-five to forty years old, predating most of the terms presently used.

In this regard, this paper considers some of the innumerable sources of primary historical documentation in Mexico City, as they relate to the historical experience of Chicanas. Some sources pertain to the colonial era, others to the period between the independence of Mexico and the Treaty of Guadalupe Hidalgo, but most have information about the second half of the nineteenth century and the twentieth century. This list is by no means complete, but it does serve to illustrate the richness of historical data in Mexico and its potential applicability to Chicana history.

Archivo General de la Nación

The Archivo General de la Nación (AGN) in Mexico City ranks among the major archives of the world, is the official depository of the bulk of Mexican government administrative units, and contains the largest concentration of federal government documents in Mexico. The AGN is located near downtown Mexico City in the old

Cárcel de Lecumberri, an impressive starfish-shaped building constructed during the Porfiriato as a modern, progressive prison. While its reputation as a prison is tainted, the applicability of the building to storing historical documents is remarkable. Each arm of the starfish-shaped building is called a *galería*; each *galería* contains a related group of documents.

Papers housed in the AGN include those routinely deposited by successive presidential administrations, executive branch offices and departments, some personal papers of historical figures, some judicial and ecclesiastical material, as well as those documents resulting from periodic reorganizations of the government. The organization and content of the documents vary considerably from *galería* to *galería* and record group to record group. Some *galerías* have very detailed catalogues for some record groups, while other record groups have only recently been made available for research and consequently have only the most general inventory. Moreover, materials from the period 1910-1920, the period of the Mexican Revolution, are very sketchy. It should also be noted that the Archivo does house some visual material, such as old photos.

Fortunately, records and materials at the AGN are quite accessible. Serious researchers with appropriate identification can gain admission to the AGN. Although anyone from any discipline or level of education can find useful information about Mexico or related topics in the AGN, it is most important that any researcher bring as much data as he/she can find to the Archivo. Those data (i.e., names, dates, places, etc.) will greatly assist in locating appropriate documents. AGN personnel who work with the documents in the various *galerías* are exceptionally knowledgeable about the material and generous about sharing their experience.

The following areas of the AGN are some of those relevant to Chicana history.

Galería Noroeste—Fondo Departamento de Trabajo. From 1911 to 1923, the Departamento de Migración was part of this office. Although much of the information pertains to male Mexican nationals working in the United States and some to repatriation in the 1930s, there is also material about *sociedades protectoras del trabajador mexicano*, whose benefits often affected workers' wives and families. There is a considerable amount of correspondence from inspectors working in Mexican border states and along the border, about insurance and death benefit claims for wives and widows of Mexican workers. Undoubtedly, some of these wives and widows may have gone to the United States to live and work. This Fondo also contains lists of individuals who migrated within Mexico in search of work, including those who went to the border and to the United States—one of the variables in these lists being sex. The Fondo de Trabajo is one of the groups of documents that has only the most general inventory at present.

Galería Noreste. The documents from presidential administrations are deposited in this *galería*. Most of the earlier administrations have detailed card catalogues, although it is necessary to be careful and thoughtful in using them to locate information about Chicanos. The presidential papers, in particular, contain some correspondence from the Secretaría de Relaciones Exteriores about Mexican citizens living in the United States. Fondo Alvaro Obregón-Plutarco Calles (1920-1928) contains a series entitled "Migración y Repatriación." Reports and related material pertain to the repatriations of the 1930s and attendant problems. Many Mexican women, some with their children, were isolated in the United States during the repatriation, sometimes without their husbands. There are many reports about consuls assisting Mexican women suffering from the consequences of the repatriations.

Fondo Pascual Ortíz (1930-1932) has a number of requests for various kinds of assistance in solving problems arising from the repatriations, as well as many other documents from Mexican consuls in San Francisco and Denver not necessarily found in archives of the Secretaría de Relaciones Exteriores. Some of these documents concern Mexican women living in the United States.

Fondos Abelardo L. Rodríguez (1932-1934) and Lazaro Cardenas (1934-1940) both contain a series on reports submitted by the Secretaría de Relaciones Exteriores, many of which were submitted by Mexican consuls in the United States. One of the reports, for example, was about a complaint submitted by a Mexican woman against the Mexican consul in Chicago, who actively interfered in her divorce proceedings.

Galería Este. The Fondo Patronato Eclesiástico contains extensive church records from all Mexico for extended periods time. Of relevance to Chicanas are church records for those parts of Mexico that became the American Southwest and today's Mexican border areas. Since the church as part of its missionary work documented rites that were performed (i.e., baptisms, marriages), many churches accumulated extensive statistical and clerical material about their parishioners. For example, there is a series on *matrimonios* and another on *viudez* (widowhood). Statistical information about the church in the Californias, in Texas, and in New Mexico before the Treaty of Guadalupe Hidalgo contains interesting data about the population of females of Mexican descent that later became Chicanas.

Galería Sureste. Fondo Gobernación: here we must remember that from 1821 to 1861 the Secretaria de Gobernación with a Ministerio de Relaciones Exteriores acted in the capacity of SRE today, and that a substantial amount of information remains to be classified.

From 1830 to 1853, there was an office of Censo and Estadística, which was charged with development of statistical information about the country. It contains lists of inhabitants, property owners, and so forth. Those sections pertaining to what is today the American Southwest contain some interesting information about the populace of that region. Fondo Gobernación also has *cuadros estadísticas* about migration developed by *aduanas* (customs), some of which are located at the border, for the years 1911 to 1919.

Fomento de las Californias, active from 1823 to 1853, contains reports about the region.

From this brief list it is obvious that the Archivo General de la Nación contains rich and diverse sources of information pertaining to Chicana history. We must remember, however, that primary historical material in the AGN pertinent to Chicanas is not readily apparent. A researcher must have a working knowledge of Mexican institutional history, as well as an understanding of the historical experience of Mexican women living in the United States, to be able to identify and retrieve documents.

Archivo Microfilmeco de Genealogía y Heráldica

Associated with the Academia Mexicana de Genealogía y Heráldica, and with the Mormon church, this vast collection of microfilm of parish registers in Mexico from the sixteenth to the twentieth centuries makes it a major source of social and demographic data for Mexico. Most complete coverage is for the seventeenth, eighteenth, and nineteenth centuries. Records include baptisms, marriages, *informaciones matrimoniales*, confirmations, and deaths, in some cases supplemented by civil registers. Mexican states that have been filmed include the border states of Coahuila, Tamaulipas, Nuevo León, and Chihuahua. Although it does not contain information about Mexican women in the United States per se, it can provide indispensable historical demographic data about Mexican females in border cities that have sent immigrants and workers to the United States.

Hemeroteca Nacional de México

One can certainly not overlook the Hemeroteca Nacional de México in Mexico City as a source of information on Chicanas. It is the central depository for newspapers published in Mexico City, and contains complete runs of many of the major newspapers, such as *Excélsior,* and some regional papers as well. There is a catalogue for the newspapers, and if the researcher is prepared with names, dates, and places, it is possible to locate material relevant to Mexican women living on the border and in the American Southwest.

Archivo de la Secretaría de Relaciones Exteriors

The most accessible source of primary information for Chicana history in Mexico City is the Archivo de la Secretaría de Relaciones Exteriores in Tlatelolco. It serves as the official depository for the Secretaría's documents and houses those documents which it generates and those it receives from other governments and groups as well as from its own personnel located in other countries. The range of information is vast, including confidential memos about high-level diplomatic negotiations, interdepartmental correspondence, and specialized reports (*informes*) about a variety of topics.

Of particular value to the history of Chicana and Mexican women in the United States are the various *informes* and other paperwork local Mexican consuls were required to perform as part of their job. Indeed, the Mexican consul in his capacity as the representative of the Mexican government was delegated certain obligations by the Secretaría de Relaciones Exteriores toward the local Mexican community, and it is no coincidence that there were consuls in areas with large Mexican communities, at least in the early part of the twentieth century.

A principal function of Mexican consuls was and is *protección*. This means that the consul's responsibility was actively to protect the rights of Mexican citizens while they resided in another country, even if that entailed acting in the capacity of liaison with the host society. As it was explained in an interview with an official of the Dirección de Protección of the Secretaría de Relaciones Exteriores, certain rights bestowed by Mexican citizenship are not negated by residence in another country. Local Mexican consuls theoretically constitute the legal conduit between Mexican citizens living abroad and their home government, and between them and the host society's infrastructure.

Most consuls routinely submitted reports about their activities in the area of *protección*, the nature of which varied with the demands of the circumstances and the location. But it does seem that they often assisted Mexican women and officiated on their behalf in a variety of situations. For example, they often helped female members of the local Mexican community recover insurance and pension benefits for injured and killed workers, generally their husbands or fathers. Paperwork expediting these claims often required additional procedures when noncitizens were involved; since the wives were usually the beneficiaries, many reports were sent to Mexico about consuls processing insurance benefits.

Mexican consuls, moreover, were required to compile statistical and demographic data about Mexican citizens living in their district. First, Mexican citizens were supposed to register their names and so forth with the local consul. These lists, called *matrículas* or *registros civiles*, were then submitted to Mexico City. Mexican consuls also maintained lists of local marriages of Mexican citizens, and of *nacimientos* or births. To be sure, it can be said that significant groups of Mexicans—in particular women, especially nonaffiliated women—did not register this information with the local consulate and that these data might well be biased against poor and uneducated women; but the fact remains that they do provide an important source of information.

Significantly, Mexican consuls also transmitted reports to Mexico City at other times, apart from their scheduled ones about many different topics. Therefore, one finds interesting, albeit sporadic *informes* about miscellaneous topics. For example, the consul in Los Angeles around 1930 submitted *informes* about the activities of a group called Madres Mexicanas. Another Mexican consul took the initiative to write an *informe* about married Mexican women in the United States (1932). In 1918, another consul sent one about the deportation of Mexican women from the United States for prostitution. Interestingly, Cipriano Hernandez submitted a report to the Secretaría de Relaciones Exteriores in 1931 about Mexican familes in Chicago. The consul in San Antonio informed the SRE in 1929 about a group of families who wanted to be repatriated as *colonias*. Moreover, most consuls reported quite regularly on mutual aid societies.

Paperwork submitted to Mexico City by Mexican consuls in the United States for the nineteenth century is sketchy and inconsistent on the topic of Chicanas. A few *informes* about *protección* were sent, and some *matrículas* were submitted, but they are sketchy and of very limited use. Moreover, since the migration north to urban areas in the United States where consuls were stationed was limited in the nineteenth century, their reports to Mexico were infrequent.

However, the consul documents and *informes* submitted from the United States between 1900 and 1940 provide a substantial amount of information about Chicanas. There were many consuls all over the United States, at least ten in Texas alone, at least four in California and New Mexico, several in Arizona, Chicago, and St. Louis, and active ones in New Orleans, Philadelphia, and Colorado with the consul general being located in New York. Many of these cities had growing Mexican *colonias* between 1900 and 1940; in many instances, the consuls were active in the social and cultural life of the *colonias*.

This period, 1900-1940, further marks the pivotal generation of Mexican immigrant women. Migration before that time was mostly male, generally for employment on the railroads or in the mines. This period, however, witnessed some of the first sizable migrations of Mexican females to the American Southwest and to other areas; many contemporary Chicanas can point to the migration of their mothers or grandmothers from Mexico to the United States during that period.

This is not to say that there are not problems with the data. It can be argued with reason that middle- and upper-class women would be more likely to register with the consuls and maintain some kind of relationship with them. Moreover, there was probably a large gap between what appeared in the various *informes* of the consuls and what really happened. Many problems, events, and concerns may never have been given their proper place in the consul's paperwork. But the fact remains that a tremendous amount of information did make it into the consul's reports and survives in the archives of the Secretaría de Relaciones Exteriores.

Conclusion

Although this presentation refers only to archives and documents located in Mexico City, the Mexican border states also contain sources of primary historical documentation pertinent to the Chicana experience. Each state capital has an official state archive, housing its documents and papers, and other information as well. Moreover, the *municipios* along the border also have archives with potentially valuable files.

Primary historical material located in Mexico will be of use to most researchers with an interest in Chicanas, whether novices or seasoned veterans, whether social scientists or humanists. However, this kind of research is taxing and time-consuming, for at this point we are only beginning to discern the potential for understanding the Chicana that exists in Mexican historical archives. Moreover, presently available inventories for record groups do not necessarily take either Chicanos or Chicanas into consideration. Notwithstanding the obstacles, researchers of any discipline studying the Chicana who want to include a historical dimension in their work must seriously think about doing some work in Mexican archives to complement their findings.

In sum, then, sources of primary historical information in Mexico should not be overlooked for their possible relevance to the Chicana experience. They represent a very valuable source of data from a different perspective about the experience of Mexican women in the United States.

REFERENCES

García y García, J. Jesús. *Guía de Archivos, Contiene Material de Interés para el Estudio del Desarrollo Socioeconómico de México* (Mexico, 1972).

Greenleaf, Richard E. and Michael C. Meyer (eds.). *Research in Mexican History* (Lincoln: University of Nebraska Press, 1973).

Guía General de los Fondos que Contiene el Archivo General de la Nación (Mexico, 1981).

Chicana Reference Sources

Richard CHABRAN

Acknowledgments: A preliminary version of this essay appeared in *La Gente*. I would like to thank Cynthia Orozco for encouraging me to write this essay and Ady Martha Calderón, Marta Lopez-Garza, and Lillian Valadez for their assistance. I would also like to acknowledge the support of the Chicano Studies Research Center.

Serious scholarly inquiry should begin by consulting bibliographic tools. These range from library catalogues to periodical indexes to bibliographies. Most often we begin by consulting a library's card catalogue. For Chicanas it is here that a certain sense of frustration and anger begins. It does not take long to discover the few books listed in library catalogues, which usually are under the heading "Mexican American women." Although Latino bibliographic activity has a long and rich tradition, Chicano bibliography emerged in the late sixties as a response to the need to identify relevant materials on Chicanos. It has been noted elsewhere that the first Chicano bibliographies lacked a clear scope, had numerous typographical errors, and were simple enumerative listings with no subject access. However, over the years the general area of Chicano bibliographic research has become increasingly more sophisticated. It has moved from general works to specific subfields of Chicano studies. One question which might be asked is: what has been its contribution to Chicana studies? Significantly, all too often one fails to find any materials related to women in Chicano bibliographies. And even where they might exist, they are rarely treated as a general category or indexed separately.

It is the purpose of this bibliographic essay selectively and descriptively to survey the most important bibliographic and reference tools in the area of Chicana studies. First, major sources on the following topics are discussed: Bibliographic guides, general Chicana bibliographies, Chicana literary bibliographies, fact sources and compendiums, biographical sources relevant to Chicanas, historical bibliographies with reference to Chicanas, social science bibliographies, indexes, and archival guides. This is followed by a simple enumerative listing of minor sources. Finally, some concluding remarks on the direction of Chicana reference and bibliographic sources are included.

Chicana/o Bibliographic Guides

The Mexican American: A Critical Guide to Research Aids (Greenwich, Conn.: JAI Press, 1980), compiled by Barbara J. Robinson and J. Cordell Robinson, is meant to be a comprehensive bibliography of bibliographies on Mexican Americans. It contains a chapter on women. This chapter, like others, has an introductory essay to the bibliographic sources listed. There are 17 annotated reference sources noted in this section. Notably absent is Elizabeth Martínez Smith's "A Chicana Bibliography," which is noted below. A subject index provides additional reference sources which contain information on women.

Quien Sabe? A Preliminary List of Chicano Reference Materials (Los Angeles: Chicano Studies Research Center Publications, 1980), compiled by Francisco García Ayvens, is a selected bibliography of bibliographies on Chicanos. It contains five annotated entries of the most important Chicana reference works. A subject index provides access to other works.

"La Chicana: A Bibliographic Survey" (*Frontiers* 5/2 [1980]: 59-74) by Catherine Loeb is the best general literature review on Chicanas. In arguing for a feminist perspective, she notes the problems of accessing Chicana materials and their suppression by libraries and publishers. Her essay covers background materials, history, literature, economic and social profiles, the family, politics, other sources, notes, and a bibliography. While many new studies are not included, this is a fine overview and a good starting point for those interested in Chicana studies.

General Chicana Bibliographies

Bibliografía de la Chicana/Bibliography on the Chicana (Lakewood, Colo.: Marcela Cordova, 1973), compiled by Marcela Cordova, alphabetically lists works by and about Chicanas. A few of the entries are annotated. The majority of the works are taken from Chicano periodicals, but some books and a few dissertations are included. Although dated, it was nonetheless one of the first separately published bibliographies on Chicanas.

"A Chicana Bibliography" (*New Directions in Education: Estudios Feminiles de la Chicana* [Los Angeles: UCLA Extension and Montal Educational Associates, 1974]), compiled by Elizabeth Martínez Smith, sought to encourage instructional efforts in the area of Chicana studies. It is divided into the following categories: books and pamphlets, articles, government publications, unpublished materials, and films. This also was one of the early Chicana bibliographies. Unfortunately much of its material is only peripherally related to Chicanas.

Bibliography on la Mujer Chicana (Austin: Center for the Study of Human Resources, 1975), compiled by Lewis A. Gutierrez, is an unannotated bibliography organized into the following areas: art, bibliographies, business/employment, Chicano movement, ecology, economics, education, family, farmworkers, feminism, health, history, immigration, justice, labor, literature, machismo, Midwest, newspapers, politics, publications, sexism, socialism, social studies, and Third World women. This publication represents a catalogue of the holdings of the Chicano Library Project at the Center for Human Resources in Austin, Texas, including books, articles, clippings, and special editions. A few materials which are not housed in the Library Project are also noted.

La Chicana: A Comprehensive Bibliographic Study (Los Angeles: Aztlán Publications, 1976), compiled by Roberto Cabello Argandona, Juan Gómez-Quiñones, and Patricia Herrera Duran, is an extension of another work, *The Chicana: A Preliminary Bibliographic Study* (Los Angeles: Chicano Studies Research Library, 1973). The initial effort contained 273 items and was organized into the following sections: books, documents and papers, articles, theses and dissertations, films, newspapers, and a subject index. The second effort contains 491 annotated items. It is organized into the following sections: films, serials, general readings, culture and cultural processes and folk culture, demography, economics, education, family, marriage and sex roles, health and nutrition, history, labor and discrimination in employment, literature, politics, religion, social conditions, and author and title indexes. Within each section material is further divided by format: books, articles, and so forth. Brief essays precede each section. It represents the most important separately published reference work on Chicanas, with useful annotations. One criticism is that the bibliography contains many peripheral citations. The second version dropped the subject index in favor of the general subject categories. A subject index would have added to its usefulness.

La Mujer Chicana: An Annotated Bibliography (Austin: Chicana Research and Learning Center, 1976), though now dated, is one of the most important bibliographies on Chicanas. It is organized into the following categories: Chicana publications, Chicana feminism *y el movimiento*, education, health, history labor/employment, *la cultura, la familia*, machismo, politics, social issues, Third World Women, and an appendix titled "Reference List for Locating Sources." *La Mujer Chicana* contains approximately 275 annotated items. Francisco García Ayvens notes in *Quien Sabe?*: "This important work is marred by the appearance of many typographical errors and the incorrect collation of several pages in the publications."

Bibliography of Writing: La Mujer (Berkeley: Chicano Studies Library Publications, 1976), compiled by Cristina Portillo, Graciela Ríos, and Martha Rodríguez, is a catalogue of the holdings of the Chicano Studies Library at the University of California, Berkeley up to 1976. The first part of the bibliography, which contains 264 articles, student papers, observations, and books, is arranged alphabetically by author. Part 2 contains serials which relate specifically to Chicanas. A brief subject index and art work are included. This bibliography contains many so-called fugitive materials.

Chicana Literary Bibliographies

"Chicana Literature and Related Sources: A Selected and Annotated Bibliography" (*Bilingual Review* 7/2 [May/August, 1980]: 143-164), compiled by Elizabeth Ordonez, contains 198 items. This is by far the most extensive bibliography of Chicana literary production. It is divided into the following sections: bibliographies, general works, Chicana feminism, folklore, history, anthologies, poetry, fiction, drama, criticism—general literary, plastic arts, music and entertainment, films, works by men with significant women as themes, related sources, and useful addresses, periodicals, newspapers, and book distributors. This partially annotated work does not contain indexes.

"Hacia una bibliografía de poesía femenina chicana" (*La Palabra* 2/2 [Spring, 1980]), compiled by Eliana Sonntag, focuses on major Chicana poets. Each poet's books, poems in anthologies, poems in periodicals, translations, and criticism about her work are noted.

A Bibliography of Criticism of Contemporary Chicano Literature (Berkeley: Chicano Studies Library Publications, 1982), compiled by Ernestina Eger, contains a section on Chicanas. The items in this section deal mainly with the image of Chicanas in literature. Also included in this bibliography are Chicana authors.

A Current Bibliography of Chicano Literature: Creative and Critical Writing through 1984 (Stanford: Stanford University Libraries, 1984) was compiled by Roberto Trujillo and Andres Rodríguez. This bibliography contains approximately 69 separately published literary works by or about Chicanas. It is divided into the following sections: poetry, novel, short fiction, theater, literary criticism, *literatura chicanesca*, oral tradition, anthologies, literary periodicals, unpublished dissertations, bibliographies and encyclopedias, autobiographical works, and video and sound recordings. Author and title indexes are included.

Historical Bibliographies with References to Chicanas

Texas Women's History Project Bibliography (Austin: Foundation for Women's Resources, 1980) was compiled in order to "explore and recognize the contributions of Texas women to the development of their state." It contains a section on "Chicanos-Tejanos" with 152 entries listed alphabetically.

The Mexican Revolution: An Annotated Guide to Recent Scholarship (Boston: G.K. Hall, 1982), compiled by W. Dirk Raat, has a section on women's history bibliographies as well as references to other sources in the index.

Bibliography of Mexican American History (Westport, Conn.: Greenwood Press, 1984) was compiled by Matt S. Meier in order "to provide access to information necessary for a more sophisticated understanding of the Mexican American experience and its contribution to contemporary America." It is organized as follows: general works, colonial period, Mexican period, Guadalupe Hidalgo to 1900, 1900 to World War II, World War II to the 1980's, labor, immigration and the border region, civil rights and politics, culture, bibliographies and guides, collections, archives, and libraries, and journals. Author and subject indexes are included. This work contains only 45 items under the subject entry "Chicanas." This is disappointing for such a massive bibliography.

Chicana Social Science Bibliographies

"Mexican American Women in the Social Sciences" (*Signs: Journal of Women in Culture and Society* 8/2 [Winter, 1982]:259-272) is a review essay by Maxine Baca Zinn which focus on social science and historical literature on Chicanas. While not a bibliography per se, it identifies much of the recent significant literature on women not contained in other general Chicana bibliographies.

Hispanic Mental Health: A Research Guide (Berkeley: University of California Press, 1982), compiled by Frank Newton, Esteban L. Olmedo, and Amado M. Padilla, is a major research tool in the area of Latino mental health and the social sciences. Primary arrangement is by author. This research aid contains an inverted index. Selective relevant terms for Chicano research are birth control, child abuse, child-rearing practices, family planning, family rates, female, gender identity, machismo, marital stability, and marriage.

Ethnicity and Aging: A Bibliography (San Antonio: Trinity University Press, 1984), compiled by Edward Murguia et al., "deals only with American elderly ethnic and racial groups and lists titles that are readily accessible to the user, excluding unpublished papers, conference reports, in-house documents, and other such materials." Chapter 3, which covers Hispanic Americans, contains a subsection listing only 4 items on women.

Fact Sources and Compendiums

Dictionary of Mexican American History (Westport, Conn.: Greenwood Press, 1981), compiled by Matt S. Meier and Feliciano Rivera, contains a few references to Chicanas and Chicana organizations.

International Inventory of Current Mexico-Related Research (San Diego: Center for U.S.-Mexican Studies, 1982) is a compendium of advanced research progress related to Mexico. The third volume contains a subject index. There are 19 entries under the subject heading "women."

"Profile of the Chicana: A Statistical Fact Sheet" (*Mexican Women in the United States: Struggles Past and Present* [Los Angeles: Chicano Studies Research Center Publication, 1980]), compiled by Elizabeth Waldman, and *Women of Spanish Origin in the United States* (Washington, D.C.: U.S. Department of Labor, Employment Standards Administration Women's Bureau, 1976) both provide statistical information on Chicanas.

Biographical Sources Relevant to Chicanas

Chicano Scholars and Writers: A Bio-Bibliographical Directory (Metuchen, N.J.: Scarecrow, 1979), compiled by Julio Martínez, contains 97 entries on women out of over 500 total entries. Each entry has personal data, education, professional and/or community affiliation, honors and distinction, publications, papers, speeches, lectures and nonprint works, and criticism of biographee's works. The work contains a subject index with "women" as a subject term.

Rising Voices: Profiles of Hispano-American Lives (New York: Signet, 1974) by Al Martínez has short biographical sketches on six Latinas.

Mexican Americans: Movements and Leaders (Los Alamitos: Hwang Publishing Co., 1976) by Carlos Larralde contains lengthy entries for five Chicanas.

Dedication Rewarded (San Antonio: Centro Cultural Mexicano Americano, 1981) contains several entries on Chicanas. Its emphasis is on Texas.

Chicanos y Chicanas Prominentes (Menlo Park: Educational Consortium, 1974) has biographical sketches on six Chicanas.

In general, all of these biographical sources are of poor quality and cover the same individuals.

Indexes Relevant for Chicana Research

Resources in Women's Educational Equity (Washington, D.C.: U.S. Department HEW, 1976-1979). This is a major women's studies index. It is primarily a third-generation index of women's materials which exist in major bibliographic data bases. Between eleven and fourteen data bases ranging from ERIC to Medlars are surveyed. The organization of this index is by data base producer (ERIC, Psych Abstracts), subject, and author. Institution indexes are also included. The ORACLE Software was used to generate the index. Major bibliographic data bases were first searched. These searches were then scanned for relevance and stored on magnetic tape, and citations were reformatted by machine to achieve standardization across data bases. A mini-thesaurus was created to supplement existing descriptors (subject terms in the ERIC thesaurus). The index contains approximately 40 citations on Chicanas from the years 1976 to 1979. The scant number of citations is a reflection of the fact that major bibliographic data bases are based on mainstream journals which seldom contain articles on Chicanas/os. There are plans to continue this indexing service, which was a victim of funding cuts.

Women Studies Abstracts (New York: Rush Publishing Co., Inc., 1972-) is a quarterly abstracting journal organized into approximately 19 general subject categories. An index is included. There are generally 3 or 4 entries under "Chicanos" in each issue. A cumulative index would greatly enhance this reference work. The Spring, 1983, issue was consulted for articles cited on Chicanas, none of which were abstracted. Most of the items cited are from mainstream journals.

Anthologies by and about Women: An Analytical Index (Westport, Conn.: Greenwood Press, 1982), compiled by Susan Cardinale, has a keyword index in which 8 items pertaining to Chicanas are identified and 2 items are listed under "Hispanics."

Chicano Periodical Index (Boston: G.K. Hall, 1981, 1983) is a major index to selected Chicano periodicals. It includes a thesaurus which details the subject headings used for materials on Chicanas.

The first index has over 40 items on Chicanas and the second, over 191 items. The next volume will cover both Chicano and mainstream periodicals.

Archival Guides Relevant for Chicana Research

Women's History Sources: A Guide to Archives and Manuscripts Collections in the United States, 2 Vols. (New York: Bowker, 1979), edited by Andrea Hinding, is an impressive effort to identify and describe women's primary research sources. This collaborative project, which received funding from Rockefeller and NEH, apparently had no Latina consultants. Collections were identified and surveyed by questionnaires, followed by on-site visits. Primary organization is by state. Collections are listed alphabetically by name. Type of collection is noted, as are dates covered, size, accessibility, funding tools, and depository where located. Descriptions of varying lengths follow this basic information. The second volume is an index. Personal as well as corporate names are included in the index, as are geographic and topical themes. There are 24 entries for Mexican Americans. Some of the references to Mexican women are not clear. They range from personal reminiscences to the Girl Scouts. These few entries for Mexican women are an indication of the need to identify more collections in this area. This lacuna is a reflection of libraries' and archives' continuing lack of awareness of the need to collect and index these collections. This is said in light of the fact that the survey had to depend on these repositories to identify these emerging sources. This is an area which will become increasingly important for Mexicana studies. It is hoped that a clearinghouse will be established to identify these emerging sources continually. Hopefully, it will be based on networking between librarians and scholars.

"A Selective Survey of Chicano Manuscript Collections in the United States" (*Biblio-Politica: Chicano Perspectives on Library Service* [Berkeley: Chicano Studies Library Publications, 1984]), compiled by Richard Griswold del Castillo and Julio Martínez, contains several entries on Chicanas. This survey is divided into the following categories: literature, Chicano social and political history, immigration and labor, and oral history projects.

Minor Sources

Comisión Femenil. *"Chicana Bibliography"* (n.p., n.d.).

Concilio Mujeres. *Raza Women: A Bibliography* (San Francisco: Concilio, 1974).

Cotera, Martha P. *A Reading List for Chicanas Preliminary 1976-1978* (Austin, Tex.: Information Systems Development, 1976).

Duran, Daniel Flores. *Latino Materials: A Multimedia Guide for Children and Young Adults* (Santa Barbara: ABC-Clio, 1979).

García, Odalmira. *Chicana Studies Curriculum Guide: Grades 9-12* (Las Cruces: ERIC/CRESS, 1978).

Gómez-Quiñones, Juan and Alberto Camarillo. *Selected Bibliography for Chicano Studies*, 3rd ed. (Los Angeles: Chicano Studies Center Publications. 1975).

Hispanic American Periodical Index (Los Angeles: Latin American Center, 1975-).

Maciel, David. *Mexico: A Selected Bibliography of Sources for Chicano Studies* (Los Angeles: Chicano Studies Center Publications, 1976).

Mariscal, Linda. "Index to Material on la Chicana Appearing in *El Grito del Norte*" (Unpublished guide; Berkeley: Chicano Studies Library, 1976).

Ríos, Graciela. "Index to Social Conditions Sections of the Chicano Studies Library as It Pertains to la Chicana" (Unpublished guide; Berkeley: Chicano Studies Library, 1975).

Southern Colorado State College Library. *La Chicana: A Selected Bibliography of Material Concerned with the Mexican American Women in Higher Education* (Pueblo, Colo.: The Library, 1975).

Talbot, Jane Mitchell and Gilbert Cruz. *A Comprehensive Chicano Bibliography, 1960-1972* (Austin, Tex.: Jenkins Publishing Co., 1973).

Tatum, Charles. *A Selective and Annotated Bibliography of Chicano Studies.* 2nd ed. (Lincoln, Neb.: Society of Spanish and Spanish American Studies, 1979).

Woods, Richard D. *Reference Materials on Mexican Americans: An Annotated Bibliography* (Metuchen, N.J.: Scarecrow, 1976).

Concluding Remarks

Chicana bibliographies arose in response to the lack of inclusion in

Chicano bibliographies. The first Chicana bibliographies were compiled to support instructional efforts. Several of the major Chicana bibliographies were published in 1976. Many of these remain useful, despite the fact that they are all outdated. Chicana bibliographies are becoming focused on particular subtopics of Chicana studies and more research-oriented. At the same time, both major Chicano and women's bibliographic sources have begun to incorporate Chicanas into their scope and organization.

Sandra Balderama has compiled an excellent bibliographic manuscript on Chicanas, while Adelaida del Castillo is in the process of compiling one.

In the area of history, the second edition of "Pre-Twentieth Century Mexicans North of the Rio Bravo: Selected Social and Economic Sources" (*Development of the Mexican Working Class North of the Rio Bravo: Work and Culture among Laborers and Artisans, 1860-1900* [Los Angeles: Chicano Studies Research Center Publications, 1982], pp. 55-118) by Juan Gómez-Quiñones and Roberto Calderón will contain a section on women.

Julio Martínez and Francisco Lomell's *Chicano Literature: A Reader's Enycyclopedia*, published in the fall of 1984 by Greenwood Press, contains entries on Chicana writers.

Additionally, the Mexican archival work being carried out by Barbara Driscoll will most certainly enrich our knowledge of Chicana archival sources. The next few years will, hopefully, produce more sophisticated bibliographic tools on Chicanas which are necessary to support the continuing research in this critical area of study. Bibliographers and scholars must make a conscious attempt to include sections on women in their work.

Part IV. Language, Literature, and the Theater

Introduction

The very act of writing is political, as much as, if not more than, that which is written. For women this empowering act has been denied or neglected; for Chicanas even more so. A feminist analysis of literature often focuses on the work under scrutiny from a certain view of how it reflects patriarchal society, how the writer did or did not cast women in stereotypical roles, or how the work ties in to a feminist philosophy of literature. The essays included in this section reflect the concerns, views, and ideologies presented at the NACS conference *Voces de la Mujer* and the particular concerns of the participants who cast a critical eye at the various genres: Yolanda Broyles deals with *teatro*, Clara Lomas with poetry, Elba Sánchez with short fiction, and Alvina Quintana with the written word itself, in an assessment of language as a political tool that wields power, authority, and control.

In her analysis of the role of women in the Teatro Campesino, Yolanda Broyles sets forth a necessary and worthwhile revision of the Teatro's historical role in the development of Chicano theater. But the most valuable contribution of Broyles's work is not merely historical. Although her interviews with Socorro Valdez, Yolanda Parra, and Diane Rodríguez of the Teatro are certainly valuable, more important is the fact that she deepens our understanding of how the sexism that is often decried in the society at large exists even within a supposedly conscious and aware group, Chicano *teatristas*. Her paper posits a reevaluation or rather a valuation of the contributions women have made to the genre as a whole. Although she works mainly with the women of the Teatro Campesino, her findings should not be seen as an indictment of the Teatro Campesino, for other groups have also perpetuated sexism. As Chicano works are more closely scrutinized, the sexist nature of these will surely come to light; this, however, is not the only aim of feminist criticism. Broyles is laying a foundation for the study of Chicano theater that opens up new vistas for further study, for any thorough study of theater must also seriously consider the contributions by the women members of the *teatros* and the portrayal of women in the plays themselves.

Clara Lomas reexamines a poetic text, Margarita Cota-Cárdenas's "A una Madre de Nuestros Tiempos," in an effort to explicate or better understand the theme. Cota-Cárdenas is in turn explaining recurrent themes in Chicana poetry: mothers, daughters, survival (themes which Tey Diana Rebolledo has explored elsewhere in relation to *abuelitas* in Chicana poetry). Lomas, unlike Broyles, is not focusing on a wide genre in order to find a particular truth or fact; she is, on the other hand, closely examining a poetic text to find a general truth.

Lomas allows her reader to come along with her on a search for identity as she leads through both structural and semantic explorations of the text which end in a redefinition of "mother" and of "Chicana." The value of Lomas's piece lies in its total absorption of the text. The analysis becomes a text worthy of study as well, for she aptly handles the critic's tools to forge a new vision not only of the text under consideration, but of the approach used by the critic herself. Such work can easily become a mere exercise, yet Lomas manages to offer both a readable and a fruitful piece which presents insights that go beyond the poem. She explains, for example, how the very first word of the poem—"perdónanos"—establishes the tone of the poem on both structural and semantic levels, as the speaker uses the imperative mood and at the same time establishes the voice as a collective and individual one, the reader's.

Lomas holds that Cota-Cárdenas's poems provide a redefinition of the socioeconomic and even cultural role of "mother" for Chicanas. She supports her thesis by applying an eclectic literary approach that permits not only a linguistic analysis but a structural, and in some ways Marxist, analysis of the poem, which also allows the use of the communications model to explain the poems' message.

Elba Sánchez underlines the need to look beyond the deceptively simple form to rich and complex contextual content of Luz Garzón's short narrative "Un Paseo." Under such scrutiny the story emerges as a description of two coexisting realities, not merely that of the undocumented and the documented Hispanics, but of the personal and universal mother/child relationships and the socioeconomic history which have led to "un paseo."

Sánchez points to the dialogue and likens the surface simplicity of the narration to Tomás Rivera's style. She finds a complex, underlying thematic content in both. She further analyzes the textual style by focusing on the dichotomous elements as found in the characters.

As she turns her attention to the protagonists, she first notes their anonymity, which allows for their function as icons or symbols. "La madre" could be "cualquier madre" but more explicitly all mothers. Garzón's character—an undocumented mother—becomes a representative mother. Upon further analysis of the characters, Sánchez frames a contrapunctual world—the world the story presents which unites and, through shift of point of view and dialogue, makes two realities one. In so doing, Sánchez underscores the significance of the event outside the story, in the sociohistorical present where "Un Paseo" is also an indictment of a society that maligns and mistreats not just undocumented but all migrant or farm laborers. "Un Paseo" shows two mothers and their sons traveling the same road, but in extremely different vehicles. Sánchez claims that the readers can see themselves in either one and thereby further appreciate the intensity of the social commentary.

The irony of the title and the naive and innocent children's voices set against the harsh cruel voices of the authorities—both U.S. and Mexican—provides clues as to the author's real message. The adults, whose jaded, defeated lives can be gleaned from the narrator's description, as well as their own words, are also "blind" to the world outside their own predicament.

Although Sánchez mentions the cultural relevance of the thematic content to the structure or form, she fails to stress other aspects of the narrative which add to or detract from the author's message. For example, she ignores the obvious conclusion which a linguistic analysis would yield. Although this is a minor point, it is one which would enhance her analysis and could be explored in terms of her thesis. The use of the word *bomba* for "balloon," for example, presents at least one instance of a possible culture-bound vocabulary. Many of us use not *bomba* but *vejiga* or *globo*.

Aside from this omission, Sánchez's work offers us a critical view of "Un Paseo," a view which renders the story not merely intelligible, for it already is that, but perhaps more easily accessible as social commentary, a complex and serious indictment of society under the guise of a simple tale of a mother and son.

Alvina Quintana takes a very different approach, yet one which ultimately seeks to achieve a similar understanding and use. She uses the hermeneutic approach to postulate some theories of how language and power are interrelated as shown in the work of Latinas. Much of her theoretical framework comes from Hélène Cixous and other feminist theorists. Her application of these to Mexicano/Chicano authors is invaluable.

Quintana focuses on the ideologically based oppression of the female protagonists in the stories of Mexican author Kitzia Hoffman and Argentine Sylvina Bullrich. She then turns to two Chicanas—Sylvia Gonzales and Norma Alarcón—to present further proof of how masculine discourse has dominated writing and thereby subjugated or exploited female consciousness. Alarcón's prose on the Malintzin myth and Gonzales's poem "Chicana Evolution" are seen as steps in the right direction, as women's writing moves toward what Quintana calls a realistic and holistic approach, which "is needed for the gender-balanced ideology of the future."

Because language is power and because women have traditionally been relegated to powerless positions, an analysis of language can provide usable models for change. Quintana claims that women's discourse "provides the means by which to implement change in history and ideology," and that "for Mexicanas/Chicanas this change translates into the possibility of defining ourselves in history, liberating women and men from the oppressive roles which have been handed down by masculine discourse." Using a hermeneutic approach and methodically drawing parallels between usage and message, she challenges her readers to reread the texts under examination, and to make allowance for the inherent ideological bias in reading any masculine text.

Writing is political, and women writing constitute a political voice that insists on being heard. These essays provide insight and move us toward a rethinking of all writing, but more importantly, to the writing of Chicanas as critics. Our literature merits serious analysis, and these writers through their investigations provide the tools and polemical ground for a truly complete view of Chicano literature.

Women in El Teatro Campesino: "¿Apoco Estaba Molacha la Virgen de Guadalupe?"

Yolanda Julia BROYLES

Acknowledgments: The research for this and other portions of my study on El Teatro Campesino was conducted under a grant from the National Research Council/Ford Foundation.

In the summer of 1980 I witnessed a performance of El Teatro Campesino's *Fin del Mundo* in Europe. That production marked the end of the ensemble known as El Teatro Campesino, a name which had stood as a trademark representing a way of performing and a way of living—both intimately linked through a long process of common struggle. The spirit of group commitment was still alive in that production, and that energy obviously contributed to the rare power of that performance—a power which was visibly transmitted to German and French audiences in spite of language or other cultural barriers. My own dissatisfaction with the piece sprang from the portrayal of Chicanas. The women characters in the show felt like an eerie rerun of earlier Teatro plays: the saint-like wilting wife, the sleazy whore, and the grandmother figure. Compared with the male characters, the females seemed one-dimensional and relatively insignificant. Among the male characters, the most notable in terms of expressivity was the Pachuco youth nicknamed "Huesos." It was Huesos who most controlled the audiences and the motion on stage. I was astonished backstage after the performance when I discovered that the extraordinary Huesos was played by a woman: Socorro Valdez. Her performance was unforgettable. And yet her presence in the Teatro had never been described by scholars or historians of Chicano drama. Why?

History—and that includes theater history—has frequently been reduced to a chronology of the doings of "great men." Similarly, the history of El Teatro Campesino has been canonized as the history of the "life and times" of Luis Valdez. The tendency to place individuals—usually male individuals—and not groups at the center of history constitutes a radical simplification by which the dynamics of a life *process* are filtered out, leaving behind names, dates, and places. Beyond the more obvious distortions attendant to creating monuments to individuals, that conceptual framework serves to eclipse the memory of group achievement. As individuals reading history, we are more likely to feel dwarfed by all the "great men" instead of learning of the strength we have through community and collaboration.

I would like to put aside the heroic and monolithic vision of El Teatro Campesino and momentarily destabilize that image by describing facets of a struggle that has been carried on by some of the women in the group—with varying degrees of success. In the three years since the European tour of *Fin del Mundo* I have explored the dynamics of Teatro Campesino and of other *teatros*, and I have developed a closer understanding of those dynamics, based not so much on what I have read as on what I saw then and have observed since then. My understanding is also based on long conversations and interviews and on day-to-day living experiences with the women and men of El Teatro Campesino in California. During my two years of research residence in San Juan Bautista, I was able to observe and to develop an understanding of the realities behind the appearances. Day-by-day behind the scenes inquiry has opened my eyes to the creative process that predated that production of *Fin del Mundo*—and the roles of women in that process. It is the roles of these *women* and their significance within the history of El Teatro Campesino and—by extension—within the history of Chicano theater which I address here. The composite story of the roles of women in the Teatro Campesino is only one of the unwritten chapters of its history. In reconstructing that history I rely principally on those *teatristas* who have never been viewed as prominent. I have chosen to focus on the oral testimony of various Teatro women, particularly Socorro Valdez—as well as on my own observations. The present paper represents a preliminary version of a much more extensive essay. The full version includes the testimony of several more Teatro Campesino women and focuses on various other questions concerning the work of women in *teatro*. In its final form, the essay will constitute one chapter in a book on various dimensions of El Teatro Campesino.

Women in El Teatro Campesino: Boundaries of Women's Roles

It cannot escape the attention of those who have followed the development of El Teatro Campesino through the years that the female roles have remained fairly constant. In the course of the evolutionary process from *actos* to *mitos* to *corridos* to combinations thereof, from the days of the *actos* performed by farmworkers for farmworkers atop flatbed trucks to the days of *Zoot Suit* in Hollywood and on Broadway, the female characters have consisted of variations of the same three or four types. Women are first of all defined in a familial category: mother, grandmother, sister, or wife/girlfriend. All women are also divided into one of two sexual categories: whores or virgins. Depending on the circumstances of any given play—all of which have male protagonists—the handful of female traits are mixed or matched to create the desired effect. The spectrum of female characteristics is narrow; female roles are one-dimensional stereotypes. Most common are the prostitutes and the virginal wife or mother, but there can also be prostitute mothers, for example. For the sake of brevity I dispense with a discussion of examples of this form of female characterization in the Teatro Campesino repertoire.[1] Suffice it to say that female characters typically engage in activities which are accessory to those of males. Women's roles do not enjoy the dramatic space necessary for the unfolding of a character. Never is the world seen through the eyes of women, the other half of humanity.

In my interviews with Teatro women I explored the genesis of these roles and the women's views of them. In elaborating on their views of these roles, the women—without exception—placed these roles within the context of their own personal development. There is agreement among them that the stereotyped roles found in the work of El Teatro Campesino are in many ways related to the stereotyped views of Chicanas found within society at large. The women who joined the company in the 1970s basically inherited stereotypical female roles as givens. The roles had been largely preestablished and were neither submitted to scrutiny nor questioned, owing to two major factors. On the one hand, most women entered the Teatro in their teens. Therefore, their consciousness of themselves as women and of their theatrical roles as women were not highly developed. In the words of Teatro member Diane Rodríguez:

> At the beginning we were playing various types, like the "supportive wife," you know, or the "virginal" type, like an icon, literally, she was just a statue—and that was a character; that was one of the main roles. *We* were playing these roles, *we* let that happen. And we had some input. But where were we, as women, at that point? Somehow at that point we didn't have the consciousness and we played these cardboard roles. Or maybe we did have some consciousness but we didn't know how to get it on the stage. There was *something* that was not as strong as it is now, of course. There is more of a consciousness of women—in oneself—that there wasn't then.[2]

Socorro Valdez, who performed her first Teatro Campesino role at fifteen, also feels that age prevented her from questioning female roles with which the men in the company apparently felt comfortable:

> I was growing up, you know. So for me to confront Luis at that time and say: Look, your writing about women is no good . . . well, that is not where I was coming from; he was much older than me and had more life experience. But he didn't have *female* experience.[3]

A historical factor also made the roles of women appear a secondary consideration. During the 1960s the efforts to address raza and the reality of raza as a *whole* somehow precluded a special consideration of women's roles or problems. In the words of Diane Rodríguez:

> It seems that because we have always worked for a certain goal, we have overlooked some things. I admit that. I admit very much . . . we perform his [Luis Valdez's] view of women, basically. Now there is some input. But in order that the show go on . . . well, we have said: OK we'll go with this and we have performed these roles . . . We have talked about this and I think all of us are very conscious. But I don't think that we have found the answer yet either. (interview, p. 8)

Putting women's issues second, or discounting them altogether, was common among leftist groups of the 1960s in the United States and around the world. The liberation of people "in general" was considered the chief priority. Ironically, those engaged in struggles for human equality were slow to recognize that class struggles and ethnic struggles would not necessarily better the lot of women. *Movimiento* women who raised women's issues—which are, dialectically speaking, men's issues as well—were accused of being divisive.

With the passing of time and the development of consciousness as women, the sense of working within confining roles became increasingly apparent and increasingly frustrating. Socorro, the youngest of the group, described it in this manner:

> It was like walking the same path over and over. There was the mother, the sister, or the grandmother or the girlfriend. Only four. You were either the *novia, la mamá, la abuela, o la hermana*. And most of the time these characters were passive. The way those females are laid out are for the most part very passive and laid back, *y aguantaban todo*. I think that is what really chewed me up at the time. (interview, p. 4)

The women's dissatisfaction with these roles led to one of the longest and deepest struggles in the development of the Teatro Campesino. I would even venture to say that the question of women's roles became the most enduring contradiction within the company, a contradiction paralleled in various ways within the Chicano movement. It was a contradiction between what was, on the one hand, a constant process of renewal in the form of new genres and new techniques, new visions and experimentation, and what was, on the other hand, a static clinging to well-worn stereotypes of gender roles. The Teatro Campesino repertoire, with its strong progressive strides in the treatment of labor issues, of Chicano culture, of historical issues, consistently demonstrated stagnation in its treatment of women.

Resistance to change was in some ways anchored in the makeup of the company, which had been predominantly male since its founding. Socorro Valdez describes how the women struggled to be viewed and treated as equals:

> At one time there were only three women in the whole darn

> thing: Olivia Chumacero, myself, and a third I don't remember. That was a real interesting time. We were either going to remain members of the company, or just be "the women of the company." That made a real difference, you know, because I hated to be put into a mold like "These are the ladies of the Teatro." Aw, shut up! Don't gimme *that*! They would separate you without needing to. And so Olivia fought for her own, as I did. You know we were both very young. We both ended up in the role of *fighters* because that's what was needed to get the men's heads to a place where they would be able to discuss something with you. We would have open meetings where the shit would fly across the room.... But I know how important those three women were at that period, because there was no other female voice in the company. (interview, p. 30)

Administrative decision-making power was, to a large extent, in the hands of the men. In time women learned to question the division of labor along gender lines:

> We even got down to questioning who was going to be telling who what to do; because I personally got very tired of being under the thumb of a man. We had a male touring manager. We had a male booking agent. We had a male director. We had a male stage manager. We had a male everything. And there are women there that are just as strong . . . I could pick up a house if I had to, you know . . . But they just never thought I could. And it was up to me to show them that I could. There was no fault to bear; just responsibility. (Socorro Valdez interview, p. 33)

The aspect of male dominance in administrative matters was reinforced by the patriarchal organization of El Teatro Campesino. Luis Valdez typically worked with persons much younger than himself. And the relationship between the members of the ensemble, a group that *worked and lived* together, was defined as a familial one. The group was officially defined as a *familia*; Luis Valdez was the symbolic father or person in charge. The process of changing the portrayal of women, of developing fuller roles and images of women, was perceived by the women as a challenge both in theatrical terms and in terms of human dignity. Yet the men did not share that sense of urgency in the women's challenge. Perhaps it was alarming to the patriarchal structure of El Teatro Campesino. Socorro Valdez describes the challenge created by women:

> Luis has seen a lot of stuff through the work that the women have done in this group. They've always given him a little more . . . to *challenge* him. And there were times in the group that the women were just outraged. We'd say "What are you doing? I'm sick of playing mothers! I'm sick of playing sisters!" (interview, p. 7)

The question of redefining female roles, however, met with passive resistance. For one thing, it never really found acceptance as a problem. Far from being taken up as a challenge, it was treated as an unnecessary provocation. Women's efforts to dramatize a new vision of women were frequently countered by the suggestion that they write their own plays, a subtle form of ostracism. Clearly, the collective spirit suffered a collapse when gender roles were questioned. Suddenly an individual solution was suggested for what was a collective problem. That response was indicative of the lack of ensemble commitment to the creation of adequate roles for women. Women of the Teatro view that resistance—on one level—as a function of the men not having "female experience." But a more complex dimension of that resistance is also articulated: the narrowness in the perception of women by males is linked to the narrowness in the men's self-perception: "He [Luis] can't experience women any other way except as a man. And no one else can do that either, unless they are willing to *stretch their own image of themselves*" (Socorro Valdez interview, p. 7).

Male resistance to female self-determination, however, should not be personalized or considered the special problem of this or that man or group. In truth, it is not unique to El Teatro Campesino. Male supremacist ideology and practice, in all sectors of society, have been the focus of extensive discussion and investigation within the women's movement. A prime manifestation of that ideology is the inability to accept women beyond their biological roles: wife/mother/lover; it is a form of blindness which prevents many from perceiving the vast spectrum of experiences which in reality comprises womanhood. The virgin/whore dichotomization of women is the distorted projection of male supremacist ideology. Male supremacy is—at its most basic level—a power-hunger born of a weak self-image. And maintenance of male power *needs* a fragmented (i.e., nonthreatening) image of women. Although various women in the Teatro Campesino ensemble were a living antithesis to the male stereotypes of women, there is virtually no evidence of a new understanding or "stretch." The women's self-image remained at odds with the images of those unable to see women in their wholeness: the issue of women's roles was consistently deflected.

El Teatro Campesino continued to reenact all varieties of virgins, mothers, and sleazy whores throughout the decade of the 1970s. This is not to imply that the women stayed in the company in the position of martyrs. There were various other dimensions of activity that made the experience very rewarding. Truly, the flowering of creative capacities afforded by the collective process within the Teatro was seemingly limitless, as long as it did not pertain to the expansion of women's roles. Even the eventual entry of women into administrative positions did not trigger a modification of the portrayal of women on the stage.

The growing desire of some Teatro Campesino women to create and try out roles with greater depth to some extent coincided with Luis Valdez's gradual striving to assume greater power within the organization. That striving was not without implications for the women engaged in redefining the roles of women. Casting decisions became the almost exclusive right of Luis Valdez. And casting decisions became a conscious and/or unconscious tool in the perpetuation of the classic stereotypes of women. In the last Teatro Campesino ensemble production (*Fin del Mundo*, 1980) the female lead character of Vera—companion to the drug addict Reymundo Mata—was played in the highly incongruous but characteristic ingenue style. This was the result of a casting decision: a novice actress was chosen over the more experienced Teatro women. As in so many productions, a role that promised a great deal delivered very little:

> The one role that all of us women tried out for was the role of Vera, the pregnant wife-girlfriend. Unfortunately that role

> was handled by a very weak actress . . . She was *physically* maybe suited for the role: a pretty face. But in terms of the *guts* I think that Olivia or Diane were much better suited . . . It was a real hurt for us, because we would try to coach her: "Don't act like such a clinging vine!! Leave us a little bit of pride!!" It had the makings of a wonderful role, but it didn't get developed. Luis cast her in that role.[4]

The same practice of casting weak actresses in pivotal roles was repeated in subsequent productions, to the detriment of the plays as a whole. The production of *Rose of the Rancho*, which inaugurated the Teatro Campesino Playhouse (1981), featured a wilting Rose character in the play's center. That role was a result of a casting decision and of playwriting. A powerful and expressive actress in the role of Rose might well have created a character highly incompatible with the general thrust of this lightweight melodramatic comedy. The drama seeks to entertain and to attract a broad audience by offending no one. As such, it follows a stereotyped entertainment formula: the weak Mexican Rose character saves the *rancho* by marrying an Anglo. All live happily ever after.

The same novice who played the Rose character then played the principal female role in Luis Valdez's Tiburcio Vásquez play *Bandido* (winter, 1981), with predictable results. Nor did the conception of the female roles allow for character development. The three women in the cast are all defined solely in terms of men: the highbrowed Rosario is wife to Leiva and lover to Tiburcio Vásquez; California Kate is a whore madam; Rita Madrid is a "feisty camp follower" (script) in competition with Rosario for the love of Vásquez. Much of her dialogue centers around winning him.

The reality of physical and spiritual stereotyping extended to include factors such as skin color. This is even true of a play such as *La Virgen del Tepeyac*, which occupies a very special place in the history of El Teatro Campesino. Playing Tonantzin-Guadalupe was regarded as much more than a "role" by the women of the company. It was an honor and a deeply spiritual undertaking. It is not the Roman Catholic institutionalized version of Guadalupe which gives the pageant its power, but rather the adoration of Tonanztin-Guadalupe as the Native American deity that she is: the symbol of a cosmic force. The role of Guadalupe is perhaps the one female role which was loved by all the women of the company. Unlike other roles, it represented a tribute to female potentiality. Yet the role also fell prey to stereotyping. An unspoken casting taboo altered the appearance of the Indian madonna. Yolanda Parra tells of the alteration:

> In the *Virgin del Tepeyac* they should have a real Indian-looking woman because that's the *whole point*. She appears to Juan Diego in the image of an *india*, and I mean hard-core stone-ground Mexican Indian . . . But the women they pick for the role look like little Spanish madonnas. I've always thought Olivia Chumacero would make a great Virgen del Tepeyac; because there is a certain amount of ovaries that go into that part. You're talking the guts of the Universe there. You're talking somebody who can really feel the power. (interview, pp. 6-7)

Control over casting decisions provided a kind of insurance policy for the director. It assured that the roles would be played in accordance with *his* view of women. Within the three or four role types available to women, only certain predetermined women could play certain predetermined roles. Just as female roles in plays had become cemented, women also became stereotyped along rigid lines *offstage*. A vicious circle of type-casting was created. In the words of Socorro Valdez:

> As it were, the actresses that were "soft" offstage and just *muy buenas, muy muy buenas* got the "soft" roles. And the ladies that were *medias carbronas* and had a beer and a cigarette hanging out of their mouth, well you know what role they got . . . I always ended up with that other stuff. (interview, p. 6)

Women were divided basically into "soft" types and "hard" types—into good and bad. Yet this division did not go unquestioned. What is more, it deepened the women's understanding of themselves and of their roles. In the words of Socorro Valdez:

> Now I know those choices. And I know there were moments in the group when there was to be a "girlfriend." Well, can Socorro be the girlfriend? No, Socorro can't be the

> girlfriend. Socorro is either the old lady or she's the jokester. But I was never seen in this company as a "soft" woman, because they confuse softness and hardness and they attach those two things to strength or weakness. But there is no such thing in *my* mind . . . You can't put those two things together like that. They fluctuate. (interview, p. 6)

In discussing the nature of women's roles it should not be overlooked that the rigid views of gender roles both on and off the stage created a special set of problems peculiar to women in theater. These problems illustrate the close relationship between the private and public spheres in theatrical life. One obstacle the women had to overcome was the negative response of many to the presence of women in *teatro*. The prejudice against women actors manifested itself even among some Teatro Campesino supporters:

> It got wild when people started saying: Those broads are nothing but a bunch of *tú sabes . . . que actrizes ni que actrizes*. Only *guys* could be actors. For some reason we were still only women . . . Somehow or other. Critics of the Teatro, people that were close to the company, people that were around: they wondered what kind of women we were. We were just cheap broads. Now the idea is different; but traditionally women in theater—even way back to the dark ages—were considered just whores. (interview, p. 31)

In many cases Chicanas also encountered parental resistance to their work in theater. Olivia Chumacero tells of this situation: "It's been eleven years since I left the house . . . but when my parents think of theater they think of loose women. In Mexico if you are into the arts in this way *eres mujer de la calle* . . . Women have it harder and they have to be strong."[5] In the course of time, motherhood became an issue affecting the participation of women in El Teatro Campesino. Specifically child-bearing and child-raising were considered incompatible with theatrical touring. Rather than accept elimination from the company, women struggled to demonstrate that touring with children was possible and necessary:

> We wanted to have more say in certain decisions. For instance: touring and babies. How about taking babies out on

> the road? So-and-so couldn't travel because she had a baby. Now that's ridiculous. Olivia was one of them . . . the forerunners of the mothers in the company. They had their babies . . . and they proved it, not only to themselves or to their in-laws or to their parents, but to Luis, that it could be done. They proved that women—even now—with all the pressures of motherhood could be seen performing on the stage and then breast-feeding their kid in the van the next hour. It was possible. It wasn't easy . . . I use Olivia as an example because she just trudged right through it in the best way she knew how. And it wasn't always easy for her . . . I don't have any children but I do know how *I* want to be now that I've *seen* how they could do it. They proved certain things for me. And that was during the *hard* times when we had to go cross-country to New York in one van, and the baby diapers and all that . . . You know, that was a hell of a point that the women made. It affected me a great deal to see that. The company had to make it possible for children to go with us. That's what it had to do. Staying home had to be a matter of *choice* and not a matter of having children. That point was very important: the establishment of an acting mother. (Socorro Valdez interview, p. 32)

Although acting mothers became a common thing in El Teatro Campesino, a policy of equal sharing in child-care responsibilities was not established. Each couple with children had to work out its own strategy for dealing with the added responsibility of child care. Particularly in the case of infants, primary or sole responsibility usually rested with the mother. As such, acting mothers found themselves with a work-load disadvantage within the company. In the women's or men's testimony there is no mention of difficulties in the establishment of an acting father.

Breaking the Mold: New Pathways within Collective Creation

Having devoted a good deal of attention to the limitations imposed upon women and women characters on stage, I would now like to examine the other side of that long-smouldering contradiction. The efforts—of *some* women—to break through the confinement of stereotypic female roles had, to some extent, been thwarted. Yet their determination and consciousness remained unaltered and became a compelling force in other directions. New avenues had to be explored. From the backstage perspective of theater history I witnessed dramatic breakthroughs. Some of them had immediate consequences for centerstage action. Others had their impact in areas of less media visibility.

Let us briefly follow the strivings of Socorro Valdez, whose breakthroughs have been dramatically inspirational. The first role that Socorro ever played in the company was the grandmother role. I offer her own recollection of that activity:

> I was fifteen years old—my first role in the company was that of an old lady about eighty years old. And I jumped on it real quick because it was character, it was character work. It was real big broad acting. That was my point of beginning. And so when I played my first character I immediately relied on my strength. And the old lady I played was by no means a whining old lady. She was a very powerful character . . . maybe the way I'm going to be when I'm eighty, because I don't see myself coming from a weak place. (interview, p.5)

Although that performance is not noted by historians of Teatro, it is alive in the memory of all Teatristas. Olivia Chumacero recalls:

> Socorro, for example, created the mother and grandmother characters in the Teatro. She was sixteen years old and she used to do the most fantastic old lady that you had ever seen. Incredible. Really incredible: *el movimiento, la forma, el estilo de hablar, las expresiones*, everything. It was wonderful. (interview, p. 13)

In spite of the vitality of the performance process, the female roles became stagnant after they began to repeat themselves in various guises for over a decade. Socorro Valdez describes one manner in which she resolved to break the mold:

> At the time there were no men in the group who could be made to play pachucos, or old men, etc. And it was important to play the men's roles well; because the truth is that

> Luis writes for men. He always has. His point of view is male and it will always be so. But it was kind of strange that he had no men to play the men. So I figured "Hell, what's holding me back? Just let me put on a pair of pants and jump into it and see." And in fact I ended up playing men better than the men! . . . It wasn't that I was trying to get the role; I was trying to *establish* the role within the group. Those characters of men needed to be played. But unfortunately the men in the group at the time were not able or capable or free or whatever the problem was. (interview, p. 3)

Assuming a male role represented a major step in the exploration of new possibilities as a performer. And that step was an outgrowth of the living creative impulse that had become frustrated within the narrow confines of stereotyped women's roles. The male roles enjoyed a major part of the lines. For Socorro, playing a male role provided a new adventure in role-playing: as a male she was now in an *active* position. In the Teatro Campesino repertoire, action was typically centered around male protagonists, with women characters generally functioning as auxiliary figures. The women figures were those *affected by* men; they were peripheral: the ones *to whom* things happened. Not that the reverse would be desirable. The overpowering centrality of one character (usually male) creates limitations of dialogue, space, and action in the development of other characters. In Teatro Campesino plays where the main character (male) has been balanced by other characters, those other characters are invariably also male (such as in *Fin del Mundo*, 1980; or *La Gran Carpa Cantinflesca*) or they are sexless characters like La Muerte or El Diablo (such as in *La Carpa de los Rasquachis*). Women characters fill the spaces in between.

Socorro Valdez's appropriation of male roles provided an opportunity for her to stretch her own self-image, to grow.

> [The female roles] are very limiting. There is the mother type, and then there is the "mutha": the whore type, sleazy cheap. There is always the mother, the sister, the girlfriend, or the grandmother. That's very limiting. And that's one of the reasons I dove so deep into aborting the fact that I was female and only female. I needed exploration in my work. (interview, p. 4)

The exploration and imagination involved in the creation of new characters was considerable. To play a role or character did not mean to follow the script or another person's directions. It meant literally to *create* a character, to bring it to life virtually from scratch. That included the creation of the dialogue and movement through the improvisational process. Playing each role entailed a degree of creative responsibility for performers very much unlike that of drama traditions, whose fixation rests with written scripts. To perform a play was to *generate* a play. Even the classic *actos*—which have been adopted for performance by Chicano theater groups throughout the United States and in Latin America—were never rehearsed by El Teatro Campesino using a script. Contrary to popular belief—and contrary to the spirit and practice of orality—the published collection of *actos* do not represent "definitive" texts. The concept of "definitive" is not applicable within the oral tradition, which thrives on the improvisational skill of performers. Olivia Chumacero describes the process:

> When the *actos* book was done, no scripts existed. Felix Alvarez went around with a tape recorder asking people what their lines were so that he could write it down and put the *acto* book together . . . even though those lines changed a lot as we went along, depending on who was doing the character and depending on the situation. The parts would change a lot. (interview, p. 12)

Clearly, Teatro Campesino plays were collaborative exercises that changed with each performance and with each rehearsal. Much of theater criticism and theater history divorces these pieces from the human beings who created them. Yet the texts uttered did not exist separate from those people. They did not exist in "dramatic literature" fashion. The text alone is not even half the story. For much of Chicano theater it holds true that academic textual analysis cannot unfold or reveal the artistry involved. Socorro Valdez describes her view of bringing expression to a "crude image" (i.e., role):

> The roles are like an old rock, but crack that baby open and you have intricate, intricate layers of evolution. *That* is what has been my goal: it is to take these very crude images that

> were there, that have their own form of artistry, and break them open so that the inside is expressed. It makes me work harder, it makes me push more to get inside of a *cholo* or to get inside of that campesino who seems so obvious. (interview, p. 29)

Similarly, the role of "director" of El Teatro Campesino had a function very much unlike that within mainstream theater. The dynamics of collective authorship created a process in which the director was more often engaged in taking direction than in giving it. This relationship of reciprocity prompted Yolanda Parra to indicate that "Luis Valdez was created by El Teatro Campesino," when historians of theater always put it the other way around. In her words:

> He [Luis] pulled a lot of stuff out of them and they *gave* him a lot of material, tons of material in the improvisations. And you see that material appear even in shows like *Zoot Suit*. He took characters that had been developed within the group in a collective situation. As director he might come out and say: "This is the situation." But then it was the *actors* that made it happen for him . . . In a lot of ways Luis was created by El Teatro Campesino. The unquestionable loyalty of the members also created him. (interview, p. 4)

Given the extraordinary acting skill of Socorro Valdez, it would be no exaggeration to speak of her as a leading figure in the history of El Teatro Campesino. In the entire history of her work with the Teatro Campesino, however, Socorro Valdez has never played a lead female part, only numerous male leads. That is a startling fact considering not only Socorro's almost legendary talents as a performer but also her yearning to explore many roles. Yet the stereotyped casting within the company eliminated her, and other women who look like her, from various female lead roles. There is sadness in her voice when she indicates that she was never allowed to play La Virgen de Guadalupe in *La Virgen del Tepeyac*:

> I never even got close to it. They wouldn't let me . . . I could never have the role . . . because Luis doesn't see me that way. They see the Virgen de Guadalupe as a soft, demure,

> peaceful, saintly, ingenue type. The really incredible part was when it turned out that I have too many teeth. I was told "You got too many teeth. The Virgen didn't have that many teeth." It appears the Virgen de Guadalupe had no teeth. I thought to myself: "That is the stupidest thing I ever heard of!" ¿Apoco estaba molacha la Virgen de Guadalupe? (interview, p. 5)

The truth, however, was that Socorro did not meet the standards of beauty that had been set for La Virgen Morena: Socorro has strong *indígena* features and dark brown skin. That also partially explains how she and other Teatro Campesino women ended up creating numerous roles which camouflaged their natural appearance. In addition to the male roles, they created numerous sexless characters. Socorro's portrayal of La Muerte—in calavera costume—became a classic. She comments herself: "In all these years I was always under heavy makeup or under heavy costume, you know. And one role that I pretty much made my handle was the calavera because it was sexless; it was of neither sex" (interview, p. 11). The sexless roles became numerous, and they were pursued as a creative outlet for women to escape the confinement of female roles. Olivia Chumacero created the Diabla during the *corridos* dramatizations of the seventies and also the Angel role in *La Pastorela*; Yolanda Parra's performance as St. Michael in *La Pastorela* (1981) is remembered by many as one of the finest renditions of that character. Several women also played male roles, but not as consistently as Socorro. In the course of seeking new channels for creativity, Olivia Chumacero and Socorro Valdez also began directing. Socorro directed many productions of *La Virgen del Tepeyac*.

Olivia Chumacero has also developed alternative pathways for applying her acting and directing expertise. She performed with the Teatro regularly until 1980, while also pioneering in theater work with children of Chicano migrant workers. She continues to do that work today, while also conducting a program of drama workshops for women in battered women's centers and for youth in drug prevention centers, and while evolving the performance genre of *teatropoesía* together with Rogelio Rojas.[6] Currently she also teaches dramatic techniques to future bilingual teachers at the University of California at Santa Cruz. Olivia's work can serve as a model for the application of theater skills in ways which directly benefit disenfranchised sectors of society. Her theatrical commitment is tailored to fit the needs of the community in which she lives. The paths taken by Socorro Valdez and Olivia Chumacero provide us with but two examples of the new roles that women have assumed and created, in an effort to break the mold of distorted and fragmented images of Chicanas. But at different times and in different ways virtually all the women have consciously engaged in the effort to create new spaces and models in which they and other women—and men—can move. Many have managed to transform old frustrations into new options. These are women who are keenly aware of the possibilities within themselves—as performers and as human beings. The history of El Teatro Campesino must include the history of its contradictions and of the emergence of women who have charted new territory for subsequent generations.

An Epilogue: Chicanas Onstage into the 1980s

The long history of El Teatro Campesino's collective work had ceased entirely by 1980. When Luis Valdez went to Hollywood and then to Broadway, the members of the ensemble for the most part went their separate ways. Many of them continue to fuse performance and life, in classic Teatro Campesino fashion. Most of them apply their skills within the processes of everyday activities: be it in schools, with community groups, in workshops, or also in theater productions around the Bay area. Although El Teatro Campesino still exists on paper, the name no longer stands for an acting *ensemble* that is strongly committed to specific cultural and social ideals; Luis Valdez has long since left the arena of alternative theater and is committed to mainstreaming—a process he sometimes likens to a narcotic injection: "I see it as mainlining into the veins of America."[7]

I would like to focus attention on Luis Valdez's major creation of the past two years: a production entitled *Corridos*. The show has enjoyed considerable box office success both in San Juan Bautista and at the Marines' Memorial Theater of San Francisco. *Corridos* harvested the critical acclaim of the establishment press and received virtually all Bay area theater awards for the 1983 season. A brief examination of *Corridos* corresponds with the trajectory of the present inquiry: the stated goal of *Corridos* is "to explore the relationship between men and women."[8] Let us examine the results of this exploration, especially as they pertain to women.

The *corridos* chosen for performance are *Rosita Alvirez, Cornelio Vega, Tierra sin Nombre, Delgadina*, and a Luis Valdez weaving of *La Rielera/La Valentina/La Adelita* entitled *Soldadera*. What, then, is the nature of the relationship between men and women? One prominent feature common to these *corridos* is the murder of a woman. One exception is Cornelio Vega, where a man is murdered "por amar a una mujer." Valdez himself indicates in an interview: "Hay un tema central que tiene que ver con la violencia en contra de las mujeres que desgraciadamente es real, hasta hoy en día. Es parte de nuestra historia como es parte de nuestro presente."[9] The theme of violence against women, however, is in no way treated as an issue or a problem. To the contrary: it is used as a comic element or simply as a dramatic climax. And through the very choice of *corridos*, violence against women occupies a prominent and almost exclusive role in "the relationship between men and women." In fact, men/women relationships seem to exhaust themselves in violence. In the San Francisco production, the *corrido* of Doña Elena y El Frances was added; Doña Elena is of course shot by her husband. In an effort to establish a kind of equality between the sexes, a *corrido* in which a woman murders her husband was also added: *El Corrido de Conchita la Viuda Alegre*. The heavy focus on shooting and blood project the image of Mexicans as a bloodthirsty, vengeful crowd. In spite of the abundance of existing *corridos* in which no one is murdered, only *corridos* with violence between men and women are dramatized. The desire to exploit the dramatic tensions of violence takes precedence over the desire to provide a balanced portrayal of a people and of their ballad tradition.

In his role as narrator, Luis Valdez states that the *corridos* portray types such as "la coqueta" or "el valiente." The type that emerges in the course of staging a *corrido*, however, is very much a result of dramaturgic interpretation. Attaching one label to a *corrido* figure involves a choice by which one characteristic, among many possible ones, is singled out. It is the essence of stereotyping. One example of this procedure can be seen in the decision to characterize Rosita Alvirez as a coquette. Instead of focusing upon the *hija desobediente* (i.e., the mother/daughter relationship), she emerges as a loose and reckless woman. Highlighted action includes, for example, Rosita seductively lifting her dress in front of a mirror and flashing her legs. At the dance, Rosita is lewdly flirtatious and then seems to "get what she deserves." In other words, her provocative behavior seemingly justifies Hippolito's violence against her. To boot, the traditional Mexican value of a mother's advice is reduced to ashes: the mother is portrayed as a stumbling drunkard.

Another example of the exploration of relationships between men and women is the dramatization of *Tierra sin Nombre*. Its plot consists of a love triangle; a woman loves two men and finally chooses one over the other. At the wedding she is murdered by the man she did not choose. The dramatized *corrido* distorts the text in various ways. For example, the successful suitor is portrayed as a rich, "handsome" Spanish-type gentleman whereas the rejected man is a barefooted *indio*-campesino type. Thus, through a dramaturgic sleight of hand, the woman character is subtly maneuvered out of legitimately choosing between two men based on emotional considerations. She bases her decision on money (class) and looks (race): she chooses the rich, tall, "handsome" man, who symbolically throws around a bag of coins. But is it really *her* decision? Cast in the ingenue mold, the female character cannot resist the advances of the good-looking rich man. He actively pursues her and she passively submits, her eyes lowered in shyness. We are left with the stereotype of the passive Mexican woman. None of that is in the original *corrido* text. As a comment on the nature of relationships between men and women, and as a comment about women, it projects a male fantasy of female submissiveness. Throughout the show the narrator emphasizes the point that "*corridos* are macho in viewpoint." Commentary such as that would appear to indicate that the images of men and women we see before us simply represent a retrograde Mexican tradition. That is also what the script indicates to us when we are told that "the *corridos* are reproduced with loyalty to the *corrido* tradition." Such statements seek to equate what corridos are with what is in reality one interpretation of them. A sharp distinction between the two must be drawn, however. Otherwise, not only a number of female and male *corrido* characters are stereotyped but the entire *corrido* tradition. The images of women for sale, women as passive victims, women as drunkard mothers are not a creation of the *corrido* tradition but a projection of the *Corridos* production.

Although most public *corridistas* have been male, the excesses witnessed in the *Corridos* production are a result of dramaturgy and direction. The supposedly "macho" viewpoint could easily have been mitigated through the inclusion of *corridos* such as *Juana Gallo, Agripina, El Corrido de las Comadres*, or *María y Julián*, all of which provide a multifaceted narrative portrayal of women. Such *corridos*, however, were entirely passed over.

In his attempt to do justice to the "true role of women" Luis Valdez created a pastiche entitled *Soldadera*. It is of special interest because it is conceived as a corrective to the *corrido* tradition:

> In search of some justice to the true role of women in Mexican history, we now go to the period most aficionados consider to be the high point . . . of the corrido: the Revolution of 1910 . . . And there we find three legendary songs about three legendary women—La Adelita, La Valentina and La Rielera . . . These, together with a character inspired by the dispatches of an American journalist riding with Pancho Villa back in 1914, a man by the name of John Reed, now combine to give us a portrait of Mexican woman at war.[10]

Soldadera is of further interest because Socorro Valdez plays a lead female role. For Socorro the piece marks another breakthrough in her career as a performer. After 1980 she went to Hollywood in search of other acting opportunities. Her return to San Juan Bautista was not unconditional. She demanded to play a role that she had long been denied. In her words:

> He [Luis Valdez] put the *corrido* together and he wanted me to play the role, because I had been after him for a length of time. You know, I wanted to play a young girl. And I didn't want makeup on my face. I didn't want lipstick. I didn't want false eyelashes or fake boobs or nothing. I just wanted to be myself up there, just wanted to be the Indian person that I am . . . I came back to him [Luis], but I said: "That's it. No more masks, no more calavera face, no more calavera bones on my face. None of that shit. I'll go out there in a plain cotton dress and I'll have those people going." (interview, p. 12)

She did, in truth, have *Corridos* audiences going. Her stage presence and commitment to the work at hand was unique within the cast. Yet the strength of her performance was diminished by the script's vision of women. What is Valdez's vision of women of the Mexican Revolution? One of the striking features within *Soldadera* is that it is not female characters such as La Adelita, La Valentina, and La Rielera who address women's role in history. The production does not draw from even *one* female testimonial source. Nor were historians of women consulted. The character of John Reed (*Insurgent Mexico*) does most of the talking in the piece entitled *Soldadera*. John Reed, the only Anglo in the production, also functions as white savior: he is the only male in the production who does not engage in violence against women. He is a heroic man who speaks gently and protects Elizabeta (Socorro Valdez) from her surly Mexican companion.

Reed's manner stands in strong contrast to that of the three *soldaderas* and the Mexican men. The verbal exchanges between these men and women are almost exclusively aggressive and/or abusive. Men and women fall into the categories of conqueror or conquered. Some effort is made within *Soldadera* to demonstrate diversity in women—but that diversity is external: La Valentina is the hip-swaying hard-nosed companion to the colonel. In the San Juan Bautista production she also displays a strong inclination toward attire highly unsuited to the rigors of the Mexican Revolution: she wears spiked-heel boots and tight pants. La Adelita carries a rifle; La Rielera (Socorro Valdez) is a gentle-souled Indian woman who follows. The attempt at diversity, however, collapses entirely when the women engage in dialogue. Their contribution to the narrative line consists entirely of discussions concerning the finding and losing of men, about following men, about holding on to men. There is nothing in their dialogue or actions to reveal the depth of their character or their understanding of the Revolution around them.

John Reed, for all his talking, provides no insight into the social forces within the Revolution. He has been edited in such a way that he portrays battles without causes. The Mexican Revolution, and history in general, is reduced to a backdrop, a foil for song numbers and centerstage chatter. La Rielera engages in two activities: sleeping with her man Juan and making tortillas. It is fair to conclude that Luis Valdez's "search of some justice to the true role of women in Mexican history" produced meager findings. Notwithstanding the vast critical acclaim that greeted the piece, with it the stage portrayal of Mexican women has reached a new low.

There is a paradox about the *Corridos* production which is to some extent characteristic of commercial theater as a whole. The shortcomings in the script and in the acting skills of the cast stand in strong contrast to the engaging flow of the spectacle. One enjoys the visual effects, the dancing, the fast pace, the colors, and the excellence of the musical direction (F. González) and musical performance, which sustains the momentum of the production throughout. And it is next to impossible not to love hearing the familiar *corridos*, in spite of their dramatization. Those are the undeniable entertainment qualities of the production. And some audiences seek only lighthearted entertainment. Indeed, spectacle without substance is one of the best-known formulas for success in the theater business, especially in times of economic crises. The show *Corridos* provides entertainment without being thought-provoking. It affirms Hollywood images of men in sombreros and on horseback engaged, for the most part, in violence with colorful señoritas defined in terms of men. The tradition of such images and their marketability in the entertainment business was recently described by Luis Valdez:

> Now there was a time when this country reveled in Latino images—commercially—and that was in the 1940s of course, parallel with the Zoot Suit era . . . The U.S. . . . turned its attention to Latin American and said "How can we sell more movies in Latin America?" and obviously they said "Let's put more Latin images on films, but let's make them 'safe' images." So what we ended up with was Carmen Miranda. What we ended up with was the Latin Night Club and Rhumbaing down to Rio or what have you . . . Desi Arnaz came out of that era, you know. But nothing came from the Mexican Revolution . . . at least not during World War II.[11]

With *Corridos*, the Mexican Revolution has now entered the ranks of safe (i.e., caricature) commercial "Latino" images such as those projected by Desi Arnaz, Carmen Miranda, and various others. The media may well revel in these well-worn images, now marketed as "New American Theater." Some may thrill at the visibility the show provides for so-called Hispanics. Others may take pride in seeing Mexican Americans perform in what is known as legitimate theater in show business circles. But, El Teatro Campesino in the 1960s set the standard to demand more than that.

Within the new commercial mode of theater that Luis Valdez has adopted, there is a constant turnover of hired actors. Improvisational creation and collective creation are things of the past. The professional division of labor, with its hierarchy of personnel, does not foster discussion or the development of a critical consciousness, let alone disagreement or a challenge to patriarchy. The model for the new organization comes from business administration. Theatrical production is streamlined: actors act, the director directs, administrators administrate. The spirit of group commitment and the performance energy so characteristic of the Teatro Campesino ensemble has been displaced by actors who do their jobs and then return to Los Angeles in search of the next gig. The production team recruits from a generation of entertainment actresses/actors for whom the portrayal of Mexicans on stage is not an issue. In my conversations with the cast members of *Corridos* it became apparent that the images of women (or men) they project are not a matter of particular concern. In the absence of a group of actresses who have learned to question and reject shallow roles, the emergence of a broader vision of women within the new Teatro Campesino production company seems unlikely. In the arena of glittering lights, the struggle to establish new women's roles has dissipated. Yet from the backstage perspective and far from the limelight we can perceive the efforts of Chicanas who continue to explore and create dramatic alternatives for women. The dream to reflect the vast spectrum of Chicana womanhood on the stage will in time find creative expression. After the *Corridos* production, Socorro Valdez described this aspiration:

> I'll tell you what my dream is—one of my dreams. And I know I'll get to it because it's a driving thing in me . . . My dream is to be able to do a theater piece on the phases of womanhood. It's something that has not been done yet. All the times that I've seen women's programs or women in this or women in that, it somehow has never been quite satisfactory for me, you know. No one can take womanhood and put it into *one* thing. But that is precisely what I want to do. I want to put womanhood into every form that I can express:

> in singing, in crying, in laughing, everything. That role is not yet there. That role has not been written. Maybe it has been written in a Shakespearean way. But I don't relate to those European images of women . . . Women are obviously in a type of great void. They are balanced, but in terms of the way the world looks at us they've put us in this position where we've accepted the condition of doing one role instead of many. If there were some way of taking that and putting it into words that are theatrical, I would like to do that. I don't believe a man is going to write that. I don't believe that for one single minute. And I sure can't wait for Luis to write that role. (interview, p. 36)

The activities of several of the women from El Teatro Campesino—Olivia Chumacero, Socorro Valdez, Yolanda Parra—and the work of Sylvia Wood in Tucson, Arizona; Nita Luna and El Teatro Aguacero in New Mexico; the women and men of El Teatro de la Esperanza; the now dormant Valentina Productions; Cara Hill-Castañon's one-woman shows; and the plays of Estela Portillo Trambley all mark the entry into a new cycle of theatrical activity for Chicanas. We are not without inspirational models, nor without the example of women who question and who strive to reclaim a fully human female identity on stage. We do well to acknowledge that activity in the writing of theater history.

NOTES

1. The characterization of women in the Teatro Campesino repertoire is discussed in the full version of this paper. Also, selected examples of writings on Teatro history are scrutinized.

2. Personal interview with Diane Rodríguez (TS), Core Group Member, El Teatro Campesino, Strassbourg, France, June 7, 1980, p. 5.

3. Personal interview with Socorro Valdez (TS), Core Group Member, El Teatro Campesino, San Juan Bautista, California, March 1, 1983, p. 6.

4. Personal interview with Yolanda Parra of El Teatro Campesino, San Juan Bautista, California, December 31, 1982, pp. 6-7.

5. Personal interview with Olivia Chumacero and Diane Rodríguez (TS), El Teatro Campesino, Strassbourg, France, June 7, 1980, p. 13.

6. An interesting account of *teatropoesía* and of other recent theater work of Chicanas in California's Bay area is Yvonne Yarbro-Bejarano's "Teatropoesía in the Bay Area: *Tongues of Fire*," *Revista Chicano-Riqueña* 11/1 (Spring, 1983): 78-94.

7. Interview with Luis Valdez by María Emilia Martín for California Public Radio, May 5, 1983.

8. Luis Valdez's statement in the role of narrator during the San Juan Bautista workshop production run of *Corridos*, September 16, 1982, through October 31, 1982. The San Francisco production ran from April 20 to July 4, 1983.

9. Interview by María Emilia Martín, May 5, 1983.

10. *Corridos: A New Music Play* (final draft), p. 59.

11. *Final Report to the National Endowment for the Humanities*, "Califas, Chicano Art and Culture in California," Oakes College, April 18, 1982, p. 43.

REFERENCES

Chumacero, Olivia. Personal interview, January 19, 1983.

Chumacero, Olivia and Diane Rodríquez. Personal interview, June 7, 1980.

Condon, Frank (dir.). *Rose of the Rancho*. By David Belasco. Adapted by Cesar Flores and Luis Valdez. El Teatro Campesino Playhouse, San Juan Bautista. 1981.

Final Report to the National Endowment for the Humanities. "Califas, Chicano Art and Culture in California." Oakes College, April 18, 1982.

Interview with Luis Valdez. María Emilia Martín. California Public Radio, May 5, 1983.

Parra, Yolanda. Personal interview, December 21, 1982.

Rodríguez, Diane. Personal interview, June 7, 1980.

El Teatro Campesino. *Actos*. San Juan Bautista: Menyah Productions, 1971.

______. *La Carpa de los Rasquachis*, TS. El Teatro Campesino Incorporated. San Juan Bautista, California.

______. *La Gran Carpa Cantinflesca*, TS. El Teatro Campesino Incorporated. San Juan Bautista, California

Valdez, Luis. *Bandido! The American Melodrama of Tiburcio Vásquez Notorious California Bandit*, TS, Second Draft, El Teatro Campesino Incorporated, San Juan Bautista, California.

______. *Los Corridos*. El Teatro Campesino Playhouse, San Juan Bautistia, California. September 16 through October 31, 1982.

______. *Corridos: A New Music Play*. Marines' Memorial Theater, San Francisco. April 20 through July 4, 1983.

______. *Fin del Mundo*, 1980 TS. El Teatro Campesino Incorporated. San Juan Bautista, California.

Valdez, Socorro. Personal interview, March 1, 1983.

Yarbro-Bejarano, Yvonne. "Teatropoesía in the Bay Area: Tongues of Fire." *Revista Chicano-Riqueña* 11/1 (Spring, 1983): 78-94.

Libertad de No Procrear: La Voz de la Mujer en "A una Madre de Nuestros Tiempos" de Margarita-Cota Cárdenas

Clara LOMAS

El poema "A una Madre de Nuestros Tiempos" por Margarita Cota-Cárdenas (publicado en *La Palabra* en 1980) trata de una de las preocupaciones predominantes un el análisis femenista sobre la función productiva y reproductiva de la mujer en la sociedad: la libertad de procrear o no. El tratamiento literario de este asunto por Cota-Cárdenas cuestiona las limitaciones culturales y sociales que afectan gravemente la libertad de la mujer de decidir sobre su propio cuerpo. La estructura y elaboración particular del poema revelan un proceso evolutivo que se torna una posible fuente de concientización tanto para una madre como para todo un grupo social. Este estudio es un intento de explorar las cualidades formales del poema para examinar sus posibilidades semánticas.

A UNA MADRE DE NUESTROS TIEMPOS

perdónanos
        sé que éramos tus lotos
    beso tus arrugas   no llores ya
        todas aguantaron
        y yo
            yo no pude
        fracasé
            qué tan frágil es el honor
        y yo
            yo no quise
        no acepté
    dejaste tu imagen en mi sedita bordada

dame un beso y perdóname
deja de lágrimas
madre raza
y yo
no quería que una débil tarde
vieras tus antiguas penas bordadas en mi cara
repetidas
cinceladas
mientras yo
yo quise conocer al ID
volar altísimo
definir estas entrañas
que he dejado
y librarme de leyendas
yaaaaaaaaaa
corté los hilos de gasa
sécame la sangre
porque yo
sin vientre ahora
yo ya no pude
que mis hijas y sus hijas y sus hijas no
dolorosa danos tu sonrisa de niña
quinceañera
di que comprendes
resucita conmigo
ya era tiempo
de abortar los mitos
de un sólo sentido

El título del poema nos señala el destinatario del poema: "una madre." El empleo del artículo indefinido "una" a la vez denota a un destinatario singular, quizá conocido, e indeterminado. Esta madre-receptora indefinida, no obstante, es puesta dentro de un marco histórico definido/determinado: uno de nuestros tiempos. La referencia a este espacio temporal específico indica la separación que se establece con el pasado. El mensaje, por lo tanto, se dirige a la generación actual. Mientras al principio se podría suponer un intencionado destinatario singular, esta madre indefinida se extiende, casi a mediados del poema, a todo un grupo social más amplio: "madre raza"

Aunque carece de estrofas, el poema se divide por tres secciones temáticas. La primera consiste en la ruptura consciente con el pasado tradicional opresivo. La segunda enfoca en la explicación al destinatario de las razones por las cuales se hace esa ruptura, y la tercera es la invitación hacia el cambio, hacia el desarrollo de una nueva perspectiva, de una nueva conciencia en cuanto a la función de la mujer en la sociedad.

Desde la primera palabra del poema se establece el tono de la voz poética, tanto formal como semánticamente: "perdónanos..." De modo imperativo la hablante asume una voz colectiva y se dirige al colectivo destinatario de manera informal y directa, exigiendo urgencia. Este primer mandato que demanda perdón al destinario conocido, familiar, y de confianza, nos sitúa dentro de la circunstancia dialéctica que gobernará el resto del poema en torno a la voz poética individual/colectiva y el destinario individual/colectivo. A un nivel, la voz que habla aparenta ser una sola voz íntima, muy personal, única, un llamado solitario emitido por una sola persona que se ha desviado de la norma: "todas aguantaron / y yo / yo no pude..." Esta desviación solitaria es recalcada por la reiteración constante del pronombre en primera persona singular, "yo", cuyo uso en la lengua española pone énfasis en esa primera persona como actor, ejecutador único de la acción: "y yo / y no pude...y yo / yo no quise... y yo / no quería...yo / yo quise...yo ya no pude..." No obstante, a otro nivel, el poema mismo está encuadrado por el empleo del imperativo de primera persona plural; se inicia: "perdónanos / sé que éramos tus lotos" y hacia el final empieza la clausura con un "danos tu sonrisa de niña." Por lo tanto, mientras la voz poética busca revelar los sentimientos netamente individuales de un personaje, a la vez, dialécticamente revela lo que podría ser su antítesis o contradicción—el carácter colectivo que asume esa misma voz. Se desarrolla, entonces, una interrelación mutua, aunque contradictoria, entre las dos voces que se torna una individual incluida dentro de una colectiva. El mensaje que aquí se emite, aunque aparenta ser de una sola mujer, es compartido por muchas otras mujeres. La línea, "se que éramos tus lotos" nos sugiere que esa voz colectiva son las flores y frutos, o sea las hijas. Por lo tanto, hacia la madre/raza individual/colectiva se dirige la hija individual/colectiva.

Ahora pues, ¿cuál será el posible mensaje que busca emitir la hija individual/colectiva hacia la madre/raza individual/colectiva? Desde el principio se plantea la antinomia central cuyo conflicto busca el cambio: la noción de pasado en contraposición a la de presente. Los vocablos de acción del pasado enuncian las acciones ejecutadas por la hablante y marcan el punto de partida de rechazo de la situación de las hijas/lotos: "sé que *éramos* tus lotos" (subrayado nuestro). Esto es, en el pasado éran como flores, fruto de belleza, cuya larga vida era precisamente para reproducirse.

Históricamente, vemos que con la división del trabajo y la consecuente creación de la familia patriarcal, y el nucleo familiar monógamo, la función de la mujer se va definiendo como una de exclusión de la producción social y limitación al servicio privado dentro del mundo cerrado del ámbito hogareño. Ideológicamente, se desarrollan códigos sociales que dictan que la mujer encuentra su expresión superior—dentro de esta esfera privada—en la reproducción física de la especie humana: el producir hijos. Las instituciones religiosas, sociales y políticas legitiman y santifican esta "profesión" a tal punto de definir a la mujer "completa" como aquella que es madre reproductora, y de condenar al ostracismo y categorizar como deficiente a aquella que no lo es, ya sea por gusto o incapacidad física. La aceptación por el elemento femenino de esta imposición socio-económica y moral se traduce a su participación "armónica" dentro de la sociedad patriarcal. Sin embargo, la limitación al servicio privado no-asalariado dentro del hogar ha tenido repercusiones serias como la historia ha atestigado: entre otras cosas, aislamiento, dependencia económica y esclavitud doméstica.

Dentro de nuestras comunidades, los códigos éticos heredados a través de nuestras tradiciones culturales, profundamente enraizados en la tradición religiosa católica, han contribuido a la esclavitud doméstica de la mujer. La voz poética de nuestro poema busca transmitir la toma de conciencia de esta situación opresiva fundada en la definición reproductiva impuesta a la mujer. Esta voz denomina la reacción de las hijas como un acoger, tolerar y resignarse a los códigos morales impuestos socialmente: "todas aguantaron . . ." Inmediatamente después contrapone su propia negación, rechazo y resistencia consciente ("yo no pude . . .yo no quise / no acepté") a la perspectiva del elemento establecido y respetado que ve su disensión como un malogro, una desgracia, un fiasco: "fracasé . . ." Sin embargo, en seguida la hablante proyecta, mediante una interjección, su respuesta desdeñosa que cuestiona el supuesto requisito de dignidad propia, de buena reputación impuesto por la sociedad: "qué tan frágil es el honor." Son precisamente este rechazo a la observación de los códigos morales establecidos a un nivel, y su amor, respeto y veneración a los sentimientos de la madre/raza por otro, que sitúan a la hablante en un aparente dilema de verse obligada a rechazar también a la madre/raza por ser ésta elemento perpetuador de la tradición cultural que oprime a la mujer. Recuérdese, sin embargo, que ya desde el principio se establece veneración y respeto hacia la imagen procreadora de vida física y social, la madre/raza a quien se le pide perdón, se le besa las arrugas, y aun metafóricamente se le reconoce el sacrificio que ha dejado una impresión en la hablante: "dejaste tu imagen en mi sedita bordada . . ." Aquí, donde por unos instantes la alusión alegórica a la escena religiosa pareciera afirmar la aceptación de culpabilidad y deseo de conversión, la alusión adquiere un significado irónico pues la súplica por perdón no busca la conversión de sí misma sino, primero la comprensión y después la renovación de ideas y perspectiva de la madre/raza.

Después de hacer clara la ruptura con el pasado y su rechazo, la segunda sección revela las razones, la explicación de la voluntad de resistir, a la madre/raza ("no quería que una débil tarde / vieras tus antiguas penas bordadas en mi cara / repetidas / cinceladas").

El desplazamiento de debilidad en la tarde sugiere los momentos difíciles, angustiosos, y plagados de duda en la vejez de la madre después de toda una vida de sacrificios. La hablante explica que en esos momentos no desea que la madre vea la continuación y perpetuación del mismo sufrimiento ya labrado profundamente en la vida de la siguiente generación. Las penas sufridas por la madre no son sólo viejas sino que aluden a la antigüedad del dolor transmitido por generaciones a través de la cultura. Así, por extensión se sugiere la tradición heredada, bien elaborada e inculcada que deja su marca en relieve, en las vidas de las futuras generaciones, cuando se continúan las mismas tradiciones sin cambio. Por lo tanto, explica la voz que habla que ella proponía un cambio basado en un ahondamiento introspectivo de sí misma, "yo quise conocer el ID . . ." Ella busca conocer hasta lo más profundo de sus propios instintos inconscientes para discernir estos de los elementos externos impuestos socialmente. Con este profundizar introspectivo se propone a la vez, "volar altísimo," esto es, sobresalir y superar las barreras impuestas para tomar acción concreta: "definir estas entrañas."

El movimiento ascendente en el poema llega a su punto culminante con la revelación de la acción concreta; ya con ésta, se moviliza hacia la toma de control decisivo de su propio cuerpo, de su función como mujer tanto personal como socialmente. Con la adquisición de este poder decisivo para definir su propia función, se empieza el proceso de liberación de leyendas, que se habían fabricado con el fin de definir y controlar a la mujer. El "ya" prolongado enfatiza el grito de ¡basta! En este momento la ruptura, el corte con la tradición en abstracto, cobra corporeidad con la imagen del corte de "los hilos de gasa."

De nuevo regresa la voz imperativa de la hablante a pedir la participación del destinario ("sécame la sangre") después que la decisión—de definir las entrañas y quedarse sin vientre—ha sido tanto tomada como ejecutada. Con esta acción se rompe la tradición que seguirían las siguientes generaciones: "yo ya no pude / que mis hijas y sus hijas y sus hijas no . . ." El calificativo que describe esta experiencia, inicia la última división del poema: "dolorosa..." Cambia el tono después de la sección explicativa para ahora pedir a la madre/raza, no sólo su aprobación, sino su comprensión franca y natural, así como la de alguien que apenas empieza a vivir: "danos tu sonrisa de niña . . . / di que comprendes . . ."

La voz poética se torna aún más enfática, decisiva, poderosa e imperativa en su invitación al destinario, la madre/raza, a nacer de nuevo, con un nuevo entendimiento, una nueva concientización de que la mujer debe asumir el control de sí misma para definir su propia función reproductiva: "resucita conmigo / ya era tiempo / de abortar los mitos / de un sólo sentido." Se invita a la madre/raza a interrumpir el proceso y desarrollo de una tradición opresiva—que no había reconocido, ni mucho menos respetado el punto de vista de la mujer—y desecharlo, abortarlo.

Por medio de la expresión poética, Cota-Cárdenas ahonda en los sentimientos íntimos de la hija individual/colectiva en cuanto a su función social. Con la selección de vocablos que indican persona singular o plural y la elaboración que se hace con ellos, creando una tensión dialéctica interna, el poema alude a la dicotomía de este fenómeno que es tanto individual como social, de esta voz que es a la vez de una hija y de muchas mujeres. Es de notarse que esta selección y combinación de vocablos, que constituyen y elaboran la unidad poética, puede o no ser producto consciente de la escritora.

Lo fundamental es el mensaje emitido por el poema en su totalidad y, como hemos visto, la estructuración formal y las tensiones temáticas internas proveen la dinámica para la elaboración poética de una preocupación principal de la mujer: tener la libertad de procrear o no procrear. El desarrollo del poema a través de las secciones temáticas—ruptura con el pasado, explicación, invitación hacia el cambio—se destaca particularmente por el delineamiento de un proceso de concientización, sutil mas efectivamente articulado. El llamado hacia el destinario, madre/raza, no es uno que inspira resentimiento rencor, ni antagonismo. Al contario, la voz poética proyecta un llamado que manifiesta respeto, voluntad de informar/explicar, y, por último, que invoca la revalorización de la tradición cultural que impone mitos represivos a la mujer.

La capacidad biológica de reproducción de la mujer, aunque por sí sola no es la causa de la explotación y posición social inferior de ella, sí se ha utilizado a través de la historia como pretexto y justificación de su opresión. Nosotros, las madres, las mujeres, la raza, la sociedad en general, perpetuamos la ideología dominante patriarcal al no brindarle la oportunidad a la mujer de que ella misma defina su función productiva y reproductiva dentro de la sociedad. Así como cualquier grupo étnico subyugado lucha por auto-determinación, la mujer lucha, entre otras cosas, por la libertad de no tener sus funciones reproductivas controladas por una sociedad que no se hace responsable por las consecuencias de ello. "A una Madre de Nuestros Tiempos" es un llamado al cuestionamiento de la ideología opresiva que a momentos se hace evidente en las actitudes individuales de "una madre" y en otros en las acciones sociales y políticas de la "raza" y la sociedad en general.

Reproductive Freedom: The Voice of Women in Margarita Cota-Cárdenas's "A una Madre de Nuestros Tiempos"

Clara LOMAS

The poem "A una Madre de Nuestros Tiempos" by Margarita Cota-Cárdenas (published in *La Palabra* in 1980) deals with one of the predominant concerns in a feminist analysis of the productive and reproductive function of women in society: reproductive freedom. The literary treatment of this issue by Cota-Cárdenas calls into question cultural and social constraints that deeply affect women's freedom to decide about their own bodies. The particular structure and elaboration of the poem reveal an evolutionary process that becomes a potential source of consciousness raising for both a mother and an entire social group. This study is an attempt to explore the poem's formal quality and to examine its semantic possibilities.

A UNA MADRE DE NUESTROS TIEMPOS

perdónanos
sé que éramos tus lotos
beso tus arrugas   no llores ya
todas aguantaron
y yo
yo no pude
fracasé
qué tan frágil es el honor
y yo
yo no quise
no acepté
dejaste tu imagen en mi sedita bordada

dame un beso y perdóname
deja de lágrimas
madre raza
y yo
no quería que una débil tarde
vieras tus antiguas penas bordadas en mi cara
repetidas
cinceladas
mientras yo
yo quise conocer al ID
volar altísimo
definir estas entrañas
que he dejado
y librarme de leyendas
yaaaaaaaaaa
corté los hilos de gasa
sécame la sangre
porque yo
sin vientre ahora
yo ya no pude
que mis hijas y sus hijas y sus hijas no
dolorosa danos tu sonrisa de niña
quinceañera
di que comprendes
resucita conmigo
ya era tiempo
de abortar los mitos
de un sólo sentido

The title of the poem designates the addressee: "una madre." The use of the indefinite article "una" simultaneoulsy denotes a singular addressee, perhaps known, and another, undetermined addressee. This indefinite mother/receptor, however, is placed within a definite/determined historical framework: "de nuestros tiempos." The reference to a specific temporal space indicates the separation established with the past. The poem, then, addresses the present generation. While at the beginning, one could assume the existence of an intended singular addressee, this indefinite mother unfolds, almost midway through the poem, into an entire social group: "madre raza."

Although the poem does not follow any stanzaic conventions, it is divided into three thematic sections. The first consists of the conscious rupture with the oppressive past. The second focuses on the explanation to the addressee of the reasons for that rupture, and the third is the invitation to change, to the development of a new perspective, to a new consciousness in terms of the role of women in society.

From the first word of the poem, the tone of the poetic voice is established both formally and semantically: "perdónanos." By using the imperative, the speaker assumes a collective voice and directs herself to the addressee in an informal, yet direct and urgent manner. This first command requesting forgiveness—from the known, familiar addressee who inspires confidence—places the reader within the dialectical structure that will govern the rest of the poem: the relationship between the individual/collective poetic voice and the individual/collective addressee. At one level, the speaker appears as a single, unique, and very personal voice, a solitary call articulated by one person who has deviated from the norm: "todas aguantaron / y yo / yo no pude." This solitary deviation is accented by the constant reiteration of the singular first person pronoun, "yo," whose use in the Spanish language places the emphasis on that first person as the actor, the sole agent of the action: "y yo / yo no pude...y yo / yo no quise...y yo / no quería...yo / yo quise...yo ya no pude..." However, at another level, the poem itself is framed by the use of the imperative mood in the first person plural; it begins "perdónanos / sé que éramos tus lotos"; toward the end, the closure begins with "danos tu sonrisa de niña." Therefore, while the poetic voice seeks to reveal the genuine sentiments of an individual, simultaneously, it dialectically reveals what could be its antithesis or contradiction—the collective character who assumes that same voice. A mutual, yet contradictory, interrelationship develops between the two voices as they function as an individual within a collective. Although the message emitted may appear to be that of a single woman, it is in fact shared by many women. This collective voice is suggested in the line "sé que éramos tus lotos." The flowers, the natural off-spring, the female children are in fact the many speaking as one. Therefore, the individual/collective daughter addresses the individual/collective/raza.

What, then, could be the message sought by the individual/collective daughter to be transmitted to the individual/collective mother/raza? A search for change is designated by the central antinomy posed from the beginning of the poem through the notion of past juxtaposed to present. The verbal forms in the past tense enunciate the actions performed by the speaker and suggest a will to reject that situation of the "hijas/lotos": "sé que *éramos* tus lotos" (my italics). In other words, in the past we were like flowers and offspring of beauty whose long life's goal was precisely to reproduce.

History reveals that with the division of labor and, consequently, the creation of patriarchal and monogamous nuclear family, the role of women is defined by exclusion from social production and limitation to services rendered inside the closed and private sphere of the home. At an ideological level, specific social codes are developed which maintain that women find their most fulfilling expression—within this private sphere—in the physical reproduction of the human race: the production of children. Religious, social, and political institutions legitimize and sanctify this "profession" to the extreme of defining a "complete" woman as one who has given birth. Consequently, women who are not mothers—whether due to physical incapacity or by choice—may be ostracized and categorized as somehow incomplete, deficient women. Acceptance by women of this socioeconomic and moral imposition is translated into "harmonic" participation in patriarchal society. History has witnessed, however, that limiting women to unsalaried services within the private sphere has had serious repercussions: among many others, alienation, economic dependency, and domestic slavery.

In our communities, we find that ethical codes inherited from our cultural traditions, some deeply rooted in the Catholic church, have contributed to women's domestic slavery. The poetic voice in this poem transmits a consciousness awakening to this oppressive situation, which is based on the reproductive definition imposed on women. This voice refers to the daughters' reaction as welcoming, tolerating, and resigning of themselves to the socially imposed moral codes: "todas aguantaron." Following immediately, she counteracts this with her own negation, rejection, and conscious resistance ("yo no pude... / yo no quise / no acepté") to the perspective of the well-established and respected sector of society that sees her dissension as a disappointment, a disgrace, a failure: "fracasé." However, through the interjection which follows, "qué tan frágil es el honor," the speaker projects a contemptuous reply that questions the moral codes of dignity, self-worth, and good reputation set forth by society. It is precisely the rejection of these fixed moral codes on one level and her love, respect, and veneration for the mother/raza's feelings at another that create a dilemma for the speaker. She could find herself also forced to reject her mother/raza for constituting a perpetuating element in a cultural tradition that oppresses women. One must remember, however, that at the beginning of the poem, the line "beso tus arrugas" metaphorically alludes to honor and respect for the procreating image of physical and social life, the mother/raza whose forgiveness is sought. Also metaphorically conveyed is the imprint left on the speaker by the mother's sacrifice, "dejaste tu imagen en mi sedita bordada." The allegorical allusion to a religious scene could seem to affirm acceptance of guilt and a possible desire for conversion; however, it acquires ironic significance as the poem evolves and it becomes evident that the plea for forgiveness is primarily asking for understanding and secondarily for a renewal of ideas and perspective of the mother/raza: "no quería que una débil tarde / vieras tus antiguas penas bordadas en mi cara / repetidas / cinceladas."

The displacement of weakness, frailty, onto the evening insinuates those difficult moments of uncertainty in the mother's old age. The qualification of the mother's suffering as not only old but ancient alludes to the antiquity of the pain transmitted for generations. By extension, the image makes reference to the inherited and inculcated cultural tradition which leaves its mark on the lives of the following generations as these same traditions are consistently practiced without substantial change. Therefore, the speaker proposes change founded on an introspective look at herself, "yo quise conocer el ID." She longs to know her deepest unconscious instincts to discern and separate these from those external elements which are socially imposed. With introspective exploration she proposes to overcome the imposed obstacles, "volar altísimo," and take concrete action, "definir estas entrañas."

The poem's ascending movement reaches its culminating point with the revelation of concrete action. The poetic voice manifests a move toward decisive control over her own body, her own function as woman, at both the personal and social levels. Having acquired decisive power to define her reproductive needs, the process of liberation from legends—fabricated to define and control women—is begun. The prolonged "ya" emphasizes the cry of saturation. Here the rupture, the break with abstract tradition, materializes with the image of cutting "los hilos de gasa." This image also suggests the end of sterilization surgery.

The imperative voice again speaks directly to the addressee, this time asking for participation: "sécame la sangre." The tradition that could have been followed by future generations is broken with this conscious action, "yo ya no pude / que mis hijas y sus hijas y sus hijas no." The qualifying adjective that describes this experience initiates the poem's last section: "dolorosa." Following this explicatory section, the tone changes to requesting of the mother/raza, not only approval, but understanding, frank and natural, as if renewing life: "danos tu sonrisa de niña / di que comprendes."

The poetic voice becomes even more emphatic, decisive, and powerful in its invitation to the addressee to be born anew, with new comprehension, new consciousness of women's right to assume control of themselves, to define their own reproductive function: "resucita conmigo / ya era tiempo / de abortar los mitos / de un sólo sentido." The mother/raza is asked to interrupt the process and development of an oppressive tradition—that has not recognized, much less respected, women's perspective—to destroy it, abort it.

By means of her poetic expression, Cota-Cárdenas penetrates the intimate sentiments of the individual/collective daughter regarding her social function. With the selection of words that indicate singular or plural person and the elaboration made with them—thereby creating an internal dialectical tension—the poem alludes to the dichotomy of the concern of this voice, both individual and social, as it belongs to a daughter and to all women as well. It should be noted that the selection and combination of words—which constitute and elaborate the poetic unity—may or may not be a conscious effort by the writer. The fundamental message of the poem in its totality and, as discussed, in its formal structure and internal thematic tensions also provide the dynamics for poetic expression of one of women's primary preoccupations: the freedom to procreate or not. The development of the poem throughout the thematic divisions—rupture with the past, explanation, and invitation for change—is particularly important, due to its delineation of a process of awareness, subtly yet effectively articulated. The call toward the addressee, mother/raza, is not one that inspires resentment, hatred, or antagonism. On the contrary, the poetic voice is a call manifesting respect, a will to inform/explain, and finally, it invokes reevaluation of cultural traditions which impose repressive myths on women.

Although women's biological capacity to reproduce is not by itself the only cause of women's exploitation and inferior social position, it has been utilized throughout history as pretext for and justification of their oppression. Mothers, women, ethnic groups, and society in general perpetuate the dominant patriarchal ideology by not offering the opportunity for women to define their own productive and reproductive roles within society. As any subjugated ethnic group struggles for self-determination, women struggle, among many other things, for the freedom not to have their reproductive function controlled by a society that does not assume responsibility for the consequences. "A una Madre de Nuestros Tiempos" questions the oppressive ideology that becomes evident, at times, in a mother's individual attitudes and, at other times, in the social and political actions of the "raza" and society in general.

La Realidad A Traves de la Inocencia en el Cuento: Un Paseo

Elba R. SÁNCHEZ

Editors' note: The option to translate Spanish text to English in this volume was left to the authors' discretion.

Empleando un lenguaje sencillo, cotidiano, el cuento de Luz Garzón titulado "Un Paseo"[1] nos presenta las experiencias opuestas de dos madres y sus hijos. Después de una primera lectura el cuento se podría describir como sencillo, breve, sensible. Y aunque el título implica un paseo turístico, se encuentran desde el principio ciertas contradicciones, o más bien claves que no concuerdan con un reposo placentero y además contradicen esa idea. Es más, al examinar este relato más cuidadosamente y dentro de un contexto actual veremos como la temática presentada tiene una fuerte relación con la forma y a la vez la forma exige atención al contenido. Es así como en esa interrelación entre forma y contenido encontramos relevancia cultural en la temática. El tema del cuento narra eventos aborrecidos y temidos por los pobladores y trabajadores indocumentados de innumerables comunidades hispanohablantes en los Estados Unidos. Este cuento relata el paseo forzado, es decir, la deportación de una madre y su hijo de seis años quienes como pasajeros involuntarios se encuentran en un autobús rumbo a San Ysidro. La deportación de estos protagonistas se contrasta con un paseo verídico de otra madre e hijo en su coche.

Como mencioné previamente, desde un principio existe una antinomia entre los diálogos iniciados por los niños, la narración y el título mismo. En el primer párrafo, por ejemplo, el narrador omnisciente nos indica que éste no es un paseo común y mucho menos turístico. La voz que se escucha por micrófono instruye a los padres en el autobús: "...Hagan favor de mantener a sus niños sentados en sus lugares. No queremos que anden como chivos corriendo por todo el autobús" (p. 67). Es obvio que ésta no es la voz de un guía turístico pues no insultaría tan obviamente a su clientela.

El primer diálogo que nos introduce a los protagonistas en el autobús es un intercambio entre la madre y la voz ingenua y curiosa del niño quien nos transmite mucho de su realidad.

> —Mira, amá, esas casitas tienen vacas afuera y mira, ¡allá están unos becerritos pintos!
>
> —No son casas, hijo, son establos.
>
> —¿Y eso qué es, amá?
>
> —Es un lugar especial para vacas, allí viven, comen y duermen.
>
> —Allí viven siempre, ¿no tienen que andar buscando casa?
>
> —Sí, allí viven siempre.
>
> —¡Qué chistoso!
>
> —¿Por qué?
>
> —Pos porque ellas tienen casa y nosotros tenemos que dormir en el campo. (p. 67)

Por lo tanto nos enteramos del estado de ánimo de la madre que contesta las muchas preguntas de su niño, "Y el niño siguió...haciendo un torbellino de preguntas que la mamá contestaba nerviosa y agitada en la mejor manera posible" (p. 67). Inmediatamente después continúa el niño con su sencilla candidez proporcionándonos más de su vida: "—Ay, amá, qué bueno que vamos de paseo, nosotros nunca salimos de vacaciones" (p. 67). Cuando llegamos al pie de esta primera página, la inocencia y el ánimo del niño que se nos contrapone con la descripción narrativa y el título nos hace cuestionar más profundamente lo que está sucediendo.

En el mismo autobús, sentado al lado de la madre que se nos dice iba "preocupada con sus pensamientos," se encuentra un señor conocido quien "con mirada triste y cansada se apretaba las manos nerviosamente." Éste lamentaba no haberle podido comprar a su viejita los zapatos que ella quería para que la protegieran en los campos agrícolas: "Pobrecita, tanto tiempo que anduvo batallando en los 'files' con lo duro que están los huisaches" (p. 68). Tan pronto como leemos que este señor trabajaba en los campos sabemos que estamos hablando y tratando con un sector muy específico de nuestra población hispanohablante. Indubablemente, después de examinar estas claves desde un punto socio-histórico, sabemos que se habla de un trabajador migratorio mexicano y que la inquietud, ansiedad y preocupación de los dos protagonistas adultos revelan que ésta no es otra cosa que una deportación. La experiencia de estos pasajeros en el autobús de Servicio de Inmigración y Naturalización, más bien conocido como "la migra," es muy común para un sin-número de trabajadores quienes sufren las represalias de un sistema económico que busca constantemente la mano de obra barata para garantizar la continuación de sus beneficios económicos; y de esa manera su continuación en el poder. Históricamente, al sufrir sus ciclos de desplomes económicos, el capitalismo estadounidense desata su propoganda repleta de nacionalismo y racismo con el fin de desviar el antagonismo del pueblo trabajador blanco, en contra del sistema mismo y así señala a los diferentes grupos minoritarios como los chivos expiatorios; como la causa de la situación económica. Es así como en este ambiente se pretende elevar a un grupo de trabajadores para reprimir a otro grupo aún más severamente explotado—los trabajadores indocumentados. A estos trabajadores, quienes supuestamente amenazan con quitar los empleos se les trata como criminales. A la vez que surgen las recesiones y depresiones surgen también las campañas de hostigamiento en contra de las poblaciones hispanohablantes.

Al conocer la importancia de la temática decidimos leer aún más cuidadosamente. En vez de recibir pasivamente las claves que se nos proporcionan, ahora las buscamos ávidamente. Luz Garzón logra exponer claramente una situación grave, experimentada por las poblaciones pobres e hispanohablantes del sudoeste. Su relato nos recuerda el estilo de Tomás Rivera pues en el trabajo de ambos late una complejidad subyacente de contenido, debajo de una aparente forma sencilla.

Una clave fundamental del cuento es la anonimia de los protagonistas. Cuando se refiere a ellos simplemente como el "hijo" o la "madre" se puede pensar que es cualquier persona, cualquier madre, pero más bien puede ser muchas personas, es decir, una madre representativa.

Mientras miran los protagonistas, la madre y el niño, desde las ventanas del camión, les llama la atención un niño que viaja con su mamá en coche. Este desplazamiento a mediados del cuento, desde el autobús hacia el coche cuyos pasajeros andan verdaderamente de paseo es significativo puesto que nos introduce a otro mundo. En esa misma carretera viajan dos experiencias opuestas y ahora el enfoque narrativo cambia a un coche particular donde conversan la madre y su hijo sobre su paseo al parque. Mientras que la madre en el autobús se encuentra nerviosa y preocupada, la madre en el coche "para calmar la insistencia del niño que la venía distrayendo" [volteó a mirar el autobús que éste le señalaba] pero siguió manejando "despreocupadamente." Es el niño en el coche quien primeramente señala el autobús "chistoso" a su mamá.

—Mami, ¡fíjate, dale recio para que veas qué raro autobús!

—Qué niño tan necio. ¿Por qúe raro?

—Mira, allí está, fíjate bien. ¡Ves como lleva fierros en las ventanas! (p. 68)

Una vez más es la voz de la inocencia quien despierta la atención de la persona adulta y supuestamente consciente. La madre es forzada a mirar el autobús y choca allí con "la mirada fascinada [del niño en el autobús] que seguía la bomba, que su hijo llevaba volando fuera de la ventanilla." A través del contacto visual que se establece entre el niño en el autobús y la madre en el coche se logra cierta concientización en el lector. He aquí un punto primordial ya que un buen número del público lector se identificaría con el mundo y experiencia de la mujer/madre en el coche.

Las dos madres que viajan lado a lado en la carretera se enteran de sus diferencias mientras la narración entrelaza sus conversaciones respectivas y hace hincapié en la injusticia de la situación de una de ellas.

—Ves, mami, te dije que estaba raro ese camión.

—Sí, hijo, ya veo.

—Amá, amá, yo quiero una bomba como la de ese carro donde viene esa señora volteando. La ves, ¡qué grandota y cuántos colores!

—Sí, mijo, ya la vi, que a gusto viene ella con su hijo.

—¿Me la compras, amá? ¿Te gusta?

—Sí, mijo, luego que lleguemos te la compro.

—¿Ya vamos a llegar? (p. 69)

La misma forma obliga al lector a detenerse a leer más de una vez para discernir las diferentes voces. Tan rápidamente como se establece el contacto visual entre todos los personajes se desplaza y continúan los viajeros cada quien por su camino, pero ahora llevan con ellos imágenes nuevas, fuertes. Se han dado cuenta de las vivencias de otra clase, de otro mundo diferente del de ellos. Ahora se aprecia mucho más el título pues es sugestivo porque es engañador. El título engaña porque cualquier lector interpreta un paseo como una excursión frívola, tranquila, agradable, y es este significado y evento el que se contrasta con el temido y aborrecido viaje forzado por "la migra." Hay mucha ironía en este cuento en la manera como las voces de los dos niños—voces ingenuas, curiosas e insistentes—nos sacuden, despertándonos a las contradicciones flagrantes de los dos. La injusticia de las grandes diferencias entre los dos niveles de vida y las acompañantes repercusiones sociales para las víctimas de este sistema económico no pueden representarse más efectivamente que en el relato de dos niños quienes con su candidez y sencillez exponen tanto.

Hacia el fin del cuento, la voz por micrófono, la voz autoritaria, fría y despersonalizada interrumpe para advertir a los pasajeros:

> No se muevan de sus asientos hasta que paremos en San Ysidro. Esperen a que llame su número para que pasen a la oficina para tomar huellas digitales de cada uno. Tenemos que esposarlos hasta que estén fuera de nuestras manos y de nuestra responsabilidad. Las autoridades mexicanas se encargarán de ustedes. (p. 69)

Estos pasajeros anónimos ahora adquieren un número y ese número se adjunta a las miles de cifras y estadísticas que se distorsionan y utilizan por el gobierno estadounidense para "comprobar" la fabricada amenaza laboral. Además de convertirlos en números, a estos trabajadores se les considera personas *non-grata*. Como si fueran criminales, las autoridades de inmigración los esposan para expulsarlos del país. Estas autoridades en ambos lados de la frontera, son los intrumentos del estado para disponer de los trabajadores migratorios cuando no se necesita ya de su mano de obra barata. Es bien sabido que el mismo hostigamiento desatado por los agentes estadounidenses se encuentra al lado mexicano.

A través de estas voces se nos pinta el nivel de vida de las familias migratorias en los Estados Unidos. Sabemos muy bien que este sector laboral ha sido uno de los más oprimidos y marginados. Las contradicciones económicas crecientes en México, en conjunto con las demandas por la mano de obra superexplotable han resultado en la continua inmigración de miles y miles de nacionales mexicanos en busca de mejoramiento económico. Al llegar a las cuidades o las áreas rurales de este país, se encuentran con pocos trabajos no-calificados y pésimamente mal pagados, condiciones de vivienda insalubres y apiñadas, y el siempre presente racismo como un órgano engendrado por el sistema económico existente. Los deseos y sueños que espolearon a los miles a arriesgar hasta sus propias vidas para cruzar la frontera sin documentos, son pulverizados por las situaciones reales a las cuales se enfrentan antes y después de su llegada a este país. Cada día corren el riesgo de ser detectados, acorralados y deportados por el Servicio de Inmigración y Naturalización quienes se comportan como una especie de cazadores. Las víctimas de las desigualdades inherentes en este sistema económico sufren el maltrato y hasta la muerte a manos de ambos agentes mexicanos y estadounidenses, con el fin de vencer sus situaciones socio-económicas. El cuento señala muy claramente que no hay diferencia en el tratamiento del trabajador por "la migra," ya sea mexicana o estadounidense.

> Al pasar por la migración mexicana los oficiales barrieron de arriba a abajo a la gente que iba entrando a Tijuana.
> —Quihúbole, mojaditos, más vale que no se vuelvan a regresar porque tenemos nuevas medidas para castigarlos. (p. 69)

A pesar del hostigamiento constante en los dos lados de la frontera ese sector significante representado por los trabajadores indocumentados continúa luchando por el derecho a sobrevivir. Este sector reprimido necesariamente busca y encuentra cada día nuevas maneras para circunventar los muchos obstáculos a los que se encara.

El análisis de este cuento nos hace cuestionar la noción o el mito que un lenguaje sencillo no puede expresar algo complejo. "Un Paseo" emplea el habla cotidiana para exponer muy efectivamente una temática relevante y compleja y sirve como excelente ejemplar de la interrelación cohesiva entre contenido y forma.

NOTES

1. Publicado en *Requisa Treinta y Dos*, ed. Rosaura Sánchez (La Jolla: Chicano Studies Program, University of California, San Diego, 1979).

Women: Prisoners of the Word

Alvina E. QUINTANA

Language, when viewed as a set of intricate symbols used to define or symbolically represent existence, preserving knowledge as well as providing an outlet for aesthetic pleasure and intellectual thought, appears to represent a nonthreatening and essential form. It is, however, interesting to take language a step further, using it as a tool with the power to enforce specific value systems, representing and, more dangerous still, dictating, controlling, and categorizing. Language, in this sense, can be seen as a violent force, ripping through individuals as well as cultures, in order to create units of preservable information. Ralph Ellison illuminates the paradox created by the word when he states "For if the word has the potency to revive and make us free, it also has the power to blind, imprison, and destroy."[1] When Lévi-Strauss represents primitive cultures (the other), he is effectively giving birth to them, in the Western academic context, so that we may experience or understand them. Those cultures exist for us because he has recorded and interpreted them, textualizing them, and thus making them exist. This process is the same practiced in most developed industrial cultures, where an individual's existence is recognized after being textualized by birth records, naming, christening, and so forth. In many of these cultures, the word speaks to individuals the moment they are born, defining parameters according to gender. For women, the word then takes on a pervasive quality at the moment of birth, since it defines on one hand and alienates on another. Women are constantly confronted with the problem of the misrepresentation masculine desire and discourse bring about, with the problem of seeking definition within a male framework. As Hélène Cixous points out, "even at the moment of uttering a sentence, admitting a notion of 'being,' a question of being, an ontology, we are already seized by a certain kind of masculine desire, the desire that mobilizes philosophical discourse."[2] We are thus caught by the word's power to blind and imprison. How do we move from this language of misrepresentation to the language of self-understanding, move away from the word as an imprisoning and alienating force to the word in its liberating sense? One way of becoming more conscious of language as both a repressive and a liberating force is through writing.

Literature provides the medium to voice female concerns much as current ideology provides the medium for male discourse. Writing serves as a vehicle for the demystification through self-representation of that unity we call woman. It provides the stage for a multiplicity of voices, experiences, issues which speak to the subordination of women to ideology, and thus replaces the oversimplistic stereotypes so often used to categorize and define women. We should therefore begin to look at women's literary works as not only an alternative to but a counterpart of traditional social scientific feminist theory. Women's literature is important because it allows the opportunity to articulate opposing views in a nonthreatening, nonauthoritarian form, which feels natural and is accessible to most women regardless of race or class. Literature has always reflected the ideology and social conditions of its time, yet it is usually dismissed as insignificant when historians or social scientists theorize. Literature maintains a lower status because of its fictional quality, whereas history, based on fact, is looked upon as truth in its highest and most objective form. But as Terry Eagleton, Marxist literary critic, points out, "Literary works are not mysteriously inspired, or explicable simply in terms of their authors' psychology. They are forms of perception, particular ways of seeing the world; and as such they have a relation to that dominant way of seeing the world which is the social mentality of ideology of an age."[3] Women's literary works when viewed in the way Eagleton describes are an essential part of feminist theory, as they embroider traditional feminist theory with issues and experiences rooted in the female consciousness. When we begin to move away from our dualistic way of compartmentalizing literature as false and the social sciences as true, merging the two instead, we will begin to open the doors for a more sensitive type of theorizing about cultures and individuals. Studying the social sciences and literature together sets the stage for a more realistic type of theorizing which will eventually eliminate the ineffective, outdated, and above all inaccurate type of analysis which holds women hostage today. Women's literature provides the method, the voices, experiences, and rituals involved in growing up female.

Women writers like ethnographers focus on microcosms within a culture, unpacking rituals in the context of inherited symbolic and social structures of subjugation. Women writers are acting as their own ethnographers, using the word for self-representation. This kind of self-representation marks a significant step toward the kind of liberation Ellison speaks of and Hélène Cixous refers to as the possibility for change, "the space that can serve as a springboard for subversive thought, the precursory movement of a transformation of social and cultural structures."[4]

Kitzia Hoffman and Sylvina Bullrich are two Latina writers who through their short stories show us the limitations women are confronted within Latino society. In "Old Adelina," Kitzia Hoffman weaves a tale around an old Mexican *curandera* named Adelina. Hoffman's character is preoccupied with her decision, made as a young girl, to blind herself by gazing into the sun. As the story opens, we find Adelina in a total state of powerlessness and invisibility:

> Adelina, old Adelina, was left alone, seated on the sidewalk. After a few moments, it would even have been easy to overlook her presence. She seemed to be just another unevenness in the stone pavement. That was Adelina. She had the rare gift not only of being, but of belonging to and becoming part of any place where she settled.[5]

Throughout this story Adelina reflects back over her years in an uneasy attempt to understand her tragic life. As a girl, Adelina was forced to leave town after being accused of causing many of her neighbors harm with her "mal de ojo." Because of superstition and a network of gossip that limits and defines women, the townspeople blame Adelina's psychic powers for every minor calamity. The use of language as a tool of power to subordinate women is very clear in "Old Adelina"—language in the form of gossip and superstition is used to "other" Adelina and drive her out of town. In order to ensure that she will never again be forced to flee any other town, Adelina decides to blind herself. She sacrifices her sight, family, and home, to gain acceptance; she surrenders, in a single act that denies her identity, everything for the demands of her culture. Throughout the story Adelina is haunted by one question: "Does everyone in the world have to burn something in order to be able to live among their fellows?" The obvious answer to Adelina's question is yes, but the tragedy of the story for Adelina, and for all women by implication, is that the price she pays is far too much "to be just another unevenness in the stone pavement." Walter Benjamin says that all stories are about death;[6] here we see death forcing the end of the story, and measuring an old women's life:

> The bitter taste came into her mouth when she thought of this. What a price she had paid for her place among the women in the market. Oh God what a price.
>
> If she had not burned out her eyes staring at the sun . . . if she had had the courage to be different from others and to hold on to her strong sight without running away.[7]

Hoffman's story ends with Adelina realizing the enormity of the price she has paid for "her place . . . in the market."

In "The Bridge," Argentinean author Sylvina Bullrich introduces the reader to Patricia, an aggressive, rebellious woman with a desire to escape what she calls tedious and provincial. Patricia is obsessed with the prospect of having a bridge built in her town to join the island on which she lives with the outside world. The bridge is obviously a metaphor for escape. Patricia is educated and in love with progress, yet she is confined to the obsolescence that her culture reserves for women no matter what their education. Because Patricia is a woman, she is constantly told that her dreaming of bridges is inappropriate and that she should concern herself with more womanly things such as cooking, sewing, and making babies. Finally, in an act striving for self-fulfillment, Patricia sacrifices herself, marrying an older man, an engineer she does not love, in hopes of achieving her dream. Her husband shares Patricia's vision and brings with him the method and the means necessary to transform Patricia's dream to reality. Patricia's engineer and bridge are important for her because, as she explains, "Both were an escape from a tedious and provincial home, from that which was too stable and ossified." It is clear that Patricia wants vicariously to build that bridge of her dreams, sacrificing the only thing she has as a woman, herself. Patricia reveals the extent of her dreams when she tells her husband about her visions for female liberation:

> We will be strange missionaries, we will go building links around the world, we will go around providing bridges so that no young girl with a free soul will have the feeling that the world has forgotten her.[8]

Patricia's dreams reveal her desperate desire for change and progress, especially where young women are concerned. While Patricia's husband, Eugenio, initially shares her dreams, she gradually begins to detect a change in his attitude regarding the construction of the bridge:

> Before his urgency was as great as mine; now it was tempered. When I asked for precise details—the date when work was to begin, the time required to finish—his voice wavered, and he started his answers with vague expression such as "God willing," "If time permits," "If no one objects," "If there are no obstacles," "If no unforseen cirumstances arise," "If the cabinet isn't changed," "If the next government lends its support." The threats that hung over the bridge were so many I began to feel a real anxiety. I communicated this feeling, and Eugenio ended up angry.[9]

What Patricia describes as vague expressions can be viewed as the mystification of the male-controlled bureaucracy. Eugenio soon understands that the powerful men of their town have no interest in having a bridge constructed. A bridge in their eyes, as in Patricia's, would serve to bring civilization. But, unlike Patricia, these men believe that when "civilization arrives, troubles come." Eugenio is faced with making a choice between his wife's dreams of building the bridge, which will bring a lack of work and money, or conforming to the male perception of power and social order, a choice which promises employment and survival. Eugenio's decision is in line with the men and against his wife's insistence. Patricia does not appear to understand how powerless her husband's position is and feels that with more patience and sacrifices their bridge can still become a reality. It is interesting to note the change in attitude of the townspeople once Eugenio makes his decision to put his plans for the bridge aside. His position of powerlessness and invisibility quickly becomes one of power and visibility.

> As soon as it was known that Eugenio was working with Don Aristides and Don Fortunato, we were both much sought after. After all, no one could move from Rio Dorado without the aid of those two.
>
> "It's good, Engineer, we need a bigger boat and another ferry. We know the bridge is most important, but in the meantime you have to live, right? We thought that a man like yourself, born here, wouldn't be indifferent to our needs."
>
> Eugenio smiled, flattered and surprised when he was so often stopped on the street, he who up until a few days ago seemed invisible.[10]

Unfortunately, Patricia's dreams are never realized. Instead of developing her "free soul" and cultivating more dreams for a more balanced world of gender potential, Patricia accepts her role as wife and mother, the role she once dreamed of escaping. Patricia's sacrifice is made in vain, as her dreams of progress and visions of a better world for women are simply dismissed as the irrational thoughts of a young, inexperienced, and rebellious child.

Both "Old Adelina" and "The Bridge" provide representations of women in conflict with their male-defined place in society. Hoffman and Bullrich develop rich but tragic stories about their protagonists, emphasizing the subordination of women to ideology. Although the characters in these stories differ in respect to age, ethnicity, and social position, they are both women struggling with cultural limitations and female issues. Both stories speak of the unfulfilled lives of women; they speak of the need to sacrifice oneself as a strategy for survival, of the need to conform to the dictates of the patriarchy. Julia Kristeva's concept of the socio-contract, "the sacrificial relationship of separation and articulation of differences," is acted out tragically by both Adelina and Patricia. Patricia's love for progress and desire for change are direct results of her education, her literacy.

It is her ability to manipulate complex language that reveals the limitations of the woman's role in her culture, the source of her frustration. Adelina realizes as an old lady that she has sacrificed too much, while Patricia, after conforming and sacrificing her "free soul," feels that she has not sacrificed enough. One woman begins by sacrificing her eyes, the other her soul; both women remain unhappy and unfulfilled in spite of their sacrifices.

Hoffman and Bullrich, like ethnographers, have succeeded in representing two women addressing issues of female subjugation brought about by masculine expectations and discourse, by ideology and history. As both stories are representations of women defeated by the limitations and expectations of their cultures, they illustrate how the word has the power to imprison and destroy. But on another level these stories are like springboards for transformation (using Cixous's analogy), functioning as liberating forces since they awaken and raise the consciousness of all who read them. These two storytellers are acting as counselors defining issues, articulating the female condition in their respective societies. Walter Benjamin makes a point that is relevant here:

> In every case the storyteller is a man (woman), who has counsel for his readers . . . After all, counsel is less an answer to a question than a proposal concerning the continuation of a story which is just unfolding. To seek counsel one would first have to be able to tell the story. (Quite apart from the fact that a man [women] is receptive to counsel only to the extent that he [she] allows he [her] situation to speak.) Counsel woven into the fabric of real life is wisdom.[11]

Before we can move toward the transformation of social and cultural structures, it is first necessary to understand our past and present situations. As Benjamin points out, the storyteller does not necessarily provide an answer but does offer a proposal concerning the stories' possible outcome. Benjamin goes on to explain how the art of storytelling provides us with the symptoms of the secular productive forces of history, a point which is generally overlooked by most social scientists. Both Hoffman and Bullrich are effective as storytellers because they bring to the public clear political messages regarding the limitations women are confronted with in Latino society; they awaken minds and create the urgency necessary for the kind of subversive thought Cixous speaks of, which ultimately leads to the possibility of change. In both stories the authors' writing is analogous to the bridge metaphor Bullrich elicits, reaching out to other women, linking them to one another so that no woman with a free spirit will feel the world has forgotten her, so that women who have felt trapped or imprisoned by the word can also begin to look to the word for its reviving and liberating force.

Hoffman and Bullrich have taken the first steps toward the understanding of the self-imposed sacrificial contract Latina women willingly commit themselves to; they use the literary form to diagnose the conditions of women's inequality and in the process give the world two finely crafted stories that are rich in ideological promise. For Marcelle Thiebaux, it is this kind of writing that begins to break ground for female discourse, creating balance and understanding.

> When the female reader is not central—as is usual in masculinist writing—the patriarchal discourse embraces the whole Woman/Book image and incorporates it into further discourse of its own, wrenching the woman from the book and creating a realm of knowledge from which the woman is excluded, shut out of the library entirely. The only way for woman to create her own discourse is to create her own library.[12]

Stories like "Old Adelina" and "The Bridge," while addressing current ideological concerns of women, also serve to bridge the gap between ideology and history by addressing female patterns of ultimate sacrifice. The issue of sacrifice in Latino culture is directly related to the representation of Latina women in masculine myth, history, and ideology.

Sylvia Gonzales and Norma Alarcón are two Chicanas who understand how language and writing have been dominated by masculine discourse and used to subjugate and exploit female consciousness. Mexican history and ideology are predominantly masculine in perspective, and because of this they have been used to control rather than enlighten women. Women are characterized as weak, passive, and totally dependent on men for their meaning. The masculine domination of language has therefore led to the domination of women. Norma Alarcón shows how the masculine myth of Malintzin affects male and female thought:

> Because the myth of Malintzin pervades not only male thought but ours too it seeps into our own consciousness in the cradle through their eyes as well as our mothers', who are entrusted with the transmission of culture, we may come to believe that indeed our very sexuality condemns us to enslavement. An enslavement which is subsequently manifested in self-hatred. All we see is hatred of women. We must hate her too since love seems only possible through extreme virtue whose definition is at best slippery.[13]

The language of our history becomes a corruptive force when accepted at face value, without taking into account the limitations, authority, or perspective of its textualized discourse. The poet Sylvia Gonzales must have realized the pervasive quality of masculine historical discourse. In her poem "Chicana Evolution" she cries with the pain of literacy as she speaks of a second rape:

> I am Chicana
> But while you developed
> in the womb,
> I was raped again.
> I am Chicana
> In a holocaust of sperm,
> bitter fragments of fertilization
> mankind's victim,
> humankind's burden.[14]

To understand Gonzales's poem it is necessary to understand the myth of Malintzin, to place it in its proper context. Gonzales is effective in using her poetry to transmit ideological concerns, to bring to life the ambivalent distaste and fear of women in Mexican/Chicano history and culture. She is trying to dispel the myth that Chicanas are inferior because they are women. Women's writing provides the means by which to implement change in history and ideology. For Mexicanas/Chicanas this change translates into the possibility of defining ourselves in history, liberating women and men from the oppressive roles which have been handed down by masculine discourse, which recognizes Hernán Cortés as the leader of the conquest of the Aztec civilization while Malintzin, who is associated with the birth of a people, is seen predominantly as the traitor of the race. Her gift for language, her betrayal, her intercourse, destroyed one culture and gave life to another. She is thus simultaneously held responsible for killing and creating. In this respect Malintzin has been compared by some scholars to Eve, mother of humankind and original evil woman. Malintzin served as the vehicle for Cortés's success, transmitting, translating information for the man she believed to be her savior, Quetzalcoatl, with whom she immediately aligned herself for the betterment of her people. It was largely because of Malintzin's linguistic skill that Cortés was able to move so swiftly on the Aztec empire. Because of Malinche, Mexicanos, as mestizos, are the "offspring of violation," reaffirming the belief that if La Malinche is to be demeaned and denigrated, naturally her children will have to be considered accordingly.

Women writing in their own behalf will help discard the outdated sexist ideology of the past, moving language and history to a more realistic and holistic approach which is needed for the gender-balanced ideology of the future. Unless women begin to tell their own stories, they will continue to be what all Chicanos have been called, the bastard children of the universe, in the sense that they will continue to be raped by the word of textualized representations written by the patriarch, and rationalized by society and ideology. For Hélène Cixous the act of woman writing herself

> . . . will return to the body which has been more than confiscated from her, which has been turned into the uncanny stranger on display—the ailing or dead figure, which so often turns out to be the nasty companion, that

> cause breath and speech at the same time . . . A woman without a body, dumb, blind, can't possibly be a good fighter. She is reduced to being the servant of the militant male, his shadow. We must kill the false woman who is preventing the live one from breathing. Inscribe the breath of the whole woman.[16]

Women's writing in itself does not provide the solution but rather creates a balance in written discourse and marks an important and essential step toward a more holistic approach to understanding issues concerning female misrepresentation and subordination. The problems with language will then move from the initial structural ones, involving content and form, to those more pressing concerns dealing with power, authority, and control. Writing provides a double-edged reality, as Ellison points out, with the possibility of reviving or imprisoning a people. When will we move from the language of rape? How do we move from the violence of the word onto the intellectual and aesthetic pleasure of the letter?

NOTES

1. Ralph Ellison, "Twentieth Century Fiction and the Black Mask of Humanity," in *Images of the Negro in American Literature* (Chicago: University of Chicago Press), p. 155.

2. Hélène Cixous, "Castration or Decapitation," in *New French Feminisms* (Amherst: University of Massachusetts Press, 1980).

3. Terry Eagleton, *Marxism and Literary Criticism* (Berkeley: University of California Press, 1976).

4. Hélène Cixous, "The Laugh of the Medusa," in *New French Feminisms.*

5. Kitzia Hoffman, "Old Adelina," in *Latin American Literature Today* (New York: New American Library/Mentor, 1977).

6. Walter Benjamin, "The Storyteller," in *Illuminations*, ed. Hannah Arendt and trans. Harry Zohn (New York: Schocken, 1969).

7. Hoffman, "Old Adelina."

8. Sylvina Bullrich, "The Bridge," in *Latin American Literature Today.*

9. Ibid.

10. Ibid.

11. Benjamin, "The Storyteller" (emphasis on gender mine).

12. Marcelle Thiebaux, "Foucault's Fantasia for Feminists: The Woman Reading," in *Theory and Practice of Feminist Literary Criticism* (Ypsilanti, Mich.: Bilingual Press, 1982).

13. Norma Alarcón, "Chicanas' Feminist Literature: A Revision through Malintzin/or Malintzin: Putting Flesh Back on the Object," in *This Bridge Called My Back* (Watertown, Mass.: Persephone Press, 1981).

14. Sylvia Gonzales, "Chicana Evolution," in *The Third Woman* (Boston: Houghton Mifflin Company, 1980).

15. Adelaida del Castillo, "Malintzin Tenepal: A Preliminary Look into a New Perspective," *Essays on La Mujer*, ed. Rosaura Sánchez and Rosa Martínez Cruz (Los Angeles: University of California, Chicano Studies Center Publications, 1977), p. 144.

16. Cixous, "The Laugh of the Medusa."

Contributors

Yolanda Julia Broyles is currently teaching German studies and Chicano studies at the University of California at Santa Barbara. She is a well-known scholar in Germany, having published books and articles in both the Federal Republic of Germany and the German Democratic Republic. Her cross-cultural work is exemplified in *The German Response to Latin American Literature* (Heidelberg: Carl Winter, 1981). She received her Ph.D. in German studies and comparative literature from Stanford University and is currently doing research on El Teatro Campesino.

Roberto R. Calderón is a doctoral candidate in the history department at the University of California, Los Angeles. His area of work includes oral history, labor, and political history of the late nineteenth and early twentieth centuries. He has published one anthology, *South Texas Coal Mining: A Community History* (n.p., 1984).

Teresa Carrillo is pursuing graduate work in the department of political science at Stanford University. Her research interests center on Latin America, with special interest in Third World women in development and in politics. She is an active member of the Stanford Central American Action Network (SCAAN) and the Chicano Graduate Student Association.

Richard Chabran is a founder and current editor of the Chicano Periodical Index Project. He is co-director of the Chicano Data Base, a contributing editor of *Critica: A Journal of Critical Essays* (San Diego: Third College, 1984), an advisory board member of the Instituto de Lengua y Cultura, and the author of several book reviews and bibliographic guides. He is co-editor of *Biblio-Politica: Chicano Perspectives on Library Services in the United States* (Berkeley: Chicano Studies Research Library Publications Unit, 1984). Currently, he is the coordinator of the Bibliographic Research and Collection Development Unit, of which the Chicano Studies Research Library at UCLA is a subunit. Additionally, he is an adjunct lecturer at UCLA's Graduate School of Library and Information Science.

Barbara A. Driscoll is a visiting scholar at CEFNOMEX. She did her undergraduate work at Boston State College and received her M.A. and Ph.D. from Notre Dame University. She is active in border studies, both academically and in the community.

Alma M. García is an assistant professor of sociology/ethnic studies at the University of Santa Clara. Her teaching interests include Chicano culture, the Chicano family, minority women, the sociology of development, and political sociology. Currently, she is conducting research on the development of Chicana feminism, 1970-1980. She is also interested in Mexican peasant movements. Her study "Peasant Revolts during the Mexican Revolution: A Social-Structural and Political Approach" appeared in *History, Culture and Society: Chicano Studies in the 1980's*, ed. Mario T. García et al. (Ypsilanti, Mich.: Bilingual Press/Editorial Bilingüe, 1983). García has been active in NACS, serving as the Northern California regional representative and national treasurer.

Clara Lomas recently completed her doctoral dissertation entitled "A Critique of Social Institutions in Mario Vargas Llosa's *La Ciudad y los Perros, Conversación en la Catedral*, and *Pantaleón y las Visitadoras*." She is on leave from the University of California, Santa Cruz, conducting research at the University of Texas, Austin. Her research interests focus primarily on women writers in the United States and Latin America.

Marta C. Lopez-Garza received her Ph.D. in the department of sociology at UCLA where she completed a dissertation on the informal labor sector in the City of Mexico. She has taught courses on Chicanas and Women and Development in the Third World at California State University at Northridge. Her previous work has covered Mexican/U.S. relations, social and economic conditions of Chicanas, and Gramsci's notion of ideological hegemony.

Cynthia Orozco is a Ph.D. candidate in history at UCLA. She is the author of "Rancho Women's Social Relationships in Nineteenth Century Alta California: Friends, Family, and Servants," forthcoming in *Women's History in Transition: Content, Theory, and Methodology in Chicana/Mexicana History*, edited by Adelaida del Castillo. She has also written "Chicana Labor History: A Critique of Male Consciousness in Historical Writing," *La Red* 77 (February, 1984). She was the 1982-1983 Institute of American Cultures Fellow at the Chicano Studies Research Center at UCLA. She has conducted extensive research on the history of LULAC, has been an active participant in NACS, is a founder of the Chicana Caucus of NACS, and has been active with Raza Women's Organization and *La Gente* at UCLA.

Devon Peña is an assistant professor of sociology at Colorado College, where he is developing courses on the comparative sociology of the Third World. He received his Ph.D. in 1983 from the University of Texas at Austin. Currently, he is working on a book-length manuscript, *The Terror of Production: Women and Global Fordism in Mexico*. He has published articles and monographs on Mexican border industrialization, women in the labor process, immigration, and social welfare policy issues. His current research interests include women's struggles in the global electronics industry, mental health and workplace organization, and immigration and social work.

Alvina E. Quintana is working on her doctorate in the History of Consciousness Program at the University of California, Santa Cruz. She teaches writing and literature at the School of Ethnic Studies, San Francisco State University. Her research is concerned with the evolution of Chicana feminist thought in literature.

Elba Sánchez received her B.A. in Latin American studies and her M.A. in literature from the University of California, Santa Cruz. She is presently working with the Spanish for Spanish Speakers program. She is an editorial member for *Revista Mujeres*, a publication for Latinas at UC Santa Cruz.

Denise A. Segura is a Ph.D. candidate in sociology at the University of California, Berkeley. She is working on her dissertation, "Chicana/Mexicana Labor: A Study of Social Stratification and Mobility." She is currently interested in the interplay among race, class, and gender that affects the options of women of color in U.S. society.

Angelina F. Veyna is a graduate student in the doctoral program in anthropology at the University of California, Los Angeles. While her area of expertise has been Aztec society, mainly use of ornamentation, she has recently begun to examine eighteenth-century New Mexican society through the use of ethnohistorical sources. Her present efforts include an analysis of the 1790 census of Santa Cruz de la Cañada and an investigation of New Mexican women's wills during the 1700s. She also works as an educational researcher at Southwest Educational Research Laboratory (Los Alamitos, California), focusing on various aspects of bilingual education and language acquisition.

Emilio Zamora is the program director of the Chicano Studies Research Center at UCLA. He has conducted work on Mexican labor history in the United States and is presently engaged in studies pertaining to the early twentieth century history of Mexicans in Texas.

Editorial Committee

Teresa Cordova (Chair) received her Ph.D. from the University of California, Berkeley where she completed a dissertation entitled "Local Communities and National Organiations: Land Use and Social Conflict in Southern Colorado." She is Vice-chair of the city of Berkeley Planning Commission and Chair of the South Berkeley Area Plan Committee. Aside from her interests in community development she is an active feminist and co-editor of *Unsettled Issues: Chicanas in the 80's*. She is a member of Mujeres en Marcha, Women of Color in Unity, and Mujeres Activas en Letras y Cambio Social. In January, 1986, she joined the department of Latin American Studies at the University of Illinois, Chicago, where she will be developing a community studies program.

Norma Cantú, Ph.D., is an assistant professor of English at Laredo State University, where she teaches courses in linguistics, children's literature, writing, and literature. She is active in various professional groups and in numerous community organizations such as a local Chicano theater group and Las Mujeres, a local women's group that advocates women's rights and sponsors an annual women's conference—Primavera.

Gilbert Cardenas is an associate professor of sociology at the University of Texas at Austin and was the 1984 NACS conference coordinator. His research interests include international migration and border studies and he is currently studying pannationalist ideology in Chicano-Mexicano relations. He is a research associate of the Population Research Center at UT and a research associate of the Centro de Estudios Fronterizos del Norte de México.

Juan R. García is an associate professor of history at the University of Arizona. He is the author of *Operation Wetback* and other publications. He has served as a member of the NACS executive boards, the site committee of NACS XI, and the Editorial Board. Currently, he is completing work on his third book, *Broken Promises: Mexicans in the Corporate Midwest, 1900-1932*, a social history of Mexicans in the Midwest.

Christine Marie Sierra will join the faculty of the University of New Mexico in the fall of 1986 after completing one year as a research fellow at the Brookings Institute in Washington D.C. Her research interests include Chicano/minority politics, Mexican immigration, and community organization. As a co-recipient of a grant from the Southwest Institute for Research on Women (SIROW), at the University of Arizona, she conducted a year-long project in 1984-85 on Integrating Women's Studies into the Curriculum at Colorado College. She is currently at work on an article on Hispanic advocacy groups in national politics. She is co-founder and member of Mujeres Activas en Letras y Cambio Social (MALCS), a group of Chicana scholars engaged in research on women and in the recruitment and support of Chicanas in higher education.